THE HALL OF HOMELESS GODS

Novels by John Michael Greer

The Weird of Hali:

I – Innsmouth

II – Kingsport

III – Chorazin

IV – Dreamlands

V – Providence

VI – Red Hook

VII – Arkham

Others:

The Fires of Shalsha

Star's Reach

Twilight's Last Gleaming

Retrotopia

The Shoggoth Concerto

The Nyogtha Variations

A Voyage to Hyperborea

The Seal of Yueh Lao

Journey Star

The Witch of Criswell

The Book of Haatan

The Hall of Homeless Gods

THE HALL OF HOMELESS GODS

John Michael Greer

First published in 2024 by
Sphinx Books
London

British Library Cataloguing in Publication Data

A C.I.P. for this book is available from the British Library

ISBN-13: 978-1-91595-212-7

Cover art by Phoebe Young
Typeset by Medlar Publishing Solutions Pvt Ltd, India

www.aeonbooks.co.uk/sphinx

AUTHOR'S NOTE

For reasons which will become clear in the course of the tale, there are plenty of Japanese words in this story. Readers not familiar with the Japanese language will want to know that every vowel is pronounced, so the last name Abe is pronounced "ah-bay," not like Lincoln's nickname. A is ah, e is eh, i is ee, o is oh, and u is oo: keep that in mind and you won't go too far wrong.

In Japanese the family name always comes first. The main character, for example, usually goes by Jerry Shimizu but his Japanese name is Shimizu Junichi. Shimizu is the family name and Junichi is the personal name—what gaijin (Westerners) think of as the "first name." His mother is Shimizu Hanako, and so on.

I've put a glossary of Japanese terms in back for reference. I tried to get Jerry to define every word when he first used it, but I won't swear that he always did so.

Chapter 1

I GOT TO THE ferry dock around half past eleven. Night had already clamped down hard over Shoreside by then, blotting out the ramshackle colors of the day, turning the hills back behind the town into ink-black shapes against the less intense black of the sky. Little constellations of lamps here and there along the beach showed where somebody or other had electricity to waste and didn't care who knew it. The ferry dock, a rickety shape of recycled lumber jutting out from the buildings past the beach and into the Atlantic, had two solar-powered lamps up on poles, high enough that you'd have to work hard to steal them and hope that none of Big Goro's boys spotted you and decided to have some fun. Me, I kept to the shadows and pretended to look along the beach toward the big hill a couple of blocks further south, which stuck up black against scattered stars. What I was really doing was watching the other passengers gather.

Not counting me, there were twelve people on the ferry dock. Four were young punks from the Habitats out on a spree, dressed for the part in shorts and sandals and loud sleeveless shirts. From their talk, they'd decided to go home for once instead of staying out until the first ferry after dawn. Three of those had company they'd hired for the night. They'd have to do some fast talking or hand over a chunk of change to get

Shoreside girls past the Habitat guards, but it happened often enough that I didn't raise an eyebrow.

Three more were older guys, more conservatively dressed in slacks and button-up shirts. Two of them I knew. One was George Morita, who lived in Habitat 3. He'd retired years ago and liked to go to a Shoreside tea house to play shoji against all comers. The way he was grinning, not to mention the smell of vodka and rum I caught from him, told me he must have met someone who beat the pants off him. The other one I knew was Big Goro's accountant, Jim Nakano, a lean man in a jacket and slacks with a briefcase in one hand. The guy with him, who I didn't know, was hard-faced and silent and had a pistol in a holster right there on his belt. Goro's organization banked its take offshore, and I had a pretty good idea the briefcase Nakano carried had a hell of a lot of money in it.

Then there was the old woman who stood all alone under one of the lamp poles, smiling to herself and looking out past the flooded ruins just offshore to the horizon and the five tall brightly lit shapes that rose from it. She had a cheap flowered blouse and dark blue slacks on, and over those a hapi coat, dark red, with four Japanese characters embroidered on the back in a bright yellow that was supposed to be gold. Her hands were together and she was holding a nenju, a string of prayer beads. She was half the reason I was in the shadows just then. Her name was Ms. Otome, I knew her and she knew me, and the last thing I wanted right then was to have her spot me and make a fuss that might let the other half of the reason know he was being followed by yours truly.

The other half of the reason stood apart from the others, a couple of yards closer to the dark shapes and scattered lamps of Shoreside. He was gaijin, stocky and nervous, with thinning blond hair. He wore a gaudy vest over a short-sleeved shirt and slacks, and the reason he wore the vest showed every time he shifted, if you knew what to look for. He had a holster tucked under his left armpit, and it wasn't a small one, either.

I'd followed him all day. I knew why he was there and what he planned on doing. My job was to stop him.

A mile or so out to sea, a point of light showed in the darkness. The ferry was on time. Its route took it past the five Habitats and then through a gap in the drowned ruins to the Shoreside dock. One of the things I knew I probably wouldn't have a chance to figure out was how the guy expected to get away. He might be planning to disappear back into the crowded alleys of Shoreside, though if he had that in mind he'd have been smarter to get moving before the ferry came in sight. He might be planning on hijacking the ferry and taking it out to meet a ship in deep water, or he might have a friend with a boat tucked into one of the ruins offshore. He might be headed for one of the Habitats, in which case all hell was going to break loose if anybody found out which one. He wasn't going to get that far this time, though. I watched him out of the corner of my eye, wondered when he'd make his move, and got my fingers around the grip of my favorite gun: a Browning .45, a fine old automatic pistol, the one I like to take with me when I'm expecting serious trouble.

That was when I saw the woman on the beach.

She was gaijin and in her early twenties, maybe, a little gawky, with lots of loose dark curly hair framing a pale face with big eyes. She wore odd clothing, a short-sleeved top and long pants of flimsy blue fabric, in a cut I didn't recognize. I hadn't seen her come along the beach but there she was, standing a dozen yards from the dock, facing me. The oddest thing about her was her expression, which I could just see by the light from the lamps. She stared at me and the dock with a wide-eyed look, like she'd never seen a guy or a dock before, and then she turned the same expression on the ferry.

A lookout? Maybe. I glanced reflexively at the guy I was following, and just then things started to happen.

One of the young punks, the one who didn't have a girl with him, turned suddenly and lunged at the guard. At that same moment my guy pulled a big revolver and went toward Jim Nakano, and I went after him. I'd judged the distance right. Before he could get to the accountant, I stuck the business end of my Browning against his back and said "Drop it."

Of course he didn't drop it. I didn't expect him to. He tried to whip around to the right to knock my gun aside and get his muzzle pointed toward me, but he didn't realize I had my pistol in my left hand. I grabbed his right wrist and yanked, and at the same moment got my foot behind his right knee and stomped down hard. He crumpled. I helped him out by pistol-whipping him a couple of times and wrenching his wrist until he dropped his gun. It was that or shoot him dead, and I don't do that if I can help it.

Crack of a pistol a little further down the dock told me that someone else hadn't been so generous. I made sure that the guard was still standing and the punk was the one who'd doubled over clutching his chest with blood making a mess all over the place. The three Shoreside girls had all ducked behind the nearest dense objects, which in all three cases amounted to their boyfriends of the night. The boyfriends played the part by standing there looking frightened with their mouths hanging open. Jim Nakano had a gun out by then and looked perfectly willing to empty it into anyone who got near him, and old George had gotten out of the line of fire and was right over at the edge of the dock, ready to drop into the water if he needed to. Meanwhile Ms. Otome was still standing there with a blissful smile on her face, looking out to sea. She hadn't moved a muscle.

The woman I'd seen on the beach was gone. I didn't see her leave, either. I shook my head, made sure of my grip on the guy I'd caught, and jabbed the muzzle of my Browning into his upper back when he tried to move.

Just then running feet pounded on the dock. I risked a glance and saw half a dozen of Big Goro's boys pelting toward us, guns out. Behind them at a more measured pace came

Big Goro himself. You didn't call him that to his face, you called him Mr. Omogawa, sir, but when he was out of earshot he was always Big Goro, and for good reason. He was one of those really fat men who had even more muscle to him than fat. He had fists the size of melons. I'd seen him kill somebody with a punch. You didn't see him strolling around at night in Shoreside very often, too many people had reason to go gunning for him, and the fact that he was out with his boys got me wondering what was up.

The guy I was holding chose that moment to try to pull free. I tightened my grip on him, jabbed him in the back with my pistol and pushed down with my foot. That occupied the time it took Big Goro to reach the rest of us, nod to Jim Nakano, and turn to me. "Jerry," he said. His voice was quieter than you'd expect from someone his size. "Your boss sent you here, eh?"

"Yeah. This kind of thing's happening too often. It's bad for business."

"Tell her I said thanks. You have any use for this?" A motion of his head indicated the guy I'd caught, who started babbling something frantic I couldn't make out.

I knew then that I probably should have put a bullet through the guy's brain. It would have been kinder than what he was going to get. I decided to take a risk. "I'm supposed to turn him over to a law officer."

Big Goro considered me. "Going to play it by the book, eh?"

"Part of my job."

"Of course." He put on a smile I didn't like. "Bill? You know Jerry Shimizu, don't you? Show him your badge."

I knew Bill Takagi, too. He was in his fifties, let's say a good twenty years older than me, a lean muscular guy with short legs and long arms. He had a scar where somebody once laid open one side of his face with a knife, and he walked with the kind of rolling gait that tells you he had more than his share of broken bones. He came over to me, and without a word showed me a county sheriff deputy's badge and the ID that went with it. If any part of Shoreside still had a county sheriff it was news to me, and I was pretty sure the county seat was somewhere out where waves off the Atlantic pound big chunks of old concrete into smaller chunks, but I wasn't about to try to pick a fight over it, not with Big Goro standing there surrounded by his toughs. I nodded and hauled the guy to his feet.

Bill took him from me and cuffed him across the face to stop his babbling. "Mako? Get his hands."

Mako was another one of Big Goro's boys, a big muscle-bound guy with a neck about as thick as his head. He always wore jeans and a tee shirt without any sleeves, no matter what the weather was like, and he kept his head shaved. He said, "Okay, boss," came over, spun the guy around and got his hands tied behind him with a bit of rope. I put my gun back in the holster and stepped back.

"You've done me a favor, Jerry," said Big Goro then. "You know I never forget a favor." He pulled a wad of bills out of a pocket, peeled off half a dozen of them, handed them to me. "Buy yourself a drink."

It would have been a hell of a drink. He'd given me more money than I usually saw in a month. I kept my thoughts to myself and said, "Thank you, Mr. Omogawa."

Big Goro smiled again, motioned to his boys with his head, and started back up the dock toward Shoreside. Most of his boys went with him, and so did the guy I'd caught, half-carried by Mako and Bill. The other guy who'd been part of the setup, the one who looked like a punk from Shoreside, wasn't going anywhere ever again. One of Big Goro's boys prodded him with a foot, shrugged, and walked away.

Two of the boys stayed behind, staying close to Jim Nakano, and one of those picked up the gun from where my guy had dropped it. He motioned with it and gave me a questioning look. I shrugged, and he grinned and pocketed the gun. I looked away and tried not to think about what was going to happen to the guy I'd caught. I hated handing him over to Big Goro, but sometimes you do what you have to do.

Off past the end of the dock, I could see the ferry to the Habitats, a low lumpy yellow shape surrounded by a diesel growl and a plume of pale smoke you could just see in the dim light. It was a hundred yards out and closing fast. Old Ms. Otome was smiling and praying. She still hadn't moved a muscle.

THE FERRY TOOK HALF an hour to get out to the nearest of the Habitats, where Jim and his three guards clambered up onto the dock and went to wait for the elevator, and another fifteen minutes or so to get to mine. I sat next to Ms. Otome, since I didn't want to be rude to Mom's best friend and number one disciple, but she smiled up at me and then went back to saying her silent prayers and counting them on the beads of the nenju.

I didn't mind. Silence was what I wanted just then. There wasn't much of it on a little passenger ferry with a diesel grumbling to itself somewhere down below and spitting smoke that smelled like fried food. It didn't help, either, that the three young punks were talking loud to try to prove to their Shoreside girls that they hadn't been scared pea green when the guns came out, but I was willing to take what I could get. So I sat there on the painted wooden bench seat next to Ms. Otome, and looked through the window at the black churning waves and the pale stars rising above them, until four huge concrete pillars and Habitat 4 above them blotted out so much of the sky that I couldn't see the stars any more.

The growl of the engine changed and changed again. I got up, helped Ms. Otome do the same thing, got another beatific smile from her, and waited while she pattered up the aisle to the front of the ferry. The three young punks and their hired girls stayed put, which was some consolation. A minute or so later Ms. Otome and I climbed onto the passenger dock and crossed over to the pillar at the other end of it.

If you haven't been out to the Habitats you have no idea how big those pillars are, and no, it doesn't matter if you've seen pictures. They invented those for deepwater oil rigs back when there was still oil to pump anywhere at all. The pillars are hollow, so you could float them out to wherever and then flood them, starting from the bottom to set them up, and they've got broad bases so they stand upright on the sea floor and stick up however many hundred feet you want. The seas started rising fast about the time the oil ran out, and some rich people decided to use the same trick to give themselves homes and offices that would stay above water, except they wanted them bigger than any oil rig ever was. Five sets of four pillars each got put in place and topped with steel frameworks before the crash of '47 bankrupted the project and just about everything else, and 2062 put the icing on that particular cake. After that, sea level started rising good and fast, and not too many Americans wanted to live close to the shore any more, but there were a lot of nanmin—that's Japanese for refugees—who didn't have anyplace else to go, and there were the five Habitats sitting there half finished two miles offshore. It's three miles now, and it'll be more before long.

I heard stories growing up about what the Habitats were like when Mom first moved out to Habitat 4. By all accounts it was pretty wild then, but things are more settled now. Ms. Otome and I said hi to the two big guys in flak jackets who stood guard on the dock, went to the clerk in the little booth by the elevator and signed in. I wrote my full name in the book, Shimizu Junichi, and did it in kanji, the old fancy characters that next to nobody uses any more. That got a weary look from the clerk, who was young enough that English was probably his first language. Ms. Otome, who signed in after me—she was old enough that ladies first wasn't in her mental vocabulary—made a little clucking noise at me, signed in the same way, and then jotted English letters up above both names to give the poor kid some clue what he was reading. He gave her a look of pure gratitude, and she smiled and bowed and pattered over to the elevator. I followed her and we both waited.

It took the elevator half of forever to drop down the couple of hundred feet from Ikkai. It always does. Finally, though, the door in front of us clanked and hissed open, and we went in and I pushed the button with the up arrow on it. The other half of forever went past, along with more noises, and then the door opened again and let us into another room. There were a couple of guards there too, but they'd been called by the clerk down below and waved us through, onto what used to be the main deck and now just gets called Ikkai.

Ikkai is where you find more than half of the shops and bars and cheap restaurants on Habitat 4. It's got narrow winding streets that gap open all the way to Nikai, the next deck up, which looks like a gray corrugated sky where you can see it past the signs and balconies. All the Habitats have electricity, which is more than you can say for a lot of places these days, and Ikkai has just enough in the way of streetlights that you can more or less find your way when it's dark. The lamps hanging out in front of the bars provide more light.

I said goodnight to Ms. Otome and headed for Stair 11, which is about half a mile away. Past midnight, Ikkai gets as quiet as it ever does, which isn't saying much. The bars and nightclubs were busy, no surprises there, and I took a detour once to avoid two drunk guys in the street: they were in the middle of a shoving match that looked like it was about to become something more serious. Nobody was hanging around the foot of Stair 11, which was welcome, and noodle bars on two of the landings were still open for the night trade, which was even more welcome. I got a bowl of Hakata ramen and a bottle of beer to go and hauled them along with me the rest of the way up to where I live.

Unless you live with a bunch of other people, family or friends or what have you, you get one room in a Habitat, and there's not a lot to choose between them. Mine has one big oval window with a window seat in it, looking west across the water toward Shoreside and the hills off past it. That's its claim to uniqueness. Other than that, it's a cramped little space ten feet wide and twenty feet long with a futon in a frame, a little table, a couple of chairs, a couple of bookshelves, a closet, a tiny kitchen unit set into one wall with a one-burner stove and a little box of a fridge, and a bathroom that's almost big enough to turn around in without hitting your head. Compared to the way a lot of people live in Shoreside, it's pretty good. Compared to the way people used to live a hundred years ago—well, we don't have to get into that.

That night it felt big enough and empty enough to echo, but I did my best not to care. I called my boss and left a message on her answering machine: she's still got one of those, don't ask me how. Then I flopped on a chair and downed the ramen and the beer. Ten minutes later, maybe, my clothes went into a cloth bag. I left the bag hanging outside on the doorknob, and crawled onto the futon to get six hours or so of sleep

I dragged myself back off the futon about the time the window changed from black to gray. The clothes I'd left out had been cleaned overnight by the laundry service, folded, and put into a fresh cloth bag: one of the nice things about living in one of the Habitats, though there's a bill for it once a month and I grumble about that like everyone else when it comes due. I showered and shaved and got some breakfast going. Rice was scarce that year, so it was more noodles and a poached egg washed down with green tea.

The newspaper was sitting out in the hall right in front of my door like always, and I read it while I ate. It's about half the size of an old-fashioned newspaper—I've seen those in abandoned houses uphill from Shoreside—and only sixteen pages thick, and most of it's chatter about what's going on in the Habitats, but there are four pages of news from outside and I always read those. It was all pretty normal. There'd been another incident on the Line of Control between North and South China, one more step toward the next big war everyone knew was coming. The Central Committee of the European Union had just voted Patrice Malinbois a fourth term as president, not that they had any choice. Over in New Washington, Congress was deadlocked over a devolution bill but the heads of all four parties said they'd work it out, and the president of the Senate was up in Ohio making a speech at another canal reopening. The latest forecasts from Greenland and Antarctica called for three inches of sea level rise next year, so some of the buildings in the low-lying parts of Shoreside would have to move uphill again sooner than they'd planned. Like I said, nothing out of the ordinary.

Once I was done with the news and breakfast, I skinned into nice clothes: button-up white shirt, tan slacks, tie, blue jacket, the kind of thing you don't see people wearing anywhere these days except New Washington and some parts of the Habitats. My boss is old-fashioned and she expects her people to dress accordingly.

Before I left my room I checked myself in the mirror, made sure my tie was straight and my gun wasn't visible. My face stared back at me: long and lean, with the square chin and pointed nose I got from a father whose name I'll never know. It was a reminder, a useful one, of my place in the world: on the border, never one thing but never anything else.

At eight o'clock sharp I was waiting in the room outside my boss's office under the disapproving gaze of her secretary, a cute little item named Louise Yoshimitsu who wears close-fitting suits to show off what she's got and always looks down her nose at me. The phone rang. She picked up, got an annoyed look on her face, and in the gentlest voice imaginable said, "Yes, Mrs. Taira. I'll send him right in." A baleful look from her was all the notice I got, but it was enough. I gave her a big smile and went through the door.

The office on the other side of the door is twice the size of my room. It's got floor to ceiling windows on the far end looking west toward Shoreside and the hills past it, it's got a couple of scroll paintings on the walls that I happen to know are twice as old as the United States, and over near the windows there's an enormous teakwood desk. Behind the desk sat a tiny, round-faced, white-haired woman in a flower print dress. She looks sweet and harmless, but let me give you a hint: she's as sweet and harmless as a rocket-propelled grenade. Ruth Taira's ancestors were warlords a thousand years ago during the Gempei wars, and the old blood hasn't lost its fire quite yet. She runs Habitat 4; she's got a nephew named Ryan, a thin quiet kid who's a better shot than I am, who she's training up as her successor; and she's got people who take care of problems for her. I'm one of them.

"Tell me what happened," she said as soon as I came into the room.

I went to the center of the floor, bowed, paused for just a moment until she waved me irritably to one of the other chairs in the room. I can get away with that, sometimes. "I spotted the guy as soon as he left the place he was staying," I said. "He was using the name Richard Dart, but it's an alias. He acted like he knew someone might be looking for him. He knew Shoreside well enough to get by but not well enough to shake me, and he didn't try to hide from anybody but Jim Nakano and his guard on the way out to the ferry dock."

"And Omogawa showed up."

"Yeah. There were some other people waiting for the ferry. One of them went at Nakano's guard right before quote Dart unquote made his move. I stopped Dart, the guard shot the kid who jumped him, and then Big Goro and half a dozen of his boys came running. They took Dart away with them. Did you know that there's a county sheriff in Shoreside? Bill Takagi's one of his deputies." That got me a raised eyebrow, and I went on. "Or at least he's got the badge and the paperwork."

"Interesting," she said. "And Nakano?"

"Boarded the ferry with the guard and two more of Goro's boys, and they all got off at Habitat 5. No sign of any trouble, and I didn't think it was worth the risk to follow them."

"True." The old woman regarded me for a moment. "This is very unfortunate. It would have been better if Omogawa hadn't seen you." I braced myself, but she went on. "But that can't be helped. You'll continue looking into the robberies, of course."

"You could have Jason take over for me," I suggested.

She shook her head. "Omogawa will suspect anyone from this Habitat. No, keep looking, and I'll discuss the matter with Sam Akane and see if he can recommend someone to handle the less public aspects of this."

That rattled me, though I kept my surprise off my face. Old man Akane isn't exactly the ruler of the Habitats but he isn't exactly not that, if you get my meaning. He lives in a penthouse suite in Habitat 2 and sends out little suggestions every so often, and you jump to it and follow them if you know what's good for you. I'd seen him once before, a lean stooped man with a face like a tired scholar's and eyes that miss absolutely nothing. If my boss was bringing him into this business, there was more at stake than I'd guessed.

Ruth was silent for a little while. I waited. Then: "You're free for lunch?"

"Today? Sure."

"Good. I've met the most interesting madman. He'll be staying here for a few months. I've asked him to lunch at Kamiguchi-ya. I want your impressions of him."

Of course I agreed, partly because that's my job and partly because lunch at Kamiguchi-ya is worth having, especially on someone else's nickel. We settled the details. When I got up to go, she said, "Omogawa gave you money, I suppose."

"Of course."

"Do you need money?"

I grinned. "You know better than that."

She gave me a little precise smile in response, and I bowed and left the room. I knew exactly what she'd meant by asking, and she knew I knew. If I got in trouble and needed money, I knew I could go to her, though there would be a price. If I turned to anyone else there'd be a price, too, and part of it would be that my body would drift ashore somewhere in the northern part of Shoreside. I don't mind that. I'd do the same thing if our places were switched.

That wasn't what I was thinking about as I gave another big bright smile to Louise Yoshimitsu and went out of the waiting room into the corridor. I was thinking about the interesting madman. The Habitats don't get a lot of visitors these days but every so often one shows up, sometimes from New Washington and sometimes from somewhere else inland and now and again from overseas. If my boss wanted me to check this visitor out, it wasn't a casual visit, that was certain—and that meant I needed to pay a visit to Mom in her worship hall.

It occurs to me that if this story is going to make any kind of sense to anybody, I'm going to have to explain about the worship hall, and that means I'm going to have to explain about Mom. She was born in Japan and was one of the lucky ones in 2062, which means she spent a few years in a refugee camp outside of Vladivostok and still knows a lot of Russian swear words, though she won't use them any more unless you catch her off guard. She came to this country in 2068 and settled in Habitat 4 two years later. She was a bar girl back then, not doing sex work on any kind of regular basis but available sometimes to the right guy, which is how I happened. But about the time she got a little too old and plump to rake in the tips, she got religion.

The way she tells it, Ame no Kokoro, the heart of heaven, spoke to her in a dream and told her to purify herself, which she did the old-fashioned way by fasting and pouring twenty buckets of cold sea water over herself first thing every morning. That got her pure enough that Ame no Kokoro talked to her again and told her what she had to do to get her religion going, and then a bunch of other kami—gods, spirits, there isn't really a good English word for them—came to talk to her too. That's her version of the story and it's also the one that Ms. Otome likes to tell. I was three years old when it all started, so don't ask me.

So Mom has her own religion, but she's not the only member. Ms. Otome joined about a week after Mom got her big message from Ame no Kokoro. She was Mom's first disciple, and for a while there Daishizen no Michi, the Way of Great Nature—that's what her religion is called—was her and Mom and half a dozen other women from the bars where Mom used to work. These days there are maybe five thousand members and there are halls in three of the five Habitats, and there's also a branch hall in Shoreside, where Ms. Otome goes twice a week to conduct services. The hall in Habitat 4 is just off Stairway 11 on Nikai, the second of the steel platforms that got put in place before the original builders went broke; in case you're counting, the platforms are forty-eight feet apart, which is why you get four or five floors between them. I go to the hall when I can, partly because Mom's there pretty much all the time and partly because in my line of work I can use all the help I can get.

Mom's worship hall isn't a Shinto shrine but it looks a little like one. It's got a steel porch sticking about eight feet out from the west side of Nikai with nothing below it but ocean three hundred feet down, and there are two big bright red torii gates on the porch, one just this side of the railing and the other right up against the outer wall of the worship hall. There are doors in the wall just inside the inner torii, but those are for kami, not for human beings.

The doors for human beings are inside, off a little side corridor that juts away from the Nikai landing on Stair 11. There's a shoe rack, a temizu fountain so you can rinse your hands and mouth before you go in, and an anteroom inside with rice straw mats on the floor and double doors letting into the worship hall. I left my shoes in the shoe rack, used the temizu, went to the door of the worship hall and did the usual routine, bow twice, clap twice, bow once more, to let the kami know I was there and I appreciated that they were there too.

Then I went back into the anteroom and settled down on the tatami mats on the floor to wait. I knew I wouldn't have to wait for long. I roll my eyes sometimes at Mom's religion but she always knows when I'm going to visit the hall, even when I just happened to wake up early that morning and decided to drop by.

That day was no exception. I don't think a whole minute passed before I heard her tabi socks whispering on the narrow stairs that come down from the office above the anteroom. I got up and smiled at her as she came down the stair. Like I said, she used to be a bar girl, one of those willowy numbers that flutter their eyebrows and make your heart go pitty-pat so you buy an extra beer or two. These days she's not exactly willowy. Her face is round and so is the rest of her, her hair is graying and she keeps it shoulder length in a practical cut, and she wears ordinary blouses and slacks with a hapi coat like Ms. Otome's over the top—all the priestesses in her religion dress like that, which makes traditionalists like my boss mutter to themselves.

At any rate, I said good morning and bent down so she could hug me and kiss me on the cheek, and let her usher me up the stairs to the cramped little office with the bookshelves and filing cabinets so we could talk. Either she'd heard from Ms. Otome already or Ame no Kokoro had been snooping on me, because Mom already knew about the business at the ferry dock the night before, right down to the small details. She gave me a doleful look and told me, the way she always does, that I really should find some other way to make a living and settle down and get married, and I smiled and didn't say anything, the way I always do. Then I asked about her work and she talked about the ceremonies she'd done the day before and the new members who'd joined her religion and her big project, writing her Ofudesaki—"holy scriptures" is about as close as you'll get in English. She was getting them dictated to her by Ame no Kokoro and some other kami, a few verses at a time, and she had to purify herself and get into the right kind of trance so she could hear them, and that involved various complexities involving incense and offerings and prayers counted off on a nenju.

All that led to the main reason for my visit, and I didn't have to say a word about it. I never do. As soon as we'd run out of other things to talk about she got out the tall cup with the slips of bamboo in it that she uses for divination, and closed her eyes and murmured a prayer in Japanese so old I can't begin to follow it, and shook the cup three times. I don't know how she does it, but on the third time without fail one of the slips of bamboo jumps out of the cup. I caught it before it could hit the table between us, and gave it to her when she opened her eyes.

If you go to a Shinto shrine and ask for a divination, they'll do the same thing, look at the bamboo slip, and then give you a piece of paper from a drawer that tells you something vague. That's not how Mom does it. Mom holds the bamboo slip in both hands and closes her eyes, and it begins to twitch back and forth in her hands, and then without opening her eyes she tells you what it means. So she did that, and said, "Junichi, Junichi, be careful, be careful. Three people are coming toward you and all three of them have something in their hands. One brings knowledge and one brings love and one brings death, and you won't know which is which. Trust the one that trusts you. That's what I can see." She opened her eyes. "Be careful."

Kamiguchi-ya is a little above Yokai, the fourth of the original steel decks, over on the north side of the Habitat. It's got a whole row of windows looking out past three more Habitats into blue distance, with a line of half-demolished skyscrapers along one part of the horizon to add to the spectacle, and it's also got the best Japanese food in Habitat 4, so I don't have to tell you how busy it gets toward lunchtime. I got there about five minutes to noon and waited in the corridor outside. Lots of well-dressed people went past me into the restaurant, and the ones who knew who I was pretended not to notice me: no surprises there. A bar girl's son who makes his living with a gun in his pocket and a good eye for details is welcome down on Ikkai and Nikai but Yokai is supposed to be out of his range. I sometimes think my boss hires people like me because she wants to annoy the Yokai set. That day I certainly seemed to be doing the job.

Right on the stroke of noon my boss came down the corridor alongside two other people. One was Susan Ono, one of Ms. Taira's assistants, a stocky, hard-faced middle-aged woman in an uncompromising black suit, and it wasn't hard to tell that the other one was the interesting madman. He was gaijin, light-skinned and white-haired with big bushy eyebrows. He was stocky and not too tall, dressed in a tweed jacket with leather elbow patches, black wool slacks, a white shirt and a tie a little too bright to be tasteful. He walked with a slight limp, leaning on a walking stick of tough black wood with little stumps of branches all over it. I coveted the stick at first glance. Hit someone with that and they'd feel it for certain.

Susan handled the introductions. "Jerry, this is Dr. Michael Huddon from the National University. Dr. Huddon, Jerry Shimizu."

We shook hands and said the polite things and all the while I was sizing him up. The federal government isn't allowed to have intelligence agencies, on account of the trouble those caused under the old constitution, but of course that just means it doesn't have any *official* intelligence agencies. Since before I was born, the rumor mill's been claiming that some departments of National University fill the gap. Looking at Huddon, I decided the rumor mill might be worth listening to. He had the look you expect from a professor, a little distracted, a little clueless, and more than a little nuts, but just under that was a layer of something that felt hard and polished like a well-made gun. The hand that shook mine had the kind of muscles you mostly feel in people who know how to fight.

The moment passed and we filed into Kamiguchi-ya. Because Ms. Taira was in the party, we got the owner as well as the maitre d' buzzing around like demented bees, making sure that everything was more perfect than perfect. Finally the four of us got seated in a little private room right up against the windows, with chairs and a waist-high table—you can't expect gaijin to sit on the floor, after all. These days, you can't expect the younger generation of nanmin to sit on the floor either. That annoys me, which is how I can tell I'm getting old.

A waitress came and poured tea and took our orders—they don't hand out menus there, it's the kind of place where if you ask for it they can make it for you. I ordered chicken and vegetable tempura, which is one of the Kamiguchi-ya specialties. Mostly I sipped tea and listened to Susan and Ms. Taira make conversation with Huddon, and watched him handle hashi—that's "chopsticks" to gaijin. He knew how to use them as well as anyone at the table, which made me adjust my first opinion about him. That's not something that a lot of gaijin know how to do, not these days.

I was maybe halfway through the tempura when I ended up being brought into the talk. "You should ask Mr. Shimizu about your interest," Ms. Taira said in a lull in the conversation. "He knows more about the subject than most of us."

I turned to face Huddon and put on a smile.

"It's a little thing, really," the professor said. "One of my professional interests is new religious movements, and a friend who has contacts in Habitat 2 mentioned one of those, a religion called Daishizen no Michi." He pronounced the words flawlessly, with a trace of a Tokyo accent. "I'd be very interested to learn a little more about it."

I kept the smile just the way it was. "If you'd like to meet the founder, Dr. Huddon, I can arrange that. She's my mother."

He took that in, and beamed. "Good heavens. Thank you, and I'd be delighted if she could find the time to see me. Are you a member of her congregation?"

"I pray there when I pray anywhere," I told him, and he seemed satisfied with that.

The conversation went somewhere else. I watched Huddon and wondered what his game was. Maybe I was wrong and he was just another crazy gaijin, and maybe I was right and he was something a lot more dangerous. Either way, I knew Mom could take care of herself. She made a point of looking vague and smiling and mystical, but I knew just how much of that was a pose she'd cultivated to hide the toughness she'd learned in the back streets of Vladivostok and the narrow alleys of Ikkai. She'd be fine.

No, the question that was on my mind as I watched him was why my boss was interested in him. If he was visiting the Habitat on intelligence business, it was a safe bet that she either knew it or guessed it—the rumor mill has it that the Habitats have agents in New Washington keeping track of what the federal government's up to, and I'd bet good money that it's true. If Huddon had something else in mind, she probably knew or guessed that too, but that raised questions I couldn't begin to answer. What she'd want me to do about him, other than pass on my first impressions after lunch, was another question I couldn't answer either.

The meal wound down. We sipped tea, cleaned our hands with wet steaming towels the waitress brought us, and got up from the table. Susan Ono turned to Huddon and offered to make some kind of arrangement for him, I forget what. Off they went, leaving me and my boss in the room alone. That's just about as safe as being alone with one of those tigers they've spotted in the woods lately—the story is that someone got careless at a zoo, back when there were zoos—but I'm used to it.

"Your impressions," said the tiger.

"He doesn't need the cane to walk with," I told her. "I'm pretty sure he knows how to hit people with it. He's got a fighter's muscles. If the rumors are true about National University—"

"They are," she said.

I processed that. "Then the feds think something's going on they don't like—" I shrugged. "And if there is, he's going to be serious trouble. What do you want me to do?"

"For now, nothing," Ms. Taira said. "The other project has priority. But keep your eyes and ears open, and find out what you can about his activities. If anything comes to your attention, tell me at once."

I considered her. "Is there anything I should know about?"

She glanced up at me. She knew exactly what I was asking, of course. "No." With a little precise smile: "The government welcomed us here. They didn't have to. That entails a certain obligation, and I've acted accordingly more than once. So his presence here—" The smile faltered. "Disturbs me. That's all."

I mouthed the usual polite words and got the hell out of there.

CHAPTER 2

NOT THAT MANY MINUTES later I was down on Sankai, weaving my way through the narrow decorous streets with their little corner restaurants and their business offices with signs hanging above the doors. Habitat 4 pays its bills a bunch of different ways, all the Habitats do, but we've got a lot of little specialty import-export houses, the way Habitat 5 has banks and Habitat 1 has arms dealers. You want big cargoes of big-ticket items, you're better off going to one of the other Habitats, but if you're after something more exotic in small batches, pine tar from the new plantations in southern Greenland or religious goods from the big chunk of Tibet that India controls these days or salvaged electronics from the few corners of the world that have those and are willing to sell them, this is the place to get it.

I wasn't in the market for any of those. I wanted to know more about Michael Huddon, and I knew one way to do it without leaving a paper trail that the wrong people might be able to find. I knew perfectly well why my boss had invited me to lunch. You know how stage magicians do their tricks, waving a wand around in one hand to distract the audience while they do something else with the other hand? I was the hand with the wand. The other guys who do the same kind of work I do for Mrs. Taira—they were the other hand, the hand that might pick Huddon's pockets or stop him from going somewhere he shouldn't go or, if it came to that, stick a knife in him and chuck him into the ocean with a big lump of concrete chained to his ankles so that nobody ever found out.

I'd been the hand with the wand more than once before, and the other hand, too, much more often. This time I wasn't satisfied with being a distraction. That's why I crossed Sankai to Stair 6 and went up a couple of floors and down the kind of dim corridor that looks like nobody's gone through it in years. There was a door at the very end. I knocked and waited.

Four minutes passed—I checked—before I heard the lock rattle open and the hinges creak. Fritz peeked out the way he always does, then gave me his little uneven smile and let me in. Fritz is gaijin; he has thin arms and thin legs and a thin chest, a big round belly and a big round head, bald except for a flyaway fringe of white hair all the way around and a pair of the bushiest eyebrows I've ever seen on a human being. He always wears an old-fashioned dressing gown, dark blue, over shirt and baggy slacks and a clumsily knotted tie. He scuffs along in shapeless leather slippers that look like they were worn by all his paternal ancestors in an unbroken line back to 1586. He's far and away the smartest guy I've ever met, but I'm not sure he could tie his own shoes if he wore shoes that tied.

He lives in his own little world on the east side of Sankai, surrounded by big steel filing cabinets and shelves stacked with more books than I've ever seen in any other place. The entire population of Habitat 4 can be divided into two categories. There are a couple of dozen of us who know what Fritz can do and make sure he's safe and happy and can pay his bills and then some, and there's the other forty thousand people who live here and have never heard of him. No, we're in no hurry to enlighten them.

That's the man who let me into his warren of little rooms lined with books, mumbling something friendly. He led me back to what he calls his sitting room, which looks like all the others but it's got three overstuffed chairs and a little pentagonal table, which has just enough room for the two things he always has there, a metal box in which he keeps cookies and an antique alcohol lamp that he uses to boil water for tea. He's got a room a little further back with a bed and a little makeshift kitchen. Technically speaking, that end of Sankai is supposed to be offices and not residences, and nobody who isn't filthy rich is supposed to get that much space for themselves anyway, but nobody disturbs Fritz's little kingdom, because he never bothers anybody, and he keeps his rooms so clean you could eat off the floors, and people like me who value what he can do would make serious trouble for anyone who messed with him.

He waved me to a chair, got a kettle on the lamp, settled down in his own chair, aimed the uneven smile at me, and said in his high thin scratchy voice: "Something interesting?"

"Something a little different. A guy just came here from New Washington. He calls himself Michael Huddon and the official line is that he's a professor at National U, interested in new religious movements. He's important enough that my boss had lunch with him. Nobody's saying why he's here, and all I know is that he wants to meet Mom and talk about her religion."

Fritz didn't move so much as an eyelash until I'd been silent for a good five seconds. "What does he look like?"

I told him. He was dead still for another five seconds or so, and then nodded once. That's the way Fritz does things. I think he has to decide to take each individual breath. Another five seconds, and he hauled himself awkwardly to his feet. "Help yourself to tea and cookies," he said. "This will take a little while."

He shuffled out of the room without another word. I knew the drill, and got up to look at what was on his bookshelves while the water finished coming to a boil. Most of what Fritz has on the shelves in his sitting room are old science fiction novels, but he puts the books he's reading on a particular shelf there, and one of the ways I try to make sense of him is to look over what he's got out and guess what he's doing. I don't usually get far, and this time was no exception. There was a row of fat books written by some guy named Hegel, with iridescent green bookmarks in every one of them. Fritz always puts one of those in books he hates. He's got a whole stack of the bookmarks somewhere. He never gets rid of a book even if he hates it, so the green bookmarks are his equivalent of throwing a book across the room.

Above the books by Hegel was a whole row of twentieth-century novels, none of which I'd heard of, and right next to those was a bunch of books on comparative mythology, which I don't know from a hole in the wall. Up above those were some recent books on the history of technology—I could tell that they're recent at a glance because they've got cheap cloth bindings on them, even if I hadn't already heard Fritz talk about Boorman's *The Rise and Fall of the Space Age* and some of the other books there. History of technology is one of the things Fritz likes to read about, and it's one of the things I ask him about a lot. It's saved my life more than once. These days we've got more history than technology, but the tech is still there, and if you ignore it you can end up dead very fast.

By then the tea kettle had started making the hollow rattling noise it makes when it boils. I fished out two cups and two little plates from behind a row of squat science fiction paperbacks with garish covers, found Fritz's stash of tea bags, made myself some tea, and extracted three ginger snaps from his box. No, I didn't get any for him—you don't do that, he's very fussy about those things. I sat back and put the time into going through everything I knew so far about Huddon, which wasn't much, and then everything I knew so far about the other thing I was keeping track of for my boss, the armed robberies of Big Goro's couriers.

I finished two of the ginger snaps and half the tea before Fritz came back with a stack of papers. "Well, well, well," he said. "Interesting indeed." He set the papers down on the little table, fixed himself some tea, got four carefully chosen cookies on a plate, and settled into his chair. I waited while he did that, because that's how you handle Fritz.

"Dr. Michael Huddon," he said then, picking up the papers in one hand. "Professor of history at National University since '79. Born and raised in a Boston suburb that's underwater now. Went into the Army. Was in the last class at West Point before the academy moved to Sandusky. Saw action in California and Ireland. Purple Heart and Bronze Star in the Irish campaign. Retired from the Army in '72. Went to Purdue for his degrees. Got his Ph.D. there the year before what was left of it got consolidated into NU." He laughed, a sudden gurgling noise that sounded like he was having a fit. "Must be a habit with him, being in the last class somewhere. That's the official record."

I waited a moment and then said, "Unofficially?"

"Government intelligence. Twice now he's gone somewhere to do research. That was the claim, at least. After he was there for a while, federal police were all over the place, hustling people into planes and taking off for New Washington. One time it was an EU spy ring, a big one, with connections to an undersecretary of the Navy. The other was a network of salvage smugglers with ties to the Congolese. Oh, and people keep turning up dead when he does his research. A very dangerous man."

He sipped tea and so did I. "Any idea why he's here?" I asked.

"Not yet."

I smothered a grin. Those two words meant that Fritz was interested, and once he gets his teeth into something he doesn't let go. "What does he usually look into?"

"Hard to say." He examined one of his cookies, dipped it in his tea, bit off half of it. "His academic background is in history of technology, with a focus on computers."

"He didn't breathe a word about those."

After the usual interval, Fritz nodded. "Of course not. Will you be able to observe him?"

"Now and then. I've got other jobs that have to come first."

That earned me another of his gurgling laughs. "Watch very, very carefully." Then: "Most of what he does will be camouflage, but not all. The question is just how good he is." He was silent for longer than usual. "Pay close attention to anything Huddon says about computers," he said then. "Let me know everything you find out as soon as you can. In the meantime I'll see what I can track down."

He closed his eyes then and took a long sip of his tea. With Fritz, that means the subject is closed, and I had to be content for the time being with the hints he'd passed on to me. I ate the last of the ginger snaps and hoped it would be enough.

HUDDON WAS STAYING IN a hotel up on Yokai. That's what I found out from Louise once I got back to my room and called the office to get the details. I called Mom next, to find out what times she had free, then called the hotel and left a message for Huddon with the desk clerk. Once that was over I pulled a book I'd borrowed from Fritz off one of my shelves and started reading. I'd only gotten a few pages into it when Huddon called back.

He was just as genial as he'd been at Kamiguchi-ya, and thanked me for going to the trouble. We settled on the next morning at nine, breakfast and then a visit to Mom, and finished up the call. Once the phone hit the receiver I was on my feet.

The fancy clothes I'd worn to the restaurant had already gone back where they belonged, and I'd put on something more to my taste—canvas pants with lots of pockets, a short-sleeved shirt that could take rough handling, shoes good for running and fighting, all of them in the drab brown shades I like. My Browning went into a pocket holster on the left side. The right pocket got a length of hardwood dowel that fits perfectly in my fist and sticks out half an inch on each end. It's called a yawara stick and it's a nice little thing to have in a fight: know what to do with it and you can break bones. I learned how to use it by the time I was ten.

A few minutes later I was on Ikkai, dodging foot traffic, and not many more got me down the elevator to the passenger dock. In daylight, the other three docks were visible in the middle distance, big masses of concrete riding next to the other three pillars, with floats just visible between the concrete and the water and all the usual tackle for loading and unloading cargo. Off between two of the pillars I could see a couple of tall ships at anchor and a couple of lighters ferrying cargo in. That's a good part of how all the Habitats pay their bills. You can't get a ship close to the shore these days, not with a mile or two of drowned buildings between deep water and the beach, but the Habitats are way out past where the seashore used to be. I don't think the rich people who built them had any notion that their homes above the sea would end up being turned into seaports. Their loss was our gain.

I killed time for ten minutes or so before the ferry came by, picked me up, and started plodding across the water to Habitat 5 and then to Shoreside. With the sun high up in the west, I could see Shoreside spread out in front of me, from the big hill just south of town along the whole crescent to the sandspit on the northern end, where the cargo docks trickle away into empty beach and the travelers pull up their boats. It looked like what it was, a jumbled mess of temporary buildings marking the equally temporary border between the land and the rising sea.

Pretty soon Shoreside got close enough that the ferry had to stick to a narrow channel between concrete ruins, some of them poking up out of the water, others down below where they can rip the bottom out of a boat before you see them. More ruins, high and dry for the time being, sprawled further up the slope ahead of them. You could see past them to the beginning of farm country, smooth green rectangles of pasture, gold and green and brown rectangles of fields, rumpled green of woodlots and orchards and a farmhouse here and there. A road ran through all that and disappeared over the hills in the middle distance. I knew from maps that it kept going for hundreds of miles more or less due west, past half a dozen inland cities and a hell of a lot of farmland, but I'd never been that way, not even as far as the hills. I watched a big brown and gray armored truck with turrets on front and back, as it lurched into motion in the warehouse district a good distance north of me and started up the road, and knew the driver and the gunners would see places I'd never been.

I let thoughts like that waste some of my time while the ferry lumbered toward the shore, and then cleared my mind and brought up the day's business. The man who'd called himself Richard Dart had been the fourth outsider to show up and try to knock over a courier taking money from Shoreside to Habitat 5. Two of the others had gotten away with it, and the third had taken four bullets in the face because the guy he'd tried to jump was quicker at the draw than he was. The questions nobody could answer yet were where they came from, who was behind them, and who let them know who to go after and when. Every one of the holdups had been in the right place at the right time, and that meant somebody in Big Goro's organization was talking. What else they might be saying was another thing my boss wanted to know.

That was on my mind as I dodged the other passengers, stepped onto the dock, and walked down its length into the middle of Shoreside. It was an ordinary afternoon, meaning that the streets were getting crowded but they weren't yet to the point that you had to use your elbows to get anywhere. Voices tumbled over each other like broken shells when a wave hits them, and the familiar Shoreside smell, brewed up out of equal parts unwashed bodies, cheap booze, tobacco, weed, filth, dead fish, rotting seaweed, and sea water, slapped my nostrils silly and then settled into the background. Shoreside streets, by the way, are boardwalks laid over a layer of sand hauled up from the beach. They're good steady footing, and it's easy to move them out of the way when it's time to tie ropes to the buildings and haul them further inland.

So I dove into the crowd like a seal slipping off a ruin into salt water, and played dodge and weave for half a dozen blocks south of the ferry dock. On the way I spotted some of the regulars. There's a pickpocket named Yanni who spends most of his time waiting near the dock, propping up a wall with his back, except when he's relieving somebody of a wallet with excess weight in it. There's an old lady named Chloe who sits in a little nook where two buildings don't quite join, telling fortunes with a deck of cards older than she is, so she can make enough money for that night's bender. There are others, too, but those are the two I passed that afternoon, and I nodded to them and they nodded to me because I pay them to keep an eye on certain things for me and it's money well spent.

I went on past a gambling joint with bright red paint on the side facing the street, where the dice are so crooked I swear they've got seven sides each and all the card decks have just as many aces as the house wants them to have. On the far side of that was a big door with the word RICK'S on a sign over it. I opened it. The bouncer who was waiting just inside the door was another regular I pay from time to time. He goes by Leo, he's a foot taller than I am and not quite twice as wide across the shoulders, he's got brown skin and bleached-blond hair, and he always wears a sleeveless black leather vest and black leather pants and boots up to his knees. I grinned up at him, he glanced down at me, he stepped out of my way, and I went on past him into Rick's Café Américain.

Yeah, I've seen the movie. More to the point, so has Rick Blaine. Rick's a black guy a little shorter and more than a little rounder than me, who grew up in the city the ferry goes over on its way from the Habitats to Shoreside. His family's been in the restaurant trade for don't ask me how long, and he adores antique movies, so of course he named his restaurant after the one in *Casablanca*. It looks like the one in the movie, too, or as close to that as you're going to get when the whole establishment has to be dragged further up the beach every few years.

Like everything else in Shoreside, it's got sand for a floor, but the walls are covered in white plaster, round arches top the doorways, and Rick was able to scrape up a few bits of Middle Eastern decor to put on the walls here and there. Rick even found a pianist named Sam, though it's short for Samantha Nakaichi. She's a nanmin in her forties who stands about five foot nothing and would probably be living on Sankai or Yokai except she likes old jazz, cheap whiskey, and gaijin girlfriends. She was at the piano when I came through the door, hammering out something hard and syncopated and sharp-edged over the top of the clatter and chatter of Rick's hitting its stride.

I wove through the crowd to the bar, looking at nothing and listening to everything, and kept doing that while a cute little bar girl I didn't know fixed me a Manhattan. There's never a usual crowd at Rick's, you literally never know who's going to turn up there, but it was as close to that as the place ever got. A dozen or so sailors on shore leave leaned against the bar, downed rum drinks, and chatted up the working girls or guys, depending on which way they swung. Four beefy men who looked like truckers sat at a table well away from the bar and did pretty much the same thing. Two people from the customs office a block away washed down a late lunch with a couple glasses of gin, a trio of Big Goro's boys did the same thing with plenty of beer, and some gamblers from the Habitats sat at another table and got themselves fueled up for another night of trying not to lose more money than they could afford.

Meanwhile Rick Blaine was going from table to table the way he usually did, chatting with people, making sure everyone was happy. He had a jacket on, but that was his only concession to formality. His shirt was open halfway down his chest, his pants were baggy brown canvas, and he wore sandals instead of shoes. He circled past the bar and said hi, and we chatted a little about nothing at all before he headed off again.

The doors on the beach side of the main room were open, the way they usually were in good weather. Rick's people had hauled tables and chairs out for those who wanted to smoke something or just mix some sunlight and salt spray with their drinks. There weren't many people in either category just then and all of them were locals I recognized. So I stood by the bar for a while and sipped my drink until I'd heard all I wanted to hear about the ships anchored off by the Habitats, and I drifted past the gamblers in case they dropped a word or two that mattered to me. They didn't, so I sat down with my face to the door and my back to the truckers, sipped more of my Manhattan, and listened until I knew more than I would ever need to know about road conditions between Shoreside and the inland cities.

I didn't bother trying to eavesdrop on Big Goro's boys, they know me and wouldn't have fallen for any of the tricks I wanted to use that afternoon. I didn't bother trying with the customs clerks, either, because my boss bribes them good and proper, and if they hid anything important from her she'd have one of her people put a few awkward bits of evidence into the hands of the federal police and they'd be hauled away to New Washington so fast it would make your head spin. I didn't spend all that much time on any of the others, either. It was a routine thing, something I do because now and then it gets me a scrap of information I can't get any other way, and it didn't have anything to do with what happened next.

WHAT HAPPENED NEXT WAS that the door opened, and I didn't recognize the man who came through it. He was gaijin, a thin bald guy in his sixties with black-rimmed eyeglasses on his face, and he wore the kind of clothes you'd expect to see on a Shoreside gambler, a loud shirt with short sleeves so nobody has to worry about what he's got up them, pants with button-up pockets, and a gaudy vest that goes down past the waist and has plenty of pockets inside where the local crooks would have to put in a little extra work to get at them. It was the same kind of outfit the guy who'd called himself Richard Dart had worn. That set off one alarm bell, the fact that I didn't recognize him set off a second, and when he had to look around to figure out where the bar was, that set off a third. Everyone in Shoreside, and everyone who's been to Shoreside more than once, knows Rick's better than that.

So I stared at my drink and pretended not to watch the guy. He went over to the bar, bought a beer, took a long pull at it, and then he and the gamblers spotted each other. He looked away with a little smile, and they glared at him and went back to their conversation.

That intrigued me. Maybe there was something else going on, but my first guess was that he'd taken the gamblers for a chunk of money and they were sore about it. The man who'd called himself Richard Dart, even though he dressed like a gambler, hadn't so much as stuck a foot into any of the casinos. He'd had a job to do and he did it, or tried to. Maybe this new guy wasn't involved in the same scheme, but maybe he was, and if he took some time off to play cards or dice, my chances of finding out a lot more about the scheme might just go up fast.

I was thinking about that and trying not to grin when the door opened again, and Michael Huddon came through it.

He'd changed out of his tweed jacket and wool slacks into canvas pants and a baggy shirt, but he still had the knobby stick with him, and he still wore the same bland smile he'd had on at Kamiguchi-ya. I kept my reaction off my face, waited until his back was to me, and slipped out through the doors to the tables and chairs on the beach. I didn't like the idea of losing the guy I'd just spotted, but the last thing I wanted was to make Huddon think that my boss had people following him, especially when I knew she did. So I took my drink, made myself scarce, and found a table outside on the beach, over on the southern side of things, close to the building. It had a decent view of the bar, so I could still keep an eye on my man.

I could see Huddon, too. He got what looked like a whiskey drink, stood by the bar for a while, and then struck up a conversation with a woman I knew slightly, a late-shift bartender named Denise something who worked at one of the casinos further north. The way they met and talked looked casual, and I knew it might be casual, or it might not. They talked for a while, Denise got a drink, and then they started walking toward the doors to the beach.

I stifled one of Mom's Russian expletives, finished my drink, got up and left as quickly as I could without making it obvious that I was hurrying. Given where I was sitting, I headed south. There are only about a dozen places south of Rick's before the sand runs out and the big hill south of Shoreside tumbles down into a mess of fallen rocks and broken concrete and surf, but some of the places have tables on the sand the way Rick's does, so I had a pretty good chance of not being noticed.

I ducked through the first of those and then the second before I risked a glance back, and I was glad I'd waited. Huddon and Denise had gone down to one of the tables fairly close to the surf, away from anybody else, and the way they were sitting it was pretty clear that they were watching for eavesdroppers. It wasn't a casual conversation, then. I thought about going down to Casino Row to find out what I could about Denise, shelved the idea for the time being. I needed to know more about Huddon, no question, but Dart and the guy who dressed like him were up at the top of my to-do list just then.

South of the dock, if you want to get from the beach onto the street closest to the water—no, it doesn't have a name—and you don't want to duck through a bar and buy a drink on the way to keep the management happy, you go down to the far end, where there's a gap between the last building and the ragged cliff where the hill rises up, half plugged with some lumps of old concrete that probably meant or did something back in the day. That's the route I meant to take. I got to the gap and went around the end of the building, and found myself practically face to face with the woman I'd seen on the beach the night before.

She was wearing the same odd clothing she'd had on earlier, and her hair was still loose, framing the face I remembered. She stopped and jerked back in surprise, sucking in a sudden breath, when I came around the corner.

"Sorry," I said, and stepped back, but I caught myself before I went on past. In my business, you never ignore a witness who might have seen something you need to know about, and if she was a lookout for Dart—or for someone else—I needed to know that, too. I put on a smile. "Hey, do you mind if I ask you a question? You were down by the ferry dock last night when things happened, weren't you?"

She took that in, and I watched her. After a moment, she nodded.

"Would you mind telling me what you saw? It's important."

"Are you a detective?" she asked.

It wasn't the question I expected, but I improvised. "That's one of the things I do."

That got me a little shy smile. "Yes. I can tell you what I saw."

She glanced around, uncertain. By then I'd already taken her measure: new to Shoreside, not too sure of herself, and probably short on money. That offered an obvious angle. I gestured back the way I'd come. "Can I get you something to eat?"

The smile widened a little. "Please."

So we went back to the closest of the bars with tables on the sand, and I led her to a table well away from everyone else, waited until she sat down, and then took the seat across from her. One of the bar girls came over by the time my rump hit the chair, and I sent her for menus and made a little small talk with the woman until the menus got there. I knew the menu pretty well already, and ordered some sushi and a beer. The woman glanced at the menu, and ordered gaijin food, a hamburger and fries and a soft drink, with a nervous glance at me partway through in case I objected. I smiled at her, and the bar girl went off to get our food.

"All right," the woman said. "This is what I saw."

I'm not going to write down everything she said here, because there was so much of it: moment by moment, in more detail than you'd get from a stack of old video stills. I pulled a notebook and a pen out of one of my pockets and started jotting things down after the first couple of sentences, and I filled a lot of pages, too, some before the food came and some after. She wasn't just making things up, either. Everything I remembered from the business on the dock, from a few minutes before I noticed her standing there to the point when Big Goro and his boys took Richard Dart away, she described just as I remembered it, but she gave me a lot more, too. I've known people with photographic memories. She could have given any of them a run for their money.

With all that information, I was pretty much bound to get something useful, and I did. She didn't know Big Goro's name or who he was, but she saw him waiting with a bunch of his boys right by the foot of the dock before Dart made his move. That raised all kinds of questions. Some of them I could answer, some I couldn't, but my boss would want to know all of them. I copied down everything she said about Big Goro and his boys word for word.

She wound up about the time I finished my lunch, and I thanked her for being so observant and she smiled and blushed. "For the record," I said, "I should ask your name."

"Sophie. Sophie Ames. What's yours?"

I wrote her name down and said, "Jerry Shimizu." I looked for the bar girl, and she spotted me and came over; I got the bill and paid it with a good-sized tip, since it was business and my boss would cover it. Once she'd left again, I pulled out a twenty—more of my boss's money—and gave it to Sophie.

"Here's something for your trouble." That got me another smile. I stood up anyway. "Thanks for this. See you around sometime."

"I hope so," she said.

We said the usual and I headed back toward the place where I'd met her.

New in town, I thought, definitely, and probably from one of the cities further in from the coast, since her clothes weren't farm gear. I'd never seen anything like them on city people, either, but the newspaper talks about fashions coming and going in the inland cities now and then. You get people coming to Shoreside from inland fairly often, sometimes just to kick up their heels for a few days or weeks and then it's back home, sometimes to stay if home isn't somewhere they ever want to see again. I hoped she was planning on heading home sometime soon, because Shoreside can chew you up and spit you out if you aren't a lot more wary and a lot more street smart than she seemed to be. I'd already crossed out the notion that she might have been a lookout for Dart, or Big Goro for that matter. Nobody in their line of work would have told me the truth in that much detail, and nobody I've ever met could have gotten so many details straight if they were lying.

I went around the end of the row, and this time I didn't run into anybody worth noting, just the usual Shoreside street crowd. A Unie march was moving down the middle of it, twenty or so people heading down the middle of the street with scraps of blue cloth tied around their heads, chanting something or other about the planet. That's what the Unies always did, back when there were Unies. I wasn't sure in those days whether they were a new religion like Mom's, or a political party, or something else, but you could count on them marching down some street or other in Shoreside every couple of days, chanting about the planet. I never stopped to listen. Now—well, we'll get to that.

That afternoon I was even less interested than usual. I dodged the march and moved with the rest of the crowd, and filed away what I knew about Sophie Ames for future reference. What I needed right then was to figure out how to spot the man I'd seen in Rick's and still stay out of Huddon's way.

Sometimes you get lucky. I was still a good block away from the door to Rick's when Huddon came out of it and headed toward the ferry dock. By the time I got to Rick's he was out of sight in the crowd. I opened the door, grinned at Leo again, and went in. The thin balding man in gambler's clothes was gone, too, no surprises there, so I bought another drink, downed it, and then went back out to the street and headed for Casino Row.

That's north of the ferry dock on the beach side of the same street I was on. There are plenty of gambling joints in other parts of Shoreside, but Casino Row is where you find the serious gamblers and the games worth watching. That's because the five big houses on the row are honest. They take ten per cent of every payout and call it good, and their bouncers will beat the crap out of you if you used marked cards or gimmicked dice. Maybe the man I was looking for didn't know Shoreside well enough yet to figure that out. The gamblers who'd glared at him were Casino Row regulars, though, so I figured it was worth a try.

Once again, sometimes you get lucky. The man I wanted was in the second place I checked, a casino called The Pines. It's a big place. The walls are the ugliest yellow I've ever seen, with pines painted on them by somebody who apparently never saw a tree. There's a bar on one side, a counter where you trade your money for chips on the other, and thirty-some tables for dice and card players in between, with a couple of roulette wheels doing business down at the far end. Skylights overhead keep the bills down during the daytime, though the place has electric lamps that run late into the night. Over in the corner near the door is an old one-armed bandit salvaged from some casino that's probably full of seaweed and fish these days. It hasn't worked for years. I'd be willing to bet the old lady who owns The Pines sold the electronics in its belly a long time ago to one of the local salvage gangs, but she keeps the thing there for old times' sake.

My man was at one of the tables, playing poker. I wandered past the table, saw the stack of chips on his side of the table, then went to the bar and bought another drink and stood there with my face pointed at nothing in particular. There's an art to watching someone without letting anyone know you're looking that way. It got a workout that afternoon. If he was cheating, he was doing it without showing any sign I could see. Maybe he was just really good at poker. I watched the game finish up, and then he got up and went to the counter, where he cashed out and left The Pines.

I didn't follow him. I went to the table he'd just left, asked if they were up for a game, and when the other three guys said sure, I went to the counter to get my chips. We played for a while, I won one hand and lost two others, and then I put on my dumb smile and asked why they all looked so glum.

"That Samuels bastard," said one of them, a big burly guy with salt-and-pepper hair and a leather eyepatch over one eye. "Damn if I'm ever going to sit at a table with him again. I don't care what anybody says, he don't play fair." The other two guys called him a sore loser. I looked innocent, and it didn't take long before I had the information I wanted. The man I'd been trailing went by Rex Samuels, he'd been coming to Casino Row for a couple of months, and he always walked away with more money than anybody else he gambled with. Nobody knew where he lived, but that's nothing new. There are plenty of places to stay in Shoreside, some pretty decent and some where you get just enough floor to lay down on and a good chance of getting your throat cut while you sleep if you've got anything worth anything on you, and some of the empty houses back behind Shoreside will keep the rain off you if that's all you want.

All in all, he fit the same pattern as Richard Dart and the others I'd tracked, and that might mean I was a good couple of steps closer to whatever outfit was behind the robberies. That was worth the money I lost playing with those guys. I made sure to lose to them more often than I won, since that kept them in a talkative mood and got me more details about Samuels. I ran out of chips and they ran out of things they could tell me around the same time. I begged off another round, said my goodbyes and headed back out onto the street.

I figured it was coin-toss odds whether Samuels was at one of the other casinos or not. It didn't matter if he was cheating or just really good at poker, the bouncers would have broken a few of his bones and tossed him out the door minus his wallet if he let himself win too much too often. He wouldn't have lasted more than a few days unless he was careful. The question was whether he went to just one casino and then called it a day, or whether he risked going to more than one. Knowing the answer to that would tell me some things.

That sent me into each of the other casinos on the Row. By the time I'd done that I had my answer. He was nowhere on Casino Row, and that meant he was smart enough to take his winnings and walk away. I found myself liking Rex Samuels. In my line of work I have to cope with a lot of stupid people, and it was nice to run up against someone clever for a change, even if I ended up having to shoot him dead or hand him over to Big Goro's boys.

Once I was sure Samuels had left the Row, I headed further north, moving with the crowd past bars and brothels and the two best tattoo parlors on the entire Atlantic coast, which are right next to each other so nobody can miss the rivalry. Up that way you find a bunch of decent flophouses, and the man who called himself Richard Dart stayed in one of them, so I figured there was a chance Samuels might be there too. I didn't have a specific plan in mind, just watching the crowd and listening to the chatter and keeping an eye out for Samuels, and so it didn't take me long before I figured out that somebody was tailing me.

That's an occupational hazard in my business. Pretty often it's just somebody from one of the other Habitats who's in the same line of work as me, and who's been sent to try to figure out what my boss is up to. Pretty often, too, it's one of Big Goro's boys, because Big Goro doesn't like the fact that the bosses from the Habitats send their people to Shoreside all the time but he has a hard time getting his people into the Habitats for more than a visit now and then, and because he wants the Habitats to know who's boss on his side of the water's edge. Now and then, though, it's someone else, and that's when life gets interesting.

Life got interesting that afternoon. Once I was sure somebody was following me, I made opportunities now and again to watch reflections in windows and look out of the corners of my eyes, without doing anything to let my tail know that he'd been spotted. It didn't take too much of that before I knew the guy who was following me wasn't from the Habitats and wasn't one of Big Goro's people. He was a short muscular guy in his forties with light skin, a forgettable face, forgettable clothing, and black hair combed straight back from his forehead. He knew his business, too. He never got too close to me, never watched me too obviously, but no matter how I varied my pace, there he was, close enough to keep me in sight.

I kept going north, not too fast, and my tail followed me. Sooner or later he'd have to drop back, because you can only go about a mile past Casino Row before you get to the freight docks and the warehouse guards start giving you sideways looks if they don't know you. Not much further on, the buildings stop and you're on the sandspit where travelers pull their boats out of the water and set up their tents. Even in Shoreside, you won't find too many people who'll risk going out to the traveler camp. I'm an exception. I know them and they know me, I pay them for information and run interference for them now and then when they need help getting officials off their case, and they don't rob me or worse. I knew it might be worth my while to know whether the guy following me was an exception too.

If he was, he didn't show it. I kept going and the bars and brothels ended suddenly where the freight docks begin on one side, and warehouses with armed guards around them line the other. I walked on past like I had somewhere to go, and the guards gave me bored looks and didn't say anything. Then the last of the docks went past and I had ocean to my right, stretching out into the distance where the Habitats rose on their pillars and the tall ships swung at anchor. I turned to look out to sea, and sent a stray glance back along the street the way I'd come. There was nobody in sight. I expected that, but it was still nice to see someone being that professional.

I went the rest of the way out to the travelers' camp anyway. There were a dozen of their boats dragged up onto the beach and a dozen shabby tents huddled together around a driftwood fire, with faded ribbons fluttering in the sea wind from the tips of the tent poles. A bunch of children played some kind of game down by the water's edge, wearing exactly what they had on when they were born. Women in loose bright-colored skirts and blouses sat in front of the tents, passing around a little pottery pipe and plaiting rags together into rugs, and a big burly gray-bearded man in a leather vest and ragged knee-length pants looked up from a piece of wood he was shaping into an oar, grinned, set down the wood and the knife, and called out, "Jerry! Good to see you, man."

"Hi, Bear," I said. That's his nickname. You don't ever call travelers by their real names, it's not polite. "What's up?"

"Oh, lots of stuff. Cup of tea?"

I agreed and let myself be guided over to the fire, where the women said hi and one of them filled a cup for me from a battered metal teapot. I settled down on the sand, Bear sat near me, and the women got to work on their rugs again. One of them offered me the pipe, which I waved off, and she grinned and handed it past me to the next woman in the circle. Me, I sipped harsh black tea and mostly listened to the gossip.

Travelers know just about everything that goes on up and down the coast. They catch fish and salvage junk from the ruins and run things out to the tall ships and do a fair amount of smuggling and petty larceny, so whatever's happening, they see it. If they trust you they'll tell you a lot, but you have to let them do it at their own pace. Try to pump them and they'll clam up. So I took in all the news about who'd had a baby and what junk they'd found on offshore islands that used to be hills and where the fish were biting and what they'd brought ashore at night without benefit of paperwork from some of the ships anchored off the Habitats, and I told a few stories of my own, about the guy who called himself Richard Dart, the robbery I'd messed with, and the guy who'd tailed me north from Casino Row.

That got a reaction from Bear I hadn't expected. "Short guy with a lot of muscle, black hair back like this—" He gestured back over his head with one hand. "—and a face that don't show much?" I agreed, and he nodded and drank tea. "Guy like that came ashore two nights ago. We didn't bring him. He was on one of the Nigerian ships, not sure which one—"

"*Star of Lagos*," one of the women said. "Seagull saw him aboard."

"—and they rowed him ashore in a longboat sometime way past midnight, when the moon was down. 'Course some of our people saw them. Wonder what he's up to."

I wondered that, too, but I nodded and sipped tea and didn't say a thing.

Then one of the women, who goes by Otter, poured herself more tea, and said, "Any chance you know a guy name of Huddon? White hair, walks with a cane, likes fancy words?"

"Yeah," I said, and tried not to look as astonished as I felt. "I've seen him. He's staying in Habitat 4 for a few months. He's supposed to be a professor from National University." Their looks told me they had no idea what that meant. "How'd you hear about him?"

"Came right out here and said hi a couple of hours ago," Otter said. "Must have spent time with travelers somewhere, he was that polite. So we poured him some tea and talked for a while. A nice old guy. He had some stories from inland that were kind of fun to hear."

"I bet," I said. "Anything worth telling?"

She shrugged. "Got any idea what a 'Merlin Project' is about?"

"No clue," I admitted. "He talked about that?"

"Asked about it," said Bear. "Wanted to know if we'd heard of any stories about it. Something around this part of the country, he said. Didn't have much more to say about it, just that he collects stories about things like that."

The conversation went somewhere else after that, and finally I asked Bear if he needed anything, and he mentioned that a couple of families were hoping to pick up new sails for their boats and they'd be happy for some help with that. I gave him a couple of bills. They all thanked me, and I got up and said the usual and headed off. That's how you pay travelers. They've got their pride. Me, I had a piece of information that might be worth a little or a lot, depending. I headed back to the ferry dock by way of the beach, and nobody followed me.

Chapter 3

FRITZ LEANED FORWARD, AND his big bushy eyebrows moved way up on his forehead. "You're certain those were the words Huddon used."

I shrugged. "That's what the travelers said. I don't think they were making it up, but I can't vouch for more than that."

We were in his sitting room again. The lamp overhead splashed light across a couple of thousand books. The alcohol lamp had the kettle nearly hot enough to make rattling noises. It was evening heading toward night, though you couldn't tell that in Fritz's rooms, since he doesn't like windows and his rooms don't have any. He had a cheap notebook sprawled open across his knees, and the old fountain pen he always uses made little scratching noises across the paper, like the sounds a mouse makes when it's going somewhere in a hurry. The pen always has blue ink in it, and it's got to be the right shade of blue, too. Fritz has to have a lot of things just so. That's one of them.

"The Merlin Project," he said, sitting back in his chair. "You haven't heard about that, then." I shook my head, and he went on after the usual five seconds. "A scrap of Shoreside folklore. Maybe more than that, maybe not."

The kettle made its hollow rattle. I got up, poured hot water into one of the two cups on the little table, held out the kettle to Fritz. He took it and filled his cup, doing his usual thing with the tea bag the whole time—he moves it up and down on the little string, for reasons that I'm sure make perfect sense to him. I got my tea good and strong in a less complicated way and went back to my chair.

"Nineteen sixty-three," Fritz said. "Silver age of science fiction. Early in the Space Age, too, when people still thought there were other planets where humans could live." He laughed one of his gurgling laughs. "Space probes hadn't sent back the bad news yet. But that year a man named H. Beam Piper published a book titled *The Cosmic Computer*. I've got a copy, paperback, though it's brittle enough that it'll be sawdust in a few more years."

I nodded, sipped my tea, and wondered where all this was going.

"Not Piper's best novel, or his most popular. I doubt a dozen other people in the world still remember it. But here's the point that matters." He raised a finger, thin and crooked as an old branch. "The main plot engine is a supercomputer, big enough to handle strategy and logistics for an interplanetary war. Its name was Merlin. The characters spend the book looking for it. They finally find it."

I nodded again. You don't interrupt Fritz, but sometimes it takes an effort.

"Just a story, eh? But when I first came here you could find people in Shoreside who talked about a computer called Merlin. They didn't know about the novel. They'd never heard of Piper. They'd probably never read one word of any science fiction novel. But they thought that the old government had an installation somewhere not too far from here, back before Kikai happened. The installation had a supercomputer in it, or so they said. They always called it the same thing your traveler friends say Huddon did: the Merlin Project.

"Now." He drank some of his tea. "Maybe it's a coincidence. Maybe somebody heard somebody else talk about Piper's book and didn't realize it was fiction. Maybe a dozen other things happened. But plenty of computer professionals back in the day were obsessive science fiction fans, and people like that might have named a machine after a story like Piper's. I knew people like that in Newark before it drowned." His shrug pushed the memory aside. "The supercomputers were real. They still are. The federal government still has one of them in working order at Oak Ridge, though they won't talk about it. Two more got stripped for parts to keep that one functioning. The EU has at least one, maybe more—they used to have four, but word is they had to part three of them out to keep one running. There were others. How many? The records I have don't say, but governments in half a dozen countries sank an astounding amount of money into them. Do you know why?"

I tried to remember what I'd learned about supercomputers in school, shook my head.

"They thought they could save the world." He shook his head, and his mouth bent in a bleak hard smile. "The old government here thought the supercomputers could tell them how to get power back into the electrical grid, stop the seas from rising, end the droughts and the wildfires, shake the economy out of its coma, get on top of the insurgency out west, fix *everything*. Of course it didn't work." He finished his tea, refilled the cup with more hot water and did the thing with the bag again. "I knew a man who drank himself to death. Year after year his health got worse. Finally his liver started to fail and he went to see a doctor. The doctor said, 'It's too late now, if you'd come to me years ago I might have been able to do something.' The man begged for help and said, 'I'll do anything you ask. Absolutely anything.' So the doctor said, 'First you have to stop drinking,' and the man said, 'Anything but that.'" Fritz laughed again, and this time it was a low harsh sound, like metal foil being crumpled.

I waited until he'd stopped laughing. "Okay, let's say this Merlin Project's a real thing. Let's say it's one of the old supercomputers. Why does that matter now? Why would the feds send Huddon looking for it? If you're right, they've already got one."

He turned to look at me. "We don't know that it's the same as the one they've got. The rumors said that the Merlin Project had a supercomputer, but was that the whole project? No way to tell. It might be something else. Do you know who Merlin was?"

Most nanmin don't, though they can tell you right away who En no Gyoja was. Me, I heard some of the old stories when I was in the Army, and there's a story or two behind that, too. "King Arthur's wizard."

"Excellent. But he was more than that, much more. The offspring of a human maiden and a spirit, or maybe the Devil himself. Prophet, priest, and king, the prime mover behind the coming of Arthur. If the Merlin Project is real—" He held up one finger. "—and if the name wasn't just some fan of Piper's making a joke—" He held up another. "—and that's what Huddon is looking for—" A third finger joined the first two. "—it could be something very valuable. Or very dangerous. Or both. Most likely both."

He finished his tea again, poured more hot water into his cup, did the thing with the tea bag. I waited. "Huddon," he said then, "might be here to find it, or just to find out about it. He might be here to help someone else do either of those, or to stop someone from doing them. Whatever his intentions, he bears careful watching."

"I'll do what I can," I told him. "I'll be having breakfast with him tomorrow and then taking him to see Mom. He claims he's interested in her religion. I won't be able to keep track of him when he goes to Shoreside, though."

Fritz smiled. His teeth were yellow and jagged. "Not to worry. I can call in a few favors. This is interesting. Very, very interesting."

THE NEXT MORNING I woke up out of one of those confused dreams where everybody is two or three people at once and the scene keeps changing from a travelers' boat to a cheap Shoreside bar to the top of a volcano that's about to blow.

Nobody had any clothes on, but that happens pretty often in my dreams, so I didn't think much about it. I blinked at the vague gray light coming in through my one window, and wondered why the phrase "the Merlin Project" sounded more familiar than it should. It was in the dream, I recalled that much, but I wondered if there was more to it than that. Had I heard it somewhere before Otter mentioned it to me?

The sky over Shoreside didn't have any answers, so I hurried through my morning routine. Once I was fit for human company I climbed Stair 11 to Yokai, and got there a good half hour before I was supposed to meet Huddon. Yes, I intended to see what I could find out about him. Partly it's my job to snoop, and partly, after my conversation with Fritz the evening before, I was even more curious about the man. All three of the hotels up on Yokai have people on staff who work for my boss. That comes in handy when Mrs. Taira needs to know about a visitor from somewhere else, whether that means New Washington or points further afield.

The manager of the Akatsuki-ya, the hotel where Huddon was staying, is one of my boss's people. Her name is Audrey Miura; she's a thin, hard-faced item getting toward the far side of middle age, with a little silver in her hair and an artificial leg. She gave me a tight little smile when the girl behind the counter let me into her office. "Good morning," she said. "I thought I would see you soon, Shimizu-san."

"You weren't expecting Jason Fujita?"

The smile didn't waver. "No. He's a blunt instrument."

I didn't argue. She was right. "Then I don't have to tell you why I'm here."

She waved me to a chair. "No, of course not. You want to know all about Dr. Huddon. I can tell you what I know. I'm sorry to say it's not much."

So she told me, and she was right. It wasn't much. Huddon didn't talk freely or drink more than a glass or two at a time, and he didn't smoke anything or use any of the other drugs for sale on Habitat 4. He hadn't sampled any of the local sex workers, either, and it wasn't because the hotel had been lax about giving him opportunities. He took his tea English style, with milk and sugar, and spent the evening after dinner in his room. If he was in contact with anyone outside Habitat 4 the radio people hadn't detected any sign of it. He asked the questions you get from any casual visitor, showed zero interest in snooping around, and hadn't taken the bait when somebody dropped a casual hint about contraband. If he was what Fritz and my boss said he was, he knew his trade.

I thanked Miura for her help, and got one of her thin smiles in answer. Once out of the office, I went out the same service door I'd used coming in, went back an alley or two before circling around, and came sauntering up to the hotel's main entrance right at nine o'clock. The restaurant was just inside and through a couple of glass doors to the left. Huddon was sitting by himself at a round table over to one side, with a good view of the doors and an equally good view of the windows looking out on the street. He spotted me the moment I got within sight, no surprises there, and raised the butt end of his walking stick to catch my attention.

I wove around the tables and got to where he was sitting. "Dr. Huddon?"

He stood up and we shook hands. "Good morning," he said, and gestured to the seat across from his. I settled into it as he sat down. No, he didn't need the stick. "And I mean that. My one regret so far is that I didn't make time to come out here years ago."

I put on a smile. "I'm glad to hear that."

The waitress came over then. I ordered a fancier breakfast than I usually do, since it was on my boss's tab. Once the waitress was out of earshot again, I went on. "Would it be rude of me to ask what brought you out here?"

"Not at all. As a historian my interests cover quite a bit of ground. New religions like the one your mother founded, new community forms like the Habitats and Shoreside, new folklore traditions, stories, legends—any number of things like that. I take sabbaticals every so often and go to different parts of the country, poke around a little, see what I can turn up."

I said something about how interesting that must be, and he aimed a bland smile at me. "Oh, definitely. I meet all sorts of people. I imagine you do, too."

"Mrs. Taira must have told you a few things."

A shake of his head denied it. "Next to nothing. She called you her administrative assistant. I'd bet good money, though, that you don't do your work in anybody's office."

"You'd win that bet," I said.

His smile didn't waver. "Of course. I'd bet just as much money that you did your service in the Army. Am I right?"

"Yeah, I did two years over in England."

"Where were you stationed?"

"Outside of Carlisle with the Big Red One." If he was in the Army too, like Fritz said, he'd recognize the First Infantry Division's nickname. He nodded, and I went on: "Up close and personal with Uncle Pat's boys more than once. Any chance you were over there?"

That got me another of his smiles. "Yes, though Malinbois hadn't seized power yet when I served. I went to England with our expeditionary force straight out of West Point, and was in Bristol and then in Ireland for a while, mostly in the south."

"The invasion?"

He nodded. "I wasn't on the beaches but I saw combat later on. After that—" He motioned at the walking stick. "I'd always wanted a proper Irish shillelagh. I was lucky enough in addition to find someone who could teach me the proper way of using it."

"Martial arts interest you?"

"Now and then. It's certainly been helpful from time to time."

I took that in and fit a few more details into place. By the time I did my tour of duty, things had quieted down a lot between the US and the EU, but twenty years before that they'd tried to starve England into submission by blockading and mining the sea lanes. They didn't think the US or India would intervene. They were wrong on both counts, and that's why Ireland isn't in the EU any more. I went to Dublin a couple of times on leave when I was over there, and liked it, but Ireland isn't the kind of place you can let down your guard. You keep your mouth shut and your eyes open because it's neutral these days, and that means it's got more spies per square yard than just about any other place on the planet.

The waitress came back with our breakfasts, and that occupied us both for a while. He fixed his tea the English way, with lots of milk and sugar. I always drink one cup that way on the king's birthday every year, like a lot of soldiers who served over there, but I wash it down with gin to get the taste out of my mouth.

"I hope you didn't have any difficulty getting out here," I said.

"No, not at all. I flew in." I gave him a startled look, and he smiled that bland smile of his. "I don't get to do that very often, but I know some people and there was a flight scheduled out this way, so I talked my way on board. Fortunately you've still got an old helipad up top—is Gokai the right word?"

From the way he said it, he knew perfectly well it was the right word. "Yeah," I said. "You spent time in Japan."

The smile didn't waver. "Yes, I was in Tokyo from 2059 to 2061. When they transferred me to Canberra I thought it was wretched luck."

You hear stories like that all the time. That's no surprise, since most of the people whose luck went the other way aren't around to tell their side. I was more interested in the fact that he'd been sent to so many places while he was in the Army. "Welcome to Shinihon," I said. That's a local joke in the Habitats; it means "little Japan." I wanted to see if he would get it.

"Arigato," he said, thanking me. He had the Tokyo accent, all right.

We traded a few other useless comments like that. By the time our plates were getting empty I'd figured that he was going to keep it bland and safe the whole time, but then he finished a second cup of tea and said, "Oh, and while I'm thinking about it. There's an old story you hear in New Washington sometimes, that's supposed to have something to do with this part of the country. Stories are a good deal of what I research, of course, and this one interests me.Is there any chance you've heard about something called the Merlin Project?"

He was watching me closely when he said that, and I knew damn well that he must have seen at least a little of my reaction. I improvised. "Not before yesterday. In my line of work I spend a lot of time over in Shoreside and talk to a lot of people. I had a cup of tea with the travelers north of town yesterday afternoon, and they said somebody came up to talk to them and asked about that. Any chance it was you?"

Huddon laughed. It was a low, quiet laugh, not much more than air hissing out in bursts. "Yes, it was. So you talk to the travelers."

"And so do you," I said. His smile, bland and irritating, communicated nothing.

It wasn't much later that we crossed Yokai to Stair 11 and went down to the worship hall. The whole way Huddon asked me one question after another about the Habitat, all of them the sort of thing you'd expect from a slightly clueless visitor in a strange place for the first time. We got down to the Nikai landing and took the short corridor to the worship hall, and he glanced up at the sign over the door.

It's in grass writing, the prettiest and most illegible form of Japanese writing. I know plenty of nanmin who can't read it without taking their time and maybe getting some help from a book. Huddon took one look at it and said, "*Mushukujindo.* The Hall of Homeless Gods?" I nodded, and he went on. "Interesting. I'll have to ask your mother about that."

We shed our shoes and washed hands and mouth at the temizu and did the bowing and clapping thing at the door to the hall to say hi to the kami. I didn't have to prompt Huddon at all, but then I didn't expect to. By the time we'd finished Mom was on her way down the stairs. I spent the next few minutes introducing them while they bowed and said the usual. We all went upstairs to Mom's office, where he did without a chair in perfect comfort while Mom fixed tea for the three of us and the two of them talked theology. Mom doesn't get a chance to do that very often, and since she had an interested listener she really let go.

Pretty often when gaijin find out what the name of Mom's worship hall works out to, they get flustered, or put on the kind of squishy-faced look that tells you they're offended but don't dare admit it. It's really pretty straightforward, though. The kami got sorted out a long time ago into three categories. There are the Amatsu no kami, the kami of heaven, and the Kunitsu no kami, the kami of earth, and then there are the Yaoyorozu no kami, which basically means all the other kami who don't belong to the first two categories. The Amatsu no kami live in the High Plain of Heaven, which Mom thinks is the plane the planets orbit in, and they weren't inconvenienced at all in 2062. Most of the Kunitsu no kami were fine, too, but a lot of the minor ones had to leave Japan with the other refugees, and so did most of the Yaoyorozu no kami. There are shrines these days wherever nanmin settled afterwards, but those are mostly for the important kami. So the rest don't have shrines any more.

That's why Ame no Kokoro talked to Mom and got her to found her religion. The kami need us the same way we need them, or at least the less important ones do. So Mom and Mrs. Otome and the others started praying to the kami who don't have shrines any more, and made the usual offerings to them, and the kami's side of the deal is that they answer prayers. That happens often enough that Mom's sure they're happy with the arrangement. That's why the headquarters of her religion is called the Hall of Homeless Gods, and why it's set up like a Shinto shrine but isn't one. The other worship halls that Mom's disciples founded all look pretty much the same, though they've got different names.

So they talked theology and I sat there and sipped tea and listened to everything Huddon said and wondered what his real business was. He knew a lot about Shinto, more than any other gaijin I've ever met, more than most nanmin, maybe more than Mom. He was good at listening and good at asking questions that got her talking—I didn't have any trouble figuring out why the travelers liked him—but I didn't believe for a minute that he'd come from New Washington, by plane no less, just to listen to my mother talk about the little religion she founded.

If he was faking interest, though, he did a good job. They talked and talked, and about the time I was starting to wonder if I could figure out a way to extract myself and go do something else, Huddon suggested lunch for the three of us, his treat. We ended up at a quiet little ramen joint down on Ikkai with a nice painting of the ocean on one wall. While we ate, Huddon did a little more of the talking, but it was still about theology.

"I don't imagine you've heard about the Gnostics," he said. Mom shook her head, and he went on. "This was around two thousand years ago, mostly, though they never quite died out. But they believed that we, all of us, are homeless gods."

Mom gave him a surprised look, kept sipping tea. "How does that work?" I asked.

"The idea," said Huddon, "is that we aren't native to this world. I don't mean that we're extraterrestrials or anything like that. Our souls, our tama, came from another place, a world of light. A few of us still remember the world of light a little bit—those are the mystics and the visionaries—but most of us forgot about it a long time ago, somewhere back in all the incarnations we've lived, down through the ages of history. But that's why this world never really makes sense to us, why we all just have to get by as best we can, while we look for the clues that will show us the way back to the world of light."

"The kami wouldn't be happy if we abandoned them," Mom observed then.

Huddon nodded. "For all I know the Gnostics were just spinning daydreams. I thought the parallel was interesting."

She smiled the smile of hers that means "Yeah, whatever" in a very polite way, and we talked about something else after that. It wasn't too much later that we finished lunch. Huddon said some polite things and went his way. I walked Mom back to the worship hall, stopped at my room to pick up my gun and a few other useful things, and headed for the ferry.

I had a long list of things I wanted to do that day. I wanted to see if I could learn more about Rex Samuels and what he was up to. I wanted to see if I could spot the interesting man who'd tailed me the day before, and find out something about him. I wanted to see if Huddon showed up in Shoreside again, and if he did, who he talked to and what he did. All the way into Shoreside, too, I thought about the dream I couldn't quite remember and the sense that I might have heard of the Merlin Project before. So I had plenty on my mind, and it took me an effort to get my thoughts filed away and my eyes and ears wide open when the ferry finally pulled up to the dock and I could start the day's real work.

The streets were a little less crowded than usual for that time of the afternoon, which probably meant that there'd been lead flying on the streets not too long before. Sure enough, I heard some people talking about it not two minutes after I got off the ferry: someone shot at a bunch of Big Goro's boys in broad daylight, killed one, winged another, and got drilled full of holes as soon as Goro's people opened fire.

That had my nerves on edge, even though it wasn't exactly a surprise. You get to be boss of Shoreside by taking out the guy that holds the job before you, along with as many of his toughs as you have to. Goro got the job that way ten years back, and Al Sakamoto who was boss before him did the same thing three years earlier, and—well, I could go on. Sooner or later Goro was going to lose the job the same way, I knew that and so did everyone else, but it's bad for business and I knew there was always a risk that some of the flying lead might end up headed in random directions. Toward me, for example.

So I kept my eyes and ears wider than usual as I moved with the crowds. Chloe was still in her usual place where the buildings don't quite meet, and I wanted to talk to her, but she was telling someone's fortune just then and I left her alone for the moment. Yanni was another matter. He was in his usual place, too, holding up the wall, and all I had to do was slip a piece of paper with a couple of words on it into the back pocket of my trousers and walk past him. I didn't see or feel a thing, but the paper was gone long before I got to the other end of the block.

I kept walking, turned inland a block later, and went to the quiet little dive I'd named on the piece of paper, a nice dimly lit place full of nooks and corners where you can sit in back and sip a beer and not be noticed by anybody. That's what I did, too, until Yanni showed up. He's one of those long thin gangling guys who looks like he's got a daddy longlegs somewhere in his family tree, he's got scruffy black hair and a little mustache that you'd just about mistake for the shadow under his big nose, and he likes to wear a blank goofy look on his face so people underestimate him. There may be a better pickpocket in Shoreside but I've never met one, and Yanni's got a brain like a bear trap, too. He came in maybe ten minutes after I got there, bought a beer at the bar, strolled to the back of the place, saw me and said hi as though he had no idea I'd be there.

We sat and chatted a bit, partly just to catch up and partly to see if anybody else in the place was going to try to listen in. Nobody did, so we got down to business. "Three people I want you to keep an eye on," I said. "The first one's a gambler named Rex Samuels, the second's a guy from New Washington named Michael Huddon, and I don't know the third one's name but he tailed me yesterday." I described all three of them in as much detail as I could remember, which is a lot. "Let me know what they do and who they're with."

"No prob," said Yanni. "You want me to see what they've got in their pockets?"

I shook my head. "Don't risk it yet. Maybe not at all. Huddon's with the feds, and people end up dead way too often when he's around. The other two—" I shrugged. "No clue yet. I'll keep you posted."

Yanni nodded, and I went on. "One more thing. Ever heard about something called the Merlin Project?"

He gave me a blank look, and it wasn't the one he likes to fake. "Doesn't ring any bells. You want me to keep an ear out for it?"

"Yeah. Might be garbage, but might be worth something."

"On it," he said, and grinned. I peeled some bills from my wallet and handed them to him. It was my boss's money, of course, and I'd have to account for it like I did for the rest of what I spent on her nickel, but I knew she'd be good with it as long as I got her what she wanted. We said the usual stuff, and then I downed the last of my beer and left the dive.

Chloe was reading the cards for another customer when I went past her, so I ducked into Rick's for a drink and a look around. Sam was pounding away on the piano as usual, something slow and sentimental for a change, and she had a girlfriend sitting beside her on the bench half draped around her and more than half drunk. How she kept playing without missing a note, I have no idea. Rex Samuels wasn't there and neither was Michael Huddon, so I took just enough time with the drink to make sure I didn't look hurried, and headed back toward the front door.

I was almost there when it opened and Samuels came in. He was dressed in the same clothes he'd had on when I'd seen him the day before, not just the same kind of clothes but the identical garments, and they hadn't been slept in, either. Since I was pretty obviously leaving Rick's I kept walking, but I examined him as closely as I could without being too obvious about it. I was close enough that I can tell you for a fact that he showered and shaved that morning, and the soap he used didn't smell like any of the brands you get in Shoreside stores or out on the Habitats. He was carrying a pistol in a pocket holster, a short-barreled revolver, and something in another pocket I didn't recognize, a hard rectangle of something maybe six inches long and two across, light enough that it didn't drag the pocket down enough to matter.

I filed the details away for future reference and went out onto the street. Chloe's customer was getting up just then, and so I wove my way through the crowd and got to the nook between the two buildings before anybody else could ask for a reading. Chloe grinned up at me and gestured at the ground in front of her, and I grinned back at her and settled on the sand.

Chloe's a strange old creature. Back before all the other universities got folded up into National University, she used to be an important professor of something or other, but whatever it was had its funding cut in the last years under the old constitution and it didn't get her a place in New Washington or one of the trade schools once the new constitution was put in place. She told me once that she'd read cards for years when she was still a professor, and that kept her fed and housed and supplied with cheap booze once her job went away. I believe her, since Mom's more or less in the same business and she's always been able to pay her bills.

Chloe doesn't look anything like Mom, though. She's thin and wispy, with a big cloud of curly gray hair tumbling down onto her shoulders and little round glasses in cheap metal frames. She likes to wear long skirts and baggy blouses and a poncho of handwoven cloth thrown over everything, and she's just about the only person I know who goes around Shoreside without a gun or a knife or any kind of weapon at all. She says it's because the spirits protect her. Me, I think it's because half the toughs in town get readings from her every week and they'd make life messy and short for anyone who hurt her.

She knew I wasn't there for a reading, of course, but she's good at making sure most people never guess that half her money comes from selling information to people who'll pay for it. So she shuffled her cards in the usual way, grinning at me the whole time, and said the usual thing about crossing her palm with silver.

"I bet you'd be happier if I crossed it with some paper," I said. "With numbers on it."

"Depends on the numbers," she said. "What do you want to know about?"

I explained to her about Samuels, Huddon, and the guy who'd tailed me, and the whole time she laid out cards and pretended to look at them, and nodded as if she saw all the secrets of the world in the pictures on them. When I'd finished, she glanced up at me and said, "Well, I can tell you something about Huddon already. I did a reading for him yesterday."

That startled me. "Seriously?"

"Cross my heart. He showed up a little before ten yesterday morning, stood right over there while I finished a reading for Bobby Akira, then damn if he didn't sit down and pay for a reading himself. But he also asked some questions."

"I bet," I said. "About what?"

I knew how she was going to answer before she said a word. "Something called the Merlin Project. Said he was interested in stories about it. He collects stories, or that's what he told me."

"Did he say anything else about it?"

"Damn little." She laughed, a little harsh sound like something getting crumpled. "It was really funny. I was trying to pump him and he was trying to pump me, and we both knew it. Thing is, he didn't want to talk and I don't know a damn thing about any Merlin Project. I'm pretty sure I heard the name before but that's about it."

"You heard the name," I said. "Any idea where?"

She just grinned at me, and I took the hint, got some money out of my wallet and handed over a couple of bills. "If I heard it," she said then, "it was a long time ago, from somebody who was into the Year One thing. Long before your time, Jerry-boy. Save the world, you know? New technology, no technology, anything but what we had."

I nodded even though I didn't have the slightest idea what she was talking about. "Any of them still around?"

"The Year One people? Damn if I know. They stopped talking to me after a few of them paid for readings and I told them they were smoking their shorts. This wasn't that long after 2062, either, so we're talking ancient history."

I filed that away as a lead that probably wouldn't go anywhere. "Anything I should know about the reading you did for Huddon?"

She shook a finger at me. "Now, now, you know better than that. Secrets of the confessional and all that." Then, in a low voice: "He's in danger. The cards said that and so did his eyes. He's been there before, it's nothing new, but his nerves are on edge and he expects somebody to go after him, big time." She shrugged. "I hope he gets out of it okay. He was fun to talk to, and gave me a nice tip."

I took that hint, too, and gave her some more money. She grinned again and promised to keep an eye out for Samuels and Huddon and the guy who tailed me, and we made a little small talk before I unfolded my legs and started to get up. Before I got far she said in a low voice, "Other side of the street, by Maddie's doorway."

I gave her a little nod and acted as if I hadn't heard a thing. She gathered up her cards and put on a bland expression, and

I turned and walked away. Of course I made a chance to glance casually toward the doorway she'd named.

THE GUY WHO'D TAILED me the day before was standing there. Like I said, he was a professional. He'd put on a different style of forgettable clothes and he didn't look at me once, but once I started walking it didn't take long for me to be sure he was following me again. I considered the options and decided to try to turn the tables on him.

Shoreside's an easy place to do that if you know the place and the people. I strolled north until Casino Row was just a block further on, and went into a little storefront place called Ernie's that mostly sells salvage from the town that used to be where Shoreside is now. These days, what you find if you go into one of the old houses is junk, but that's because everything worth anything got cleaned out years ago and sold to Ernie Lobeck or one of his competitors.

Ernie himself is a little potbellied guy with eyes that bug out and short puffy hands that never stay still for long. We go way back. I used to make pocket money running errands for him, back when I was a kid sneaking out from Habitat 4 to Shoreside while I was supposed to be at school. He's a lot older and grayer now than he was then, but I drop in every week or two, and we have signals for when it's not a social visit.

I gave him one of the signals as I came through the door, and he beamed at me in the unnerving bug-eyed way he does and said nothing when I went to the back corner of the store, where somebody on the street can't see you. There's a door there, and if you go through it and hurry through the stockroom behind it and get into the little gap between Ernie's shop and the building behind it, you can duck out onto the street a block further up and get out of the way before anybody has the chance to go around the block and spot you.

That's what I did. A minute later, maybe, I was into the street, and a couple of minutes after that I'd doubled back to the street closest to the water and ducked into a nice shady gap between buildings with a good view of Ernie's. I stood there and waited. After a few minutes my tail walked past Ernie's and glanced inside oh so casually, went another half block or so, and then circled back around and went past it again the other way. I figured by then he knew I'd given him the slip, and he turned north again and started walking past Casino Row. That was when I ducked out of the gap and started following him.

The guy really knew his stuff. He stopped here and there, glanced around casually, went up to the next street at one point and then back down a block later, all the things you do when you know somebody might be watching you. The only advantage I had was that I know Shoreside like the back of my hand and it didn't take long for me to figure out that he didn't. Even so, I nearly lost him a couple of times, and I had to duck into a bar and risk losing him once when he doubled back on me.

With one thing and another, it took him about half an hour to get to where he was going. That was the Ocean, a place up past the tattoo parlors I mentioned earlier, not a flophouse but something pretty close to a genuine old-fashioned hotel. He walked past it, stopped at a bar a little further on that spilled into the street, bought a beer, stood there drinking it for a while and looking around casually. Then he ditched the bottle and went back to the front door of the Ocean as quickly as he could without seeming to hurry.

Once he was inside and had a few minutes to get past the lobby I walked past on the far side of the street, as though I'd been going that way for reasons of my own, and then went to the bar where he'd had the beer. There was a little round table on the street sitting empty when I got there, so I took it, sat facing the front door of the Ocean, and bought a beer and a bowl of edamame, hot steamed soybeans in the pod wrapped in a white cotton cloth, which you can get at every bar in Shoreside whether or not it's owned by nanmin.

Sitting there gave me plenty of chance to watch the door for a good long time and make sure my tail wasn't going to pop right back out of it. Once I was done with the beer and the edamame, I headed on over to the Ocean and went in. There wasn't much of a lobby inside, there never is in a Shoreside place, but the office door over to one side was open and when I looked in I spotted the face I hoped to see.

Roy Abeshima is someone else who grew up in the Habitats and ended up in Shoreside. We go back even further than me and Ernie—his kid brother was my best friend in elementary school, and when the kid brother got cancer and took a couple of years to die, Roy and I ended up running together a lot. He's tall and gangly, with black hair he keeps in a buzz cut and black horn-rimmed glasses and a grin that always goes up twice as far on one side as it does on the other. The moment he spotted me, that's what his face did, and he waved me in and closed the door behind me and said, "Jerry my man! How's things?"

So we caught up a bit. He surprised me a little by asking about some people we both used to know on Habitat 4—he didn't talk about old times much, and he never went back, on account of something that happened fifteen years ago that he won't talk about even when he's drunk. After that I got down to business. "There's a guy who's probably a guest of yours," I said. "Don't know his name, but it looks like he's involved in something my boss needs to know about." I described him, and by the time I got half a dozen words out Roy was nodding.

"Max Bernard," Roy said. "That's the name on his ID. Canadian, gave us a Toronto address, works in import-export. Checked in three days ago. Talked about cutting some deals with the firms on Habitat 4."

I gave him a quizzical look. "So why isn't he staying there?"

Roy grinned. "Yeah, I thought of that. He says it's cheaper here." He shrugged. "True, of course, but he's got people coming to see him who don't look like businessmen."

"Anybody I'd recognize?"

Roy shrugged again. "Good question. Nobody I know, that's for sure."

That was as much as he knew. We did a little more talking and then I headed back out onto the street.

Max Bernard, I thought, as I veered inland a block and headed south as quick as I could go without looking like I was in a hurry. Papers saying he's from Toronto, a story about import-export deals, but he came ashore from a Nigerian freighter three nights back. Smuggling, I thought. Maybe that, maybe something else. What mattered just then was that I needed to keep an eye on him but I also needed to chase down Rex Samuels and find out what he was up to. That probably meant bringing Jason Fujita in on it, and I didn't want to do that if I could avoid it. This wasn't a job for a blunt instrument.

I kept walking. My plan just then was to loop around the south end of Shoreside, get down on the beach, find a table in one of the bars and get something more substantial in me than edamame and a beer, and then sit for a while and see if I could find some way around talking to Fujita. I got to the end of the street, right up against the rubble at the foot of the hill, and started down toward the beach. That was when I realized my problem had a very simple solution, and she was sitting right there on a fallen concrete block.

Chapter 4

She was still wearing the same odd clothes of flimsy blue cloth I remembered from the other times we'd run into each other, though they looked a lot cleaner and less wrinkled than you'd expect if she was sleeping in them. To judge by the little paper dish sitting on the concrete next to her, she'd bought some food from a street vendor and taken it someplace where she could eat without being bothered by anybody. She turned my way hard and fast the moment one of my shoes crunched on the rubble, with the same wide-eyed look I remembered, too. Then her face lit up and she said, "Oh, hi, Jerry."

"Hi, Sophie. You're doing okay?"

She smiled up at me. "Oh, yes. How's the detecting going?"

My mind was already running at top speed, and that pushed it the rest of the way to its destination. "Funny you should ask that."

"Oh?"

"I need some help with a case and you might be the right person to give it. There'd be money in it for you."

That startled her. "What kind of help?"

"You've got good eyes and a good memory. I need someone who can spend a day sitting someplace and keep track of everyone who comes and goes through a door."

"I can do that," she said.

I nodded, considered her, and said, "Tomorrow work for you?" When she nodded: "Good. Let's say a hundred for the day's work, and—" I thought of a problem, figured out the solution. "It'd help if I bought you some Shoreside clothes. What you've got on is fine but people will notice it. You can keep the clothes when the job's done."

That got another startled look, and then a nod. "I'd like that. Is there a shop?"

She really, seriously didn't know much about Shoreside, I reminded myself. "In this town? There's a shop for everything. The one I'm thinking of is about four blocks from here. If you don't have anything else to do right now, maybe we can get you set up, and then I can meet you first thing tomorrow and walk you to the place I need you to watch."

She got up off the concrete block, folded up the paper dish and pocketed it. "Sure." With a little shy smile: "You're being really nice to me, you know."

"You've already helped me out once," I said. "Think of it as a thank you."

I led her up to the street I'd come south on. As soon as we got among other people Sophie went quiet and stuck close to me. That was a good idea, because the Unies were out marching again, the same twenty people with the same scraps of blue cloth tied around their heads and the same chants on their lips, "One Planet, One Future" and the rest of it. Sophie tried not to stare at them but she didn't really succeed. I watched her and decided that she must be even newer in town than I'd thought.

We got to the shop, a little storefront place on its own skids wedged in between a grocery that mostly sells to working people and a big barn of a place that has dances and music and any other public event somebody wants to pay for. I opened the door, we went in, and the old black woman who owned the place, Ella Reese, came out from behind the counter to shake hands and make us feel like old friends. I knew her the same way she knew me, by reputation, but we got the details sorted out quickly enough. I asked her to get Sophie set up in something nice and mentioned how much I wanted to pay, and then left Sophie in her hands and went out the door again and found somewhere to kill time for fifteen minutes or so.

"Nice," by the way, isn't a generality in Shoreside. The sex trade's so big in the local economy that you either dress like you're looking for customers or you dress like you're not. The clothes I wear tell anybody who looks my way that I'm not in the market for johns or janes, and that's the same look I wanted for Sophie, partly because it was pretty clear she wasn't in that trade or interested in it, and partly because I didn't want sailors or truckers to bother her while she was watching Max Bernard and the people who came to talk to him.

I spent a few minutes standing there outside the shop, because by the time I got out the door the Unies had gotten to the end of the street, turned around, and started marching back the other way, still chanting. I was close enough this time that I could see the glazed looks on their faces. The first few times I saw them I was sure they were on drugs, it was that kind of thousand-mile stare, but some people who'd been around Shoreside a while put me straight about that. Unies didn't do drugs, they didn't drink, and they had some other customs that are pretty odd by Shoreside standards. They had a boss called the Blue Elder, who didn't go out in public, and they did what he told them: that's what I heard. I finally figured out that the look on their faces is the one you see on people when they're trying not to notice that the ideas they've bought into say one thing but the world is telling them something different.

They kept going down the street, still chanting, and I went around a corner and headed a little further away from the beach. I didn't go too far—go more than a few blocks and you're in the abandoned houses, where people live when they can't afford anything better, and that part of Shoreside isn't too safe even for someone like me. I'd heard rumors that that's where Big Goro's boys take people for a bunch of ugly reasons, too, and getting too close to any of Big Goro's private business wasn't safe either. So I stayed in among the buildings on skids and the streets that were boards over sand, and nothing happened to me. My tail didn't show up, either.

Fifteen minutes later I was back at the shop. Sophie was beaming. Ella had fitted her out in an off-white blouse, brown trousers, and plain practical shoes, the sort of outfit that counts as nice in Shoreside and also looked good on her. It was perfect for what I had in mind. I paid up and walked Sophie back to where she'd been sitting, and we chatted a little and made arrangements to meet there at seven the next morning. The only odd thing that happened was that I asked her if she had a watch, and she smiled and said she didn't need one, she always knew what time it was. "It's four thirty-eight and twenty seconds," she told me. I looked at my watch, and she was right. So I laughed and told her she was talented, and we talked a little more and then I told her to take care of herself and said I'd be there at seven in the morning sharp, and headed for Rick's.

The one thing I didn't know yet was where I was going to put her. I figured that out pretty quickly, though, because about five minutes after I got to Rick's who should come in the door but Roy Abeshima. I waved him over, said, "Hey, long time no see," and he laughed, grinned his lopsided grin, sat across the table from me and ordered dinner and a beer the same way I had. We did a little more catching up, and then he asked about the business with Max Bernard—of course he didn't use the name since we were in a place where someone might have heard it, he's smarter than that.

I gave him a few scraps of info to keep him satisfied, and then said, "Got a question for you. If somebody happened to show up tomorrow morning at the Ocean, could you put her someplace where she could watch the front door all day?"

He gave me a look, one eyebrow up, the other down, and said, "Maybe."

"Would two hundred turn that to a yes?"

That got me his lopsided grin again. "Yeah, that would do it."

So I got two hundreds from my wallet and handed them to him right then and there—like I said, we go way back. He pocketed them and said, "Anybody I know?"

I shook my head. "Probably not. Her name's Sophie Ames, new in town but a quick study. You can probably give her some filing to do, or whatever."

"I'll come up with something," he said. "Hey, I don't have much time right now, but I'd like to do some serious catching up. Any chance you'll be free tomorrow evening?"

I liked the idea and said so. We settled on a time and agreed on Rick's, and about then the food showed up and we put some attention into feeding our faces.

So I WAS PLEASED with myself when I caught the ferry back out to Habitat 4 about an hour later. Once I got back to my room I called and left a message on Mrs. Taira's answering machine, telling her what I had and hadn't found out about Rex Samuels and Michael Huddon and the Merlin Project and the rest of it. Once that was done I called Fritz to make sure he was free, and then I went to Stair 11, climbed it all the way to Sankai, and made a beeline to Fritz's front door, or as close to a beeline as the Habitat streets let me.

He rubbed his hands together as he led me back to his sitting room. "Excellent, excellent," he said. "I want to hear everything you found out about the Merlin Project, and then—then I might just have something of my own to pass on."

I sat in the usual chair once he'd waved me to it, waited while he got the lamp going under the teapot, all the usual things in the usual order. Finally he settled in his chair and I said, "Huddon's asking about it all over. There's a fortune teller in Shoreside named Chloe, used to be a university professor, reads cards these days."

"I know her," Fritz said. "Keep going."

"Huddon got a reading from her and asked her if she knew stories about the Merlin Project. She didn't tell him anything, not that she knows much. The one thing she told me is that she thinks she heard about it once from somebody involved in something called Year One." Fritz sucked in a breath past his teeth. That told me right away that I'd hit pay dirt. "But that's all I found out," I finished. "I hope you had better luck."

"Did anything unusual happen?"

I considered him. "I had somebody tail me twice, yesterday and today. Not one of Big Goro's boys, either. Nobody local."

"No, it wouldn't be. Tell me everything you can."

I told him everything I'd found out about Max Bernard, and when I mentioned that the travelers said he'd come ashore from a Nigerian freighter Fritz sucked air past his teeth again. I finished, and then said, "So tell me about the Year One thing."

Once the canonical five seconds passed, that got me his wet gurgling laugh. "A good place to start," he said. "That was one of the movements that rose and fell right after 2062, when this little haven of mine wasn't much more than bare concrete above salt water." That thought seemed to delight him: he grinned and rocked back and forth, savoring it. "Year One was their way of saying that history didn't matter any more and it was time to start all over again from the beginning. Of course that simply meant that they made all the old mistakes a second time. History repeats itself, the first time as tragedy, the second as farce: that's what Marx said."

"Groucho?" I guessed.

Fritz made a little hard sound in his throat. "Might as well have been. The Year One movement was big. It had people all over this country and seven or eight others. It made plenty of noise, set off a lot of riots, did some other things to help cause the crisis that brought the old constitution down, and then collapsed. The leaders were pocketing funds that were supposed to support the organization. Nothing new there."

He shrugged, dismissing the subject. "The organization broke into half a dozen quarreling fragments, as usual. The one that's still active in this part of the country is the Planetary Unity. They have a presence in Shoreside, hold marches every few days."

I gave Fritz a blank look, and then realized what he was talking about. "The Unies. Do you think they know—"

He shrugged again. The teapot chose that moment to start rattling, so the next few minutes went into making tea. "Impossible to tell," he said then. "Membership turnover in an organization like that is upwards of ninety percent every five years or so, but there's always a few who stay. If one of them met the person that Chloe Ingram knew, you might just possibly be able to get a lead."

"But you've got one for me," I said.

It was a guess, but it earned me a smile from him. "Maybe. I found out two things. The first is that the Merlin Project definitely existed. The second is that someone besides Huddon is looking for it."

"I'm listening," I said.

"Good. The first point? Abby Kuroda found the paperwork for me. I called her right after we talked last. She sent me copies of two government letters in her files. Both of them mention the Merlin Project and talk about funding for it. One gives a couple of place names and both of them are underwater near here. I thought Abby could find something if anyone anywhere could. A fine, fine mind."

I've never met Abigail Kuroda but I've heard a lot about her. She's an old woman with a badly scarred face who lives high up in Habitat 2 and has the best collection of documents from the old government anywhere this side of New Washington. Those papers are her life. She does research for people who need it, and she did some kind of big favor for Sam Akane back in the day, so she gets everything she needs, no questions asked. I've thought more than once that if she and Fritz ever met it would be love at first sight, but neither of them ever leaves their rooms, so it's a love affair by phone and letter. Sometimes Fritz goes into a long speech about how fine her mind is, and I was afraid he was going to do that, but he didn't.

"I'll get you the copies in a few minutes. The second point—that's a little more complex. I told you I was going to call in some favors. That involved talking to certain people who spend time in Shoreside. They listen and watch for me. They told me that Huddon's been asking about the Merlin Project in Shoreside. He always says what he said to the travelers you talked to. Just interested in stories. Claims he doesn't know any more about it but the name. Pretty transparent, eh? But the one thing we know about him is that he's not transparent. He wants someone else to know that he's looking for it. The someone else has been asking about Huddon, too. He's been listening to everything anyone says about the Merlin Project. He's let it be known that there's money, lots of it, for anyone who can talk about the Project—or about Huddon. His name, as you've doubtless guessed, is Max Bernard."

"Who got here at night off a Nigerian freighter."

"Exactly. I suppose it's possible that he has an honest reason to arrive in Shoreside that way. I can't think of one offhand. What I want to know is who he's seeing."

I grinned. "I'm on it." His eyebrows went up, and I said, "I've made some arrangements. If things go the way I want I should know something by this time tomorrow."

"Good," said Fritz. "Very good. Keep me informed. That might tell us who he came to see. But be careful." He sipped at his tea. "He could be more dangerous than he looks. Much, much more dangerous, and the people behind him? More dangerous still."

THE NEXT MORNING I took the elevator down to the passenger dock maybe half an hour after sunrise, when the fog over the ocean was still thick and cold and the freighters at anchor around Habitat 4 were dim gray shapes you couldn't quite be sure were real. I didn't expect to see anybody else but the guards down there at that hour, least of all Huddon, but there he was, leaning on his stick and smiling that annoying smile of his. I said hi, and he nodded and made a little gesture with the hand that wasn't on the stick. Something like five minutes later the ferry came putting out of the fog and nosed up to the dock; we got on board, Huddon went to the back and motioned for me to come sit next to him.

We were the only people on board besides the pilot, who was in his little booth up front, but he still waited until the ferry pulled away from the docks before saying in a quiet voice, "Perhaps you can tell me a little about Mr. Omogawa."

I gave him a sidelong look, got the usual smile in response. "Depends on what you want to know," I said. "I assume you already know the basics."

A quick nod answered me. "I know he runs organized crime in Shoreside and all the legitimate businesses pay him protection money. There's someone comparable in every city I know of. I want to know more about the person."

I sent another look his way, but it was a waste of energy: the same smile met me, saying a little less than a concrete wall. "No living family," I said. "Born in Japan, grew up in a refugee camp outside of Nikolayevsk, came here as a teenager with an uncle who didn't last long. Started off as muscle for Eddie Borman, who was the boss of Shoreside twenty-something years ago, and worked his way up from there. Everyone's pretty sure he paid for the hit that took out Al Sakamoto, the boss before him."

"Habits?"

I didn't bother to look. "Likes to eat fancy dinners all by himself at a couple of top-end Shoreside places. Spends a lot of money on the upper end of the sex trade, and likes to play rough; there are bodies sometimes. Never sleeps in the same place two nights in a row. If he does anything else in his spare time I haven't heard anything about it."

"His politics?" Huddon asked then.

"Politics?" That surprised me. "None that I ever heard of. Maybe he's loyal to somebody but himself, but I doubt it."

He nodded, glanced out the window. Habitat 5 was just coming into sight then, looming up out of the fog like somebody's bad drug trip. "You get people like him in every period of crisis," he said, almost to himself. For once the smile had gone missing. "Warlords who feed the chaos and thrive on it. Sooner or later, the warlords get replaced by kings, who harness the chaos and use it to establish a new order." Then he looked at me, almost like he'd forgotten I was there, and put the smile back on. "You have a king in Habitat 4. A queen, rather."

I made a rude noise in my throat. "We have elections every four years."

His smile didn't waver. I figure he knew as well as I did just how much of a formality those elections are. "Of course. No doubt I study too much history."

Nobody got on at Habitat 5. We sat there without saying anything for a little bit while the ferry pulled out from under the Habitat and started for Shoreside. Then Huddon said words I didn't recognize: "*Facilis descensus Averni.*" He glanced at me, and then went on. "My apologies. I know Latin's an exotic taste these days. But the trip from the Habitats to Shoreside makes me think of old legends: leaving the realms of light, descending to the underworld."

"Like those people you talked about," I said. "The ones who thought that we're all homeless gods."

"The Gnostics. Yes, among others." He was quiet for a few moments. "Sparks of light, fallen down into the world of matter. Into the world of history, in a sense, and trying to find a way to wake up out of it."

Right about the time we got close enough in to spot the first concrete ruins jutting up from the sea, big bubbles started roiling the water up ahead and the ferry veered out of the way. More big bubbles came up, and then all at once a dirty gray cylinder big enough to hide a couple of bodies in came surging to the surface, flopped over on its side, and started drifting north with the current.

I recognized it, of course. A lot of the houses in the flooded town under us had septic tanks instead of sewers, and of course nobody did anything about those when the sea started rising. Every so often the dirt above one of them gets washed away by a current or something, the pipes break, and the methane inside brings it bobbing up.

"There's your world of history," I said, with a jerk of my head toward it.

Huddon laughed his quiet laugh. "True. That's history, in a certain sense: things from the past bubbling up without warning."

We both watched the septic tank for a bit, until it drifted up against one of the ruins and a stray wave wedged it into place in between a couple of pieces of broken concrete.

"Like the Merlin Project?" I asked then.

He looked at me for a long moment. "Have you heard any more about that?"

"I asked around a little," I said. "I heard from a friend of mine that you asked some other people in Shoreside about it. There's supposed to be an old science fiction story about a supercomputer with the same name. Other than that?" I shrugged. "Nothing."

"So you've heard of Piper's novel. Not a common taste in literature these days."

"I've got a friend who's into science fiction." I shrugged again. "Not something that interests me. I've got my own daydreams that didn't work out."

That got me a glance and a nod, and then he looked out the window again. Shoreside was coming into sight, vague shapes in the fog. "Daydreams are dangerous things," he said. "And the ones that didn't work out can be more dangerous than the other kind. You pass on whatever I say to Mrs. Taira, I trust."

That was blunter language than I'd expected. I kept my reaction off my face. "When it's the kind of thing she wants to know about."

"Good. Please let her know that this business around the Merlin Project is important. It's not just a matter of historical research, or money."

I decided to take a risk. "People at National University want to know about it."

He glanced my way again. I met his gaze. He nodded, and I knew what he was saying: we both knew who wanted to know about it.

The ferry slowed, veered a little, and lurched to a stop against the dock. I got up, and so did Huddon. He raised the knob end of his walking stick and smiled, I made a little bow, and we went forward and climbed onto the dock and went our own ways. He went north toward Casino Row. I went south to keep an appointment.

Sophie was sitting on the same concrete block where I'd found her the afternoon before. She had her Shoreside clothes on and her hair looked clean and combed, which was more than you could say for most of the people I passed on the way to meet her. Her face lit up when she saw me, and she stood up and said good morning and then, unnecessarily, "I'm ready." I made the right kind of noises, made sure she'd had some breakfast, and then led her through the mostly empty streets to the Ocean.

The obvious risk was that Max Bernard might come waltzing through the lobby while I was there. I'd figured out how to bluff my way through that if it happened, but as it turned out, I didn't need to. The lobby was about as busy as a tomb with a corpse shortage, and the only person in sight was Roy, sitting as usual in his office off to one side. He looked like he'd been up late drinking, which I have to admit is pretty common with him, but he blinked and gulped some tea from a big gray pottery cup on his desk and got up to greet us. I introduced him to Sophie, she smiled and looked shy and shook his hand. Roy and I got a table and a chair set up in his office facing the door, so she could see everybody who came and went through the lobby, and then I promised to pick her up that evening and got out of there. Like I said, the obvious risk was that I might run into Bernard, but I knew as well as anybody in my line of work that the obvious risks aren't the ones you really have to worry about.

ONCE I WAS WELL away from that end of Shoreside and I knew for certain that nobody was following me, I headed toward Casino Row and then veered uphill. Figuring out what Rex Samuels was up to was my top priority that day, and the first thing that meant was pumping the people who work at the casinos for everything they could tell me. They're not the most talkative bunch in the world, not by a long shot, but I know them, they know me, and I've helped enough of them out when they needed something that I can call in a favor now and then.

The casinos open at ten in the morning. Before then, if you want to find the croupiers and cashiers and waitresses, you head to a place called Betsy's a block or so uphill from Casino Row, where most of the casino workers go to gobble down some breakfast and brace themselves for another long day. That's where I went. It's a big comfortable space with salvaged windows from old houses up the hill, lots of small tables, and smells coming through the swinging doors from the kitchen that would make a wooden Buddha's belly start to growl. I got there early enough that the only people in the place who weren't waitstaff were a couple of night shift bookkeepers downing a meal before they headed home to catch some sleep. Me, I staked out a table not too far from the door, got tea and a couple of hot buns stuffed with chicken curry, wrote a single word on a scrap of paper, and waited.

Minutes passed. A few people came in and got tables, but I didn't know any of them and I guessed that none of them could tell me what I needed to know anyway. So I let my mind go where it wanted to go. Where it wanted to go as I sat there, taking my time with the tea and the buns, was the dream I'd had right before waking the other morning, where everything turned into something else and something about the Merlin Project surfaced somewhere in there, too. I tried to coax bits of it to the surface, without much luck. The only scrap of the dream that surfaced at all was a bit where I was sitting on the beach listening to somebody. That stirred a memory, too, but it wouldn't come clear either.

I was still at it when somebody I knew came through the door: a guy named Billy Balch, long and lean, with a hairline that's slid back about halfway to the crown of his head and a big black mustache that drooped down past both sides of his mouth. He works security for the Pines, and we know each other pretty well. I grinned up at him, he gave me the once-over and then said, "Hey, Jerry. Lookin' for somethin'?"

"Not here for my health," I told him. He laughed, fished out a chair with one foot, and sat down. The nearest waitress came trotting out, took his order, and went back into the kitchen. Billy gave me the kind of bland patient look you learn when you spend all day watching people lose money, and I said, "Guy named Rex Samuels, good at cards. He's sixtyish, five foot ten or so, hundred fifty pounds, getting bald, wears black-framed glasses. Know anything about him?"

"Yeah, a little. Pick up breakfast and you've got it."

I nodded, and that's where the conversation stopped until the waitress came back out with a gaijin breakfast, toast and eggs and sausages, and I paid for it.

"Okay," Billy said once she'd gone. He pitched his voice low, because other people were coming into the place by then. "We're watching him. Wins too much to be honest. Smart guy, doesn't take too much from anybody and doesn't play the same house more than once a week. Shows up around two or three in the afternoon, too, and leaves before sunset."

"So he doesn't mess with the high rollers."

"Right. The boss'd probably throw him out anyway. Problem is nobody's been able to figure out what his gimmick is, and we gotta figure that out so nobody else gets away with it. What's he done to get your people after him?"

I grinned and said nothing, and he laughed. "Okay. But if your boss finds out what he's up to, my boss would be A-number one-ppreciative."

"I'll pass that on," I said, and bit into the last of the chicken curry buns.

Billy did the same thing with part of his breakfast. He was halfway through a piece of toast when somebody else came in, a short plump gray-haired gaijin woman with a forgettable face. He looked up, made a vague noise through a mouthful of toast, swallowed, and said, "Lucy! Get over here."

She gave him a sour look, but came over. "Yeah?"

"You know Jerry here, right?"

Hard gray eyes looked me up and down. "No."

"From offshore. Wants to know about our latest slick customer. He'll pay for your breakfast, I bet."

I aimed a grin at her. The hard gray eyes looked me over again. "Let me guess. Billy-boy's shoveling smoke again."

"No," I told her. "Tell me what you know about Rex Samuels and breakfast's on me. Whatever you want."

She pulled out a chair and sat down. The waitress came over and took her order, and I said, unnecessarily, "I'm paying." That got me a smile from the waitress—she knows I tip well—and a refill on my tea a minute or so later, once she'd taken the order back.

"Okay," Lucy said then. "I do books for the Pines, in case Billy-boy forgot to mention that. I did a couple of years in college a long time ago, learned about probability, so the boss has me crunch numbers when it looks like somebody's getting away with something. So I've been watching Samuels good and close. He doesn't cheat in any of the usual ways, but you probably know that already. He doesn't do anything I can trace. What he does is he always plays exactly the way the odds point."

I tried to make sense of that. "Like counting cards."

"Way past counting cards. You've played six rounds of three-card draw and you know what everyone's put down. What's the chance that the guy across from you has ten, jack, queen, or king of diamonds? I don't mean yes or no. I mean give me a number to three or four decimal places. I don't know a way to do that. Samuels does, or he's way too good at faking it." She shrugged. "That's what I know. I hope it's worth breakfast."

I nodded, though I had no clue yet what it amounted to. The place was filling up around us by then, and the waitress came back with Lucy's breakfast, so I finished the last of my tea, paid up, told them both to have a better day than they were likely to get, and went out the door into the thinning fog. Rex Samuels was starting to interest me a lot, and I wanted to find out where he came from, where he went, and why.

THAT'S NOT ALWAYS AN easy job in Shoreside, and what I'd just learned about Samuels didn't make it any easier. By two o'clock the part of town near Casino Row is pretty crowded. Since I didn't know yet which direction he was coming from I couldn't just find a place and watch for him. I didn't have a plan yet, and it was early enough when I left Betsy's that I knew Yanni wouldn't be picking pockets yet and Chloe would still be sleeping off her bender from the night before, so I was at loose ends for a while. That was why I decided to go pay a visit to Ernie.

Like I said already, Ernie Lobeck's an old friend of mine. He's also been around Shoreside since it was a shantytown slapped together from spare junk, and the docks were a mile further out to sea than they are now. When I drop in, we talk about all kinds of stuff, but I can ask him for advice and get it. The only question I had was when he was going to open for business, because Ernie never did care much for schedules and now that he's getting old he doesn't worry about them at all.

That morning, though, I was lucky. I got there right as he was unlocking the place. He grinned at me in that bug-eyed way of his, slapped me on the back, let me help him get the place open for business, and then pulled up a second stool by the counter just inside the door and poured two glasses of a mix of grapefruit juice and cheap brandy instead of just one. I was glad I'd had some food, because you never know how much juice and how much brandy go into Ernie's jug. He's that kind of guy.

So we sat there surrounded by every kind of salvaged junk you can imagine and some you probably can't, and talked about all kinds of things. I asked about the junk trade and got to hear a lot more about it than I needed to, and he asked how things were going on the Habitats and I probably told him more than he wanted to know, too. We both sipped at our glasses of juice and brandy, and then I got around to asking him the thing I came for.

"The Merlin Project," he repeated, and nodded slowly. "Yeah, I heard of it. The Year One people liked to rant about that, and the fusey-whatsit thing that was supposed to keep the juice flowing into the power grid if they could just get it to work, and I forget what all else. You don't remember the Year One business, do you?"

"Hadn't gotten around to being born yet," I reminded him.

He let out a laugh that sounded a lot like a choking fit. I didn't worry about it, since Ernie always laughs like that. "Your timing's always been good, hasn't it? Skipped a lot of trouble. But the Year One people, yeah, they were into that. Said that the Merlin Project was either the best or the worst thing that ever was."

I gave him a blank look. "How'd they get that to work?"

Ernie shrugged. "It was supposed to figure out how to fix everything. The Year One people were sure they knew how to do that, and so either the project came up with an answer they liked or it didn't. Or something like that. But if it ever got any answer at all I never heard anything about it. So the Year One people, they made a lot of fuss for a few years and then most of 'em found something else to do with their time. Any chance you remember Ellie Kolchak, skinny old thing with long white hair, used to go around town without a stitch on and sit on the beach and talk to anyone who would listen?"

Ellie Kolchak! I hadn't thought of her for ten years, maybe more, but I remembered her all right. Shoreside was much wilder in the days when I was skipping school to go there, back when there wasn't a regular ferry yet but you could catch a ride with lighters going in with freight if you knew the right people. You had lots of prophets and preachers and strange little groups, all of them offering people something to believe in when none of the old answers worked any more, and Ellie Kolchak was one of them.

"Yeah," I said. "Yeah, I used to sit and listen to her sometimes."

"No kidding. Well, she was the last of the Year One teachers, and she kept at it all by herself when the rest of them stopped. The guy who runs the Unies these days started out as one of her followers, and he turned into the head of the franchise after hemorrhagic fever took Kolchak out. You might have met him back when he still went by Mike Glaskey."

That startled me. "Seriously? Yeah, I knew him pretty well back then. Is that who the Blue Elder is?"

"That's him. I don't think he's been out in public for years. Not even sure where he is—maybe in that big building of theirs, maybe not." Ernie shook his head. "What's got you looking into that bit of history?"

"Some people are looking for the Project. My boss wants to know why."

He nodded as if it was the most obvious thing in the world, downed a shot from his glass, and said, "Well, be careful.

Back in the day, we're talking forty, fifty years ago, right before or right after Kikai, you used to hear really weird rumors about the Merlin Project."

"Like what?"

"The way I heard it, people used to show up at the old hospital out there—" His head jerked toward the ocean and the drowned city. "Something fried their brains. No cure, just take 'em off to a nursing home and stick 'em there until they died. Rumor was the Merlin Project had something to do with it. And there was a woman I had a thing with when I was a lot younger who had a miscarriage, or that's what everyone said. That's not what she said. She said she went into that same hospital for a baby check when she was seven months along, blacked out, and the next thing she knew she was in a bed with a doctor bending over her telling her she'd lost the baby. She swore the kid was still alive, she could feel that. Said people from the Merlin Project took it. Crazier'n a hoot owl, maybe, but people believed her."

I took that in. "What's your take?"

He shrugged expressively. "No clue. Lots of ugly things happened the last fifty years or so under the old constitution, but you just never know."

We talked about other things for a while, and then who should walk in the door but Bear, Otter, and two other travelers I didn't know. They had a bunch of junk to sell, salvaged from one of the islands off the coast that haven't been stripped bare yet. They greeted me like I was their long-lost brother, of course, because travelers do that, but they were there for business and so I did the polite thing and left as soon as I could do it gracefully.

The streets were just beginning to fill up when I got back outside, but I didn't pay a lot of attention. Ellie Kolchak, I thought. Yeah, I remembered her. She must have been in her sixties when I knew her, a thin bony wrinkled thing with big blue eyes that never quite seemed to focus, but she had a little circle of followers who didn't wear any more than she did, and some of the women were young and really nice to look at. When I was twelve and just starting to figure out about sex, that was more than enough to catch my attention. So I'd sit on the beach sometimes and watch the cute little items in her crowd and listen to her talk about how history was over and we were all going to go back to living in nature, no clothes, no houses, no writing, no tools, no fire, just gathering wild plants and eating them raw. Sometimes she talked about space travel and fusion power and some of the other things that turned out not to work, saying how sad it was that people were trying those instead of going back to nature, and—yeah, that was where I'd heard of the Merlin Project, I was sure of it. I could just about remember her high thin voice saying the phrase.

Every so often somebody who was sitting there listening to her, somebody who wasn't one of her people, would take off all their clothes and just chuck them into the water. That was how you joined her group, and then you'd go live with her in an abandoned house and eat what you could scrounge or beg, and wait for history to finish being over. I didn't join them, but I'd be lying if I said I didn't think about it. I'm pretty sure that if I'd been sixteen instead of twelve and one of the cuter numbers in the group had wiggled at me I'd have shed my clothes on the spot, and maybe Ame no Kokoro knows what would have happened to me after that but I don't. But that didn't happen, my virginity lasted for another three years or so, and long before that went by the wayside I'd figured out that there was a really good reason Ellie and her followers were living in Shoreside where they could count on getting food now and then and sleeping under a roof, instead of heading out into the woods to begin the new age of the world she used to talk about so much.

I shook my head, shoved the memories aside, and paid more attention to where I was. It's a good thing, too. A murder was about to happen and I was maybe six feet away from it.

THE INTENDED VICTIM WAS about twenty feet further down the street, and the fog was thin enough by then that I could see him easily: Jim Nakano, Big Goro's accountant. He didn't have a briefcase full of money in his hand, the way he'd had the night I clobbered Dart, though the same hard-faced guy with the pistol on his belt was with him. They were being hassled by two toughs I didn't recognize, big muscular guys who dressed like sailors but moved like they'd never spent a day on deck.

They weren't the ones that mattered, though. The one that mattered was a bland little gaijin guy with a face like a well-fed rat. He was standing more than half turned away from me, facing Nakano. He had ordinary Shoreside clothes on and an automatic pistol in his hand, and he was pretty obviously waiting for a clear shot. It looked like Nakano hadn't noticed him and neither had the hard-faced guy. That's the way you do that kind of hit: the two fake sailors are distraction, the guy with the gun shoots and then makes tracks, and it's all over.

Not this time, I decided. I couldn't have told you why, not for certain, though Nakano's always been polite to me and he had a reputation in Shoreside for being tough but fair. I didn't waste any time thinking it through. The rat-faced guy raised his gun, one of the fake sailors stepped back, and right then I brought the business end of my yawara stick down hard on a spot on Rat-Face's shoulder. You do that right and it hits the nerve, and you won't be using that arm again for a couple of days at least.

I did it right. The guy's arm went into spasm and jerked down and to one side, and the pistol went off. It didn't hit anything but the street, but the sound was enough to clue in Nakano and his bodyguard, and they started shooting. Me, I dove for the ground as soon as I knew Rat-Face wasn't going to kill anyone that week, and right as I hit the street Rat-Face took two bullets in the chest and fell over. One of the fake sailors tried to draw a gun, the other one didn't get that far, and both of them hit the ground too. By then everyone else who'd been in that block was diving for cover or running as fast as they could. I scrambled over to the nearest building and flung myself through the first door I could find. The doorsill caught my foot, and I went down face first onto the sand floor.

A few more gunshots went pop-pop-pop behind me, and then things got quiet. I waited another moment and picked myself up. Five youngish women were all looking at me, and none of them had much more on than old Ellie Kolchak used to wear. Over to one side of them was a bar and some bar stools, and behind them was the inevitable door leading to the little rooms with beds in back. The girls looked at me, I looked at them, and one of them said, "You okay?"

I gave myself a quick once-over to be sure. "Yeah," I said. "Just staying out of the way."

One of the others asked, "Any idea what's up?"

"Somebody just tried to plug Jim Nakano," I said.

That got shocked looks from all of them. "I hope he's okay," said the oldest, who was about thirty. "He's a nice guy. Not like some I could name."

"I wasn't watching all that close, but I don't think he got hit." I went over to the bar, sat on one of the stools. "Any chance I can get a whiskey and water?"

"Sure." The oldest of the women went behind the bar, fixed the drink, handed it to me and took my money. I downed a good swallow and thanked her. One of the others, a blonde with a lot of curves, came over then and put her hand on my arm and said, "Maybe you've got a little time for me."

I put on a smile and said, "Thanks, but as soon as things quiet down I've got someplace to go." I got a couple of bills out of my wallet and handed them to her. "I didn't come in here and none of you ever saw me before." I didn't have to do that, nobody would care one way or the other if I'd been playing around in a Shoreside brothel, but it gave me an excuse to tip her for being friendly without spending half an hour I didn't want to waste.

The bills fielded me the kind of smile you don't expect from a working girl, soft and a little shy. I don't know, maybe she practiced it in front of a mirror every morning, but it looked genuine. "Saw who?" she said, and laughed. I grinned, raised my glass to her, and finished it off. Then I said goodbye to all of them and headed for the door.

Outside things had gotten very quiet, the kind of quiet that tells you that everyone knows there's going to be serious trouble sometime soon. The fog was gone, so were Nakano and his bodyguard, and the street was next thing to empty, except for the two fake sailors and the guy I'd clobbered. They were still there, lying in puddles of blood. They'd been headshot, all three of them. Nakano and his bodyguard clearly weren't taking chances.

I went past them and started up the street toward the wall where Yanni waits when he's not picking pockets. Before I got more than half a block, a bunch of Big Goro's boys came around the corner ahead of me. Bill Takagi was leading them, and he had Mako right next to him, big and silent and carrying a sawed-off shotgun with a pistol grip, just in case anybody got stupid. Bill spotted me, came up and said, "Well, well. If it isn't Jerry Shimizu, slumming in Shoreside again. Any chance you saw what happened?"

"Not close up," I lied. I didn't want to say more than I had to, on account of not knowing who was gunning for Nakano and who might be annoyed that he was still breathing. The other boys gathered around, watching, not saying anything. "Somebody tried to pop Jim Nakano. Jim and whoever covers him spotted the hit and shot first. I don't recognize any of the corpses, if that makes a difference."

He looked at me for a long moment. I couldn't tell what was going on behind his face but it didn't look particularly friendly. He moved his head, then, signaling to the others. Without another word he stepped around me and went on toward the mess. The boys went with him. I glanced back to make sure they weren't paying any more attention to me and got the hell out of there as fast as I could without running.

Chapter 5

By the time I got to the wall where Yanni waits for chumps, people had started coming back onto the street. Yanni was in his usual place, looking goofy and aimless and sizing up everybody who walked past. I put the piece of paper with the one word on it in my back pocket and walked by him, same as always. The paper did its vanishing act and I did mine. A few minutes later I was sitting at a little table at Rick's Café Américain, with a cup of coffee in front of me and an eye turned to the crowd, and Sam Nakaichi cranking out the mellower sort of jazz classics on the piano for background noise. The clientele was mostly sailors that morning, African and Indian, drinking coffee and joking in English and a couple of languages I don't know. I gathered from the chatter that three big freighters docked off Habitat 2 the day before and turned their crews loose on shore leave.

I sat there and listened, watching the door for Yanni. A minute passed, and then the door opened, but it wasn't Yanni who came through it. It was Max Bernard. He was wearing a different set of forgettable clothes, more pricey than the ones he'd had on when he'd tailed me, and he did a good job of checking out the crowd without looking like that was what he was up to. I wondered whether he'd seen me. I didn't have to wonder for long. He went to the bar, got a drink, paid for it, and then crossed the floor straight to the little table where I was sitting.

"Mr. Shimizu," he said with a smile I didn't trust. "Perhaps we could talk."

I motioned at the chair across from me. Up close, he looked exactly like what Roy Abeshima said he was, a well-paid sales flack for some Canadian import-export firm. His clothes were a little fussier than you'd expect to see on the American equivalent, but not much, and he had the Canadian accent, too. I started out thinking that he had to be faking it, and that's where I ended up, too.

He settled into the chair, took a sip from his glass, set it down. "You're wondering why, but you're too polite to say so. Permit me to explain. My name is Max Bernard. I represent a firm in Toronto, Laurentide Associates, international trade in electronics and technology, new and salvaged. Entirely legal, I assure you. I can have my principals forward the necessary papers any time you like."

"Go on," I said.

He smiled again. "You're careful, Mr. Shimizu. I appreciate that. The fact of the matter is that you've been pointed out to me twice by people here in Shoreside. They tell me that you're one of Ruth Taira's assistants. I would like you to take her a confidential message."

"I can do that," I said after a moment.

"Good. Excellent, in fact. Now, as to the details. You doubtless know that North and South China are on the brink of war. My principals expect both nations' allies in Africa to get involved. This is a problem for us, Mr. Shimizu. A serious problem. Much of our trade goes through Dakar and Abidjan. My principals have tried to negotiate with the African governments, but once the guns start to speak the trader's voice is drowned out." He chuckled at his own metaphor. "So we need a new entrepôt for the Atlantic trade. A location with ample capacities for shipping and not within Canadian territory, for reasons

I trust I don't have to explain. With sea levels rising as fast as they are, those are in short supply. Your Habitats have certain advantages shore-based ports don't, as I'm sure you know."

Right about then Rick Blaine came around, the way he does whenever his place is open. He grinned at me and said hi, introduced himself to Max Bernard, made a little conversation, and moved on. Bernard watched him go, and then turned back to me. I considered him, and said again, "Go on."

"Of course. It would be advantageous for us to have local agents to handle our business here. We manage our affairs in Africa that way. We would like to arrange for that with one of the trading firms of Habitat 4. It could be very lucrative, very lucrative indeed." He sipped at his drink. "Mrs. Taira's approval would be needed for any arrangement of that kind. I quite understand that. Thus this conversation."

"The message you want me to take," I said. "You want her to okay this project of yours. Anything beyond that?"

He unfolded his big smile and showed it to me again. "Not even that much. I would simply like you to tell her that I am interested in beginning a conversation. I can be found here in Shoreside, at the Red Door rooming house. You know it? Good. I would be happy to meet with her representative whenever it is convenient. With you, Mr. Shimizu, if she wishes."

It sounded plausible. That made me trust him even less. One thing you learn in Shoreside early and often is that the better a deal sounds the first time through, the bigger the catch is going to turn out to be. "Tell me one thing," I said.

"By all means." One of his hands splayed, inviting the question.

"You could have come to Habitat 4 and stayed in one of the hotels there. It would have been a lot easier to contact Mrs. Taira from there. Why didn't you?"

His smile got even wider. "Excellent, Mr. Shimizu. You are attentive. You will appreciate, I'm sure, that we researched this venture carefully. Yes, very carefully indeed. My principals were concerned that I should be able to contact them without interference or, shall we say, interception. We respect your employer far too much to expect to do that in Habitat 4. I am by no means sure I can expect that even here in Shoreside."

I let myself smile, just a little. "I'll tell her that."

He beamed at me. "Please do. By all means pass on my regards as well. Anything else? No?" He downed the last of his drink, set the glass down, and stood. "It has been a pleasure, Mr. Shimizu. A positive pleasure. A good day to you, a very good day."

I nodded and said nothing. He turned and left Rick's. I watched him go, finished my coffee, and wondered what his game was. His story was plausible, like I said, but I knew too much about him already to believe it. I started wondering what he might be up to, then caught myself and stopped. That was for my boss to figure out. My job was to tell her what I'd heard, and get back to work trying to track down Rex Samuels and figure out if he had anything to do with the robberies I was supposed to be solving.

I'D JUST FINISHED THAT when Yanni came around a little knot of sailors with a beer in his hand, gave me one of his blank looks, and we went through the little game of pretending we didn't expect to see each other. He settled down on the chair Bernard had just left, downed some of his beer, and said, "So who is he?"

I didn't have to guess who he was talking about. "He goes by Max Bernard. I don't know what he's up to."

He gave me a wry look, and then reached into a pocket and handed something to me under the table: a wallet. I took it without a word, and checked the contents without raising it above table level. It had exactly what you'd expect in it, US and Canadian money, a Canadian ID card with Bernard's name and photo on it, some other pieces of paperwork, nothing out of the ordinary, nothing that gave me a clue. The guy was a professional.

I kept hold of the wallet anyway. Some bills out of mine went across the table to Yanni. "Thanks. Doesn't help much, though."

Yanni shrugged. "Worth a try. So what do you want to know about? Same as before?"

"Start with Rex Samuels. Where does he come from, and when?"

"I see him every day between two and two-thirty," Yanni told me. "Always coming up the street from the south, all by himself. I don't know where he comes from before that, but it's always the same time and the same direction, and he heads on toward Casino Row. I went after him once but he's smart. He keeps everything in pockets inside the vest, buttoned shut."

"The same vest."

"The same clothes. If he has another set I haven't seen 'em."

"But they're always clean."

Yanni shrugged. "He usually heads back the same way sometime around four to five."

"Usually."

"Yesterday he was a couple of hours late. Six-thirty, say."

It wasn't much to go on, and we both knew it. I went on to the next thing on my list. "Okay, Max Bernard. I know more about him than I did, but not enough. Anything?"

"A few things. I've seen him around. Most of the time on his own, but sometimes with some other guys, big tough sorts packing serious heat. With 'em or without 'em, he's always going somewhere, never just dawdling."

"Any place in particular?"

Yanni shrugged again. "I never followed him. He comes here pretty often, goes down toward Casino Row almost as often, goes uphill sometimes. The one thing I'm sure of is he's busy. Places to go, things to do, people to meet."

"Okay. Michael Huddon?"

"Seen him twice. Ambling along, looks like he's not paying attention to anybody. Some dumb goose who thinks he's a pick-pocket went at him earlier this morning, not just in my space but right out in front of me." He shook his head, and I made the right sounds. "Huddon's good. He let the guy get close, and then jabbed that stick of his down at the nearest foot. The guy yelled, and Huddon turned like he didn't know what was going on and was surprised. Beyond that I couldn't tell you much."

I gave Yanni some more money anyway, we made a little talk, and he left the table and went out the door. Me, I sat there for a while, waiting for Rick to do his rounds. When he came close enough, I flagged him down.

"What's up?"

I handed him the wallet. "Mr. Bernard dropped his wallet when he was here talking with me. He's staying at the Red Door. Any chance you can have somebody run it over to the desk there sometime today?"

Of course he said yes, and of course he knew perfectly well that Max Bernard hadn't dropped anything. He knows Yanni as well as I do, and he knows Shoreside even better. He grinned at me, and I grinned at him, and he went on to the next table and I finished my coffee and left. I used the beach door since I wasn't in a hurry.

Outside the fog was long gone and the sun came down hard and bright onto the sand and the tables and me. Off in the distance, past where the waves rolled in between chunks of concrete, the five Habitats broke the horizon, gray as ghosts. I thought about the times I'd sat on the beach not far from there, listening to Ellie Kolchak talk about a future that never got around to happening, and I thought about all the other people for years and years before then who talked about futures that never got around to happening either, and shook my head to clear it. I still had a while before Rex Samuels made his appearance, and I wanted to make sure I could spot him as early as possible and follow him all day if I had to.

I SPOTTED HIM, ALL right. At two o'clock sharp he came up the street from the south, dressed in the same clothes, looking like a guy who knows where he's going and what he wants to do when he gets there. I let him go by, then left the corner where I'd been lounging around and let myself start drifting with the crowd, going the same way he was. I wasn't worried about losing him, since I was pretty sure he was headed toward Casino Row and it wouldn't be too hard to spot him in one of the casinos once he got there. Still, there's something called professional pride. I followed him as though he was about to pull every trick there is to shake me off.

It's a good thing that I did that, because he wasn't heading for Casino Row, and he wasn't a professional by any means but somebody had taught him a few tricks. He went uphill a block, ducked into a shop for a few minutes, came back out and started going the other direction for a while, then doubled back suddenly and paid attention to everybody he passed. Now of course I knew all the same tricks and what to do about them, so I kept him in sight the whole time. I figured out quick that he wasn't just going to Casino Row, but it took a while before I guessed that he might be heading for the Ocean.

I gave him plenty of space once I figured that out. Maybe it was just a coincidence that he was headed for the place where Max Bernard was staying, but I wasn't going to bet on that. If they were meeting there, for that matter, Bernard was good enough that I knew he'd have somebody watching the area the whole time. The crowd just then wasn't too thick, so I crossed to the other side of the street, let Samuels go on ahead half a block or so, and took a chance that he wouldn't pull one of the tricks he'd learned and shake me.

He didn't. He went right past the front door of the Ocean to the place where I'd gotten edamame the day before when I first tailed Bernard. I wondered if he had the smarts to get a table and wait a while to see if someone was following, but that wasn't his plan. He went inside. I gave him a few minutes, and was still trying to decide whether to follow him in when Max Bernard came out of a shop on the other side of the street, strolled casually over and went in after him. I hung back a while, to make sure neither of them was going to pop out again, and then I went further down the street to a bar a little further on, a place with tables out in front, and got a place to sit that wasn't too obvious and gave me a good view of the door they'd gone in and the front door of the Ocean.

A bar girl came out, wiggled at me in the automatic way so many of them do, took my money and brought me a beer. I nursed it and watched. People passed by and so did a bunch of minutes. Finally Samuels came out, looking a little shaken and a little pleased with himself, and headed back down the street toward Casino Row. I made sure Bernard wasn't on his heels, left a tip and an empty bottle on the table, and went after him.

Either he'd already forgotten the tricks he'd learned or he didn't think he needed them any more. He went straight to the Angel, the casino right next to the Pines. If anybody but me followed him, it was somebody a lot better at this business than I am. I went into the casino right after him, spotted him at one of the tables, waited for an open spot at a table closer to the door, and sat there with one eye on Samuels and one eye on my cards. I don't recommend playing that way, for what it's worth. The other guys at the table were happy to see me that day.

The problem, of course, was that I knew I might be in the middle of a game when Samuels got his winnings and left. After a couple of hours, I got up from the table, bought another beer, took my time drinking it, and then left the casino. Things were getting busy all over Shoreside by then, heading toward another night of drinking and partying, and there aren't many good places to watch the street close to Casino Row anyway. So I went a ways further south to the customs office, which has windows facing the street.

The old red white and blue flag was hanging limp on a pole up above the door. It's still got fifty stars in it, even though fourteen states got turned back into territories once the desertification set in and two more were about to follow them as soon as Congress got its act together on the devolution bill. The official line is that they kept the fifty stars there because maybe some of the territories are going to turn into states again someday. My guess? It's an economy measure. These days, not enough people can afford to keep buying new flags every time a couple of states devolve, and even government offices have to watch their budgets a lot more closely than they used to.

The clerk on duty was a stocky guy named Hassan who's got a round smiling face and a boxer's big hands. He's bald as an egg except for thick black eyebrows and a black handlebar mustache. My boss bribes him good and proper, so he's always friendly. I helped that along by handing him a couple of bills. That got me a chair and a place to sit far enough inside that I couldn't be spotted from outside but close enough to the window that I had a great view of everyone passing by. I settled down to wait for Samuels to pass by.

He never showed. I cooled my heels for a couple of hours, then left the customs office to see if he was still in the casino, and of course he was nowhere in sight. I stifled a couple of Mom's choicest Russian swear words for making a rookie mistake like that, and a couple more for putting too much confidence in what Yanni said, but there wasn't anything else I could do about it. Besides, it was getting on for time to pick up Sophie Ames and see what she had to say.

The streets were good and crowded by then. I took a roundabout route to the Ocean and got there a little below seven, when the sun was getting close to the hills behind Shoreside, and the five Habitats off in the distance were stained orange by its light. Roy was in his office and so was Sophie, perched there behind her little table with a stack of bills and a clipboard with some paper on it. She was flipping through the bills about as fast as a good dealer at a casino deals cards, and stopping every so often to write something down on the clipboard. She glanced up the moment I came into the lobby, smiled at me, and then went back to what she was doing.

I smiled back and then ducked over to the side of Roy's desk where I wouldn't be too visible if Bernard came by. Roy and I said the usual things, and then Sophie finished what she was doing, came over to the desk, and handed the bills and the clipboard to Roy. He glanced down at them, got a lightly glazed look on his face, and said to Sophie, "Thanks. You keep in mind what I said, okay?"

"I will," she said. To me: "Is it time to go?"

I said yes and got another one of her smiles, and we said our goodbyes to Roy and left the Ocean. I glanced back at Roy just before we went out the door and he was still standing there looking at the clipboard and shaking his head.

OUTSIDE THE SUN WAS right on the edge of the hills. Shoreside was getting warmed up for a lively night. Over the voices and the bustle I could hear music from half a dozen night spots, somebody shouting insults at someone else a block or so away, and then the crack of a gunshot settling the quarrel. Smoke and smells of roasting meat from I don't even want to guess how many kitchen stoves nearby reminded me just how long of a day it had been.

"Dinner?" I said. "Then you can fill me in."

That got me another smile and the answer I expected, so I took Sophie a couple of blocks uphill to the same quiet little place where I met Yanni the day before. The food there's better than you'd expect from the way it looks out front, as good as any place in town, and it's got lots of little nooks and corners and a couple of private dining rooms in back. You see a lot of couples there. We went in and got settled in one of the nooks. Our waiter was a tall skinny East African guy with skin so dark it was almost black. He handed us each a printed menu, which you don't see in Shoreside very often these days, and left us to settle things.

"I hope your day wasn't too boring," I said.

She looked startled. "No, not at all. Mr. Abeshima had me do some work on his books." With a little shrug: "I like math and I'm good at it, so it was fun."

"That have anything to do with what he wants you to keep in mind?"

The waiter came back then, so we ordered and made a little talk about nothing. Once he'd gone away, Sophie said, "Oh, yes. He says if I want a job he'll hire me."

That startled me. Roy's always having to push people away who want to cadge a job from him. "You could do worse," I told her. "If I didn't have a job, I'd work for him ahead of a lot of people I know."

"I told him I'd think about it." Another smile went my way. "He says he's known you for a long time."

"He's right. We ran together when I was a snot-nosed kid playing hooky from school."

The waiter came back with food and wine, and that kept us busy for a few minutes.

"You grew up on one of the Habitats," Sophie said then.

"I still live there. I'm commuting."

I meant it as a joke but she didn't take it that way. "I've never been out to them. I'd like to do that someday. It must be nice to be out there with the sea all around."

"When I was a kid I thought it was dull." I glanced up at her. "I bet everyone thinks that of the place they grew up."

She didn't rise to the bait. "Do you think it's dull now?"

"Not really. I'd probably spend a lot more time there than I do, but—" I shrugged. "My job brings me here to Shoreside a lot."

"Detecting."

"Among other things."

She sipped some of the wine, gave it an uncertain look, sipped again. "Mr. Abeshima told me some things about you. Or, well, I asked some questions, and he answered them."

"Between drinks."

She blushed. "Yes. But he didn't act drunk."

"He never does. Roy can drink anyone I know under the table." I drank some of the wine. "So what did he tell you?"

The blush didn't go away. "Oh, just some stories about when you two were younger."

I didn't believe her for a moment, but I let it go. "I could tell you some things about him, too, but I probably ought to let that wait until he hires you." That bait got a nibble, and pretty soon I was passing on a couple of harmless stories about stuff Roy and I did after his brother died and the two of us ended up running together.

I was in the middle of the second of those when the place suddenly got more crowded, and it wasn't waiters or couples, either. Half a dozen of Big Goro's boys went through it, checking out the clientele. I knew what that meant. I looked at Sophie and put a finger to my mouth, casually, hoping she'd notice. She did, and caught the glance I sent toward the nearest of the goons, too. So I let the story drop and she sipped a little wine and tried not to look nervous.

Of course the goons spotted me just as soon as I spotted them. They didn't say anything, just looked at me and at Sophie, and then went on to the other people in the place. A few minutes passed. I drank some of my wine and Sophie sipped at hers, and then I heard a voice I knew very, very well. It wasn't close by and it wasn't directed at me, but nobody else in Shoreside sounds like Big Goro. I caught Sophie's attention again and looked down at the table, hard. She figured that out, too, and concentrated good and hard at cutting something on her plate.

Another minute, maybe, and Big Goro passed by. I didn't look toward him. I didn't have to. My wine glass was nice and clean and the wine in it was dark red, so I could see his reflection clear as day. If he noticed me he didn't show any sign of it. He went past, the door to one of the private dining rooms in back opened and closed. One of the waiters got chairs for a couple of his boys to sit in, next to the door. The rest of the goons left, and everyone in the place started breathing again.

Sophie waited a few moments and then looked up at me. When I nodded, she said, "Is it okay to ask what that was about?"

I added that to the list of things everyone in Shoreside knows about but she didn't. "Mr. Goro Omogawa," I said. I wasn't going to call him Big Goro when there were still some of his boys around. "He runs organized crime in Shoreside, and he likes fancy dinners."

She took that in, and nodded.

NEITHER OF US SAID much for a few minutes after that. Once I was sure that Big Goro was going to be busy with dinner for a good long time, though, I wound up the story I'd been telling Sophie. By the time that was done we'd both finished our dinners. The waiter popped up again, took away the plates and poured some more wine. I got out my notebook and pen, and she told me everything she'd seen in the twelve hours or so she'd spent watching the lobby at the Ocean.

"Everything" isn't an exaggeration, either. She noticed things that I wouldn't notice, and I'm pretty good at paying attention. She described Max Bernard from the way he parted his hair down to the pattern of the tread on the soles of his shoes, and she did the same thing with every other person who passed through that lobby. Most of them were people I knew pretty well, and they probably didn't have anything to do with any of the things I was supposed to look into, but you never know: I copied down all the details. Then there was a lean muscular man with short legs, long arms, and a knife scar across his face, who came into the lobby at 10:34 in the morning and left exactly forty-one minutes later. I could give that description to anybody in Shoreside and they'd name Bill Takagi before I got halfway through it.

So something like an hour went by that way. I filled twenty pages or so in my notebook and filed away at least as many unanswered questions in my head. Whatever Bernard was up to, he was talking to Takagi, and that almost certainly meant that Big Goro was involved. He was talking to Rex Samuels, too, and that meant either that Samuels wasn't involved in the robberies I was looking into, or that I had no clue what was actually going on, or both. Probably both, I decided, and kept taking notes.

By the time we were finished I knew more than anybody ought to know about who'd gone in and out of the Ocean that day. I got out my wallet and peeled out five twenties to pay Sophie for the day's work, then added a sixth as a tip. "That's for going above and beyond," I said. "If you're interested, the next time I have a job like this I know who to ask."

She thanked me very prettily, then said, "Is there some way I can find you if I have to?"

"Sure," I said after a moment. "Any chance you know Rick's Café Américain?"

She shook her head. Even after the other things she didn't know, that surprised me. Like I said, everyone in Shoreside knows Rick's. I told her how to get to it from the fallen block of concrete where I'd met her that morning, which is easy enough. "You go there," I said, "and talk to Rick, who runs the place, or Leo, the bouncer at the main door. They can get a message to me any time, and—" I shrugged. "You might get lucky. I'm there a lot."

She thanked me again and I went on: "Now is there any place I can walk you? This late, it gets pretty wild out there."

She opened her mouth, closed it again, bought some time by finishing her wine and shaking her head when I offered her more. "If you can take me back to where we met this morning, that would be nice."

"Sure thing," I said. The waiter wasn't too far away, so I flagged him down, paid for the meal, told him to keep the change, and hauled myself out of my chair.

Outside it wasn't quite as wild as I'd expected, but it wasn't exactly tame, either. Sailors on shore leave and truckers between runs stumbled down the streets, blind drunk or headed that way as fast as they could manage, and every business in Shoreside offered to help them get rid of any unwanted cash they happened to be carrying. Noise came rolling up the hill from the bars and brothels and gambling places close to the water, the vague blurred sound you get from lots of voices saying lots of things in lots of languages, and now and again a shout or a scream or the crack of gunfire jumped out of the mess and fell back into it again. Nobody bothered us, though.

The whole way, whenever I could do it without letting her notice, I watched Sophie. More to the point, I watched her watch me. She did that most of the time, out of the corner of her eye, and it wasn't too hard to read her face. She liked me, that was obvious. She was nervous about what I might do to her, but she'd started to think about whether maybe she wanted me to do something to her, that was just as obvious.

The thought of bedding her hadn't occurred to me before then. I thought about it as we walked, and found that I liked the idea, but not that evening. Some women want to feel like they're taking risks and some want to feel safe, and I was pretty sure by then that Sophie needed to feel safe, so a little patience on my part seemed like a good idea. Besides, I'd had a long day and the horizontal action that interested me most just at the moment was seven or eight hours of sound sleep.

I LEFT HER BY the fallen lump of concrete where I'd found her that morning. I thought about circling around and tailing her for a little while to find out where she was staying, but taking the ferry home was the option that won out. The dock was a little more crowded than usual. George Morita was there, looking glum. Since I didn't have a job to do that night, I went over and talked to him, and found out he'd won every game of shoji he'd played that day. That always leaves him gloomy. I'd have offered to drop by the tea house where he spends his time the next morning and play him, but he's a lot better at shoji than I am and we both know it. So we talked, and he grumbled about how the younger generation isn't interested in Japanese culture any more, and after that he felt better.

That got us most of the way to Habitat 4, where I said goodbye and hauled myself onto the passenger dock. The guys in flak jackets waved me past, I signed in, and after the usual wait the elevator was rattling its way up to Ikkai with me and a few other people in it. It was early enough that Ikkai was just warming up and some of the daytime places were still open for business. I swung by one of those to pick up some groceries, and climbed Stair 11 past the noodle bars. I didn't want more food, but I picked up a bottle of sake and took it with me.

My room felt emptier and bleaker than usual that night. I shoved the feeling away, called my boss, and left a message on her answering machine. I thought about calling Fritz, decided to do that in the morning, then flopped down in a chair. The notebook I'd half filled with the stuff Sophie told me came out then, and I set it on the table. A mouthful of sake later, I flipped through the notes I'd taken, and made another try at sorting out the whole tangle. Yeah, it was my boss's job and not mine, but all those loose ends were beginning to get on my nerves.

Start with Max Bernard, I told myself, and start with the obvious. Ordinary businessmen trying to cut a deal don't get where they're going in the middle of the night by rowboat off a Nigerian freighter, they don't give fake addresses when they're trying to negotiate a deal, and they don't spend two days tailing the person they want to talk to. That didn't get me far, though, because too many other kinds of people might do that. Bernard could be hooked up with organized crime somewhere else, in which case he might be there to cut a deal with Big Goro. He could be there to cut a deal with one of Big Goro's underlings—Bill Takagi, say—and take over. He could be an international crook making arrangements with Big Goro before going after something big. He could be a spy, maybe a freelancer scooping up information to sell to the highest bidder, maybe working for some other country's intelligence agency. Too many choices, I thought, too little data.

Start with Rex Samuels, I told myself then. That didn't help any, because that led straight to Bernard again in one direction, and nowhere in the other. Big Goro? I knew as much about his operation as anybody in Habitat 4, and nothing I knew about connected to Bernard or Samuels. All I knew for certain was that Bernard was at the middle of a spiderweb and every thread ran to him.

Okay, I told myself. Start with the one thread that doesn't fit: the Merlin Project. Bernard wanted to find out about it. So did Michael Huddon. Fritz had hard evidence that it existed. Ernie Lobeck had heard rumors about it, and Ellie Kolchak knew enough to talk about it. If it still existed, I realized, it would explain a lot.

I got up from the table and walked over to the oval window. Off in the middle distance, across black water, the lights of Shoreside glittered cold. Past them the land rose up black and shapeless to the edge of the sky.

Suppose the Merlin Project facility's out there somewhere, I thought. Suppose it's in one of the places that's still above water. I'd heard about places up in the hills that weren't close enough to the roads or the ocean for most people to bother with. I'd heard stories of little bands of people scratching out a living up there, and other stories about places where nobody's gone for years, not since Kikai and the last couple of pandemics sent the population down hard. Suppose that there's an old government facility, all overgrown behind rusting chain-link fences, tucked away in one of the places nobody goes, some kind of computer facility that was supposed to solve all the world's problems. Suppose it's got a supercomputer or what's left of one.

Suppose Max Bernard knew about it.

It made sense. Maybe I was just shoveling moonbeams, but it would explain a lot. If Max Bernard was after whatever was left of the Merlin Project's supercomputer, no matter who was backing him, he'd have to negotiate with Big Goro. If he meant to ship it overseas, cutting a deal with one of the Habitats would make loading it a lot easier. I knew what I thought of that idea, and I had a pretty good idea what my boss would think, too, but Bernard didn't have any way of knowing that.

One way or another, that meant another long day ahead, and an evening drinking with Roy Abeshima afterwards. I finished the sake and got ready for bed.

It took me a while to get to sleep. The empty lonely feeling that my room picks up sometimes came seeping back in as soon as I lay down, reminding me of all the people I knew who probably weren't going to bed by themselves that night, bringing up questions I couldn't answer about what I was going to do with myself in the years ahead of me, if I got lucky enough to have some. I tried to tell myself that I should have gone back to the brothel I'd stumbled into when I was getting out of the way of the gunfire that morning, so I could take the little blonde up on her offer. It didn't work. I knew before I'd finished the thought that I didn't want a half hour of a working girl's time. Exactly what I did want I couldn't have told you, but it bothered me that Sophie Ames's face was the one that kept coming to mind.

THE NEXT MORNING I got up about the time the sun did, washed and dressed and downed some noodles and fish cakes, read the morning paper, and got to Ruth Taira's office at eight o'clock sharp. Louise Yoshimitsu gave me her usual disapproving look but sent me in. I went to the center of the floor, bowed, and waited.

My boss looked up from a stack of papers as I came in. She was sitting at her desk. The windows behind her showed Shoreside and the hills off past it, looking washed out under gray clouds. I wasn't expecting her to wave me to a chair, but she did. "Tell me everything you've found out about this Max Bernard."

I sat down. "Five nights ago he got rowed ashore in the small hours from a Nigerian freighter, the *Star of Lagos*. He tailed me at least twice on two separate days before he talked to me. I can tell you word for word what he said if you want, but the substance is what I said in my message. The place he said he's staying isn't the place he's actually staying. He's met at least once with Bill Takagi, and at least once with a guy I've been tailing, goes by Rex Samuels, who looks and acts a lot like quote Richard Dart unquote. What is he up to? I don't know yet. Is he what he says he is? No."

She nodded after a moment. "You don't know. What do you guess?"

I drew in a breath, went ahead. "My guess is that what's behind this whole business is the Merlin Project. Do you know about that?"

"I heard rumors, many years ago." A measured movement of one hand dismissed them. "Unverified and, to my mind, unlikely."

"Fritz Rohling says it existed. He says Abby Kuroda's got documents that mention it."

Her eyebrows went up. That's as close as she gets to a yelp of surprise. "Go on."

"Michael Huddon's asking about the Merlin Project. So is Max Bernard. If it was real, and anything's left of the supercomputer people say it had, and Bernard's here to get it—" I shrugged. "It's a guess, but it might explain some of what's going on."

She said nothing for a long moment. Finally: "Four months ago Habitat 5 was contacted by a person who claimed to represent a bank in São Paulo. The story was much the same, an international firm looking for a local agent to handle business here. Frank Yukihira approved it and had one of the banks he controls take it on. The first three transactions were perfectly legitimate. The fourth involved a great deal of money and certain mildly illegal activities that could be made to look extremely illegal if the counterparty chose."

I thought about that. "A neat little trap."

"Exactly. Of course the bank officials went to Yukihira-san at once. The bank cut its ties with the firm in São Paulo and told its representative that if they made any trouble, both governments would be informed. As far as I know that was the end of the matter. But now, this."

I waited. Outside the big windows, the clouds above Shoreside got thicker and a couple of gulls flew past.

"If you see Max Bernard again, tell him you passed on the message. Tell him I am interested but need to consult with my advisers. If he asks about it later, say the same thing." A thin little smile bent her mouth. I could imagine her ancestors smiling exactly that way when they ordered someone to be chopped into small pieces one slice at a time. "Tell him to be patient. Very, very patient."

"Will do," I said. "What do you want me to do besides that?"

"Find out as much as you can about Bernard and this Rex Samuels, but especially find out anything you can about the Merlin Project. This takes precedence over the robberies." The same cold little smile showed. "If the supercomputer still exists and this Habitat can get control of it, that will have certain advantages. If turning it over to the federal government is a wiser move, that could have certain other advantages. Find it if you can, but above all else keep Bernard from getting access to it."

"And if Big Goro's involved?"

She didn't blink. "Then it may be necessary to do something about him. Don't concern yourself with that for the time being. The Merlin Project comes first."

"I'm on it," I said.

"Good. You should be more careful than usual. Jason Fujita has been missing for two days now. Perhaps he will be found, but—" She allowed a fractional shrug.

I tried to keep my reaction off my face but I don't think I succeeded. Jason was a blunt instrument but he was as tough as me, maybe tougher. Even the worst types in Shoreside know better than to mess with people who work for the Habitat bosses. If he'd been kidnapped or killed, whoever did it was willing to take serious risks.

"Can I ask what Jason was doing?" I asked then.

"I assigned him to follow Michael Huddon."

I processed that, and didn't say anything. She nodded, the way she does at the end of a conversation, and I bowed and got out of there.

Chapter 6

I went back to my room and called Fritz. I wanted to have a chance to talk to him, but things didn't work out that way. He was busy talking to somebody I knew slightly who worked for one of the import-export houses on Sankai. That wasn't a big surprise, since the morning paper had a story about another incident between North and South China: artillery fire across the Line of Control, both sides blaming the other for starting it, both sides calling up reserves and dusting off as many antique weapons systems as they still had. The war everybody knew was coming had just gotten a hell of a lot closer. No question, it was going to play merry hob with economies all over the world. What happens to economies is one of the things that Fritz studies, and I knew that of the couple of dozen other people who know what he can do, I'm not at the top of his list. I still grumbled as I caught the elevator down to the passenger dock.

The clouds were thickening up over Shoreside by the time the ferry came along. That made me grumble some more, because a lot of the work I do gets harder when the streets are empty and you stand out like a tangerine in an egg carton. I climbed onto the ferry anyway. About a minute before we got to the dock the rain started, big fat drops landing hard against the windows and raising splashes from the sea. I gritted my teeth and braced myself for a wasted day.

The weather surprised me, though. By the time I climbed up onto the dock the rain was already getting slack, and a few minutes later the clouds blew away and a little washed-out sunshine came down onto Shoreside. It was early enough that things were still pretty quiet, and I still hadn't figured out which of the ways I was going to try that day to follow my boss's latest instructions and chase down the Merlin Project. That was why I paid attention when I heard the chanting of the Unies on the march a couple of blocks up from the shore.

I walked up to the street they were on and watched them march past. It was the same twenty people with the same blue rags tied around their heads and the same thousand-mile stares on their faces, but I had a reason to pay attention to them this time. I didn't see anyone in the group I recognized from the time I spent listening to Ellie Kolchak. That didn't surprise me too much. I followed them without making it too obvious, and after fifteen minutes or so got to their hall, a big barn of a place well up the slope that had been bright blue a long time ago and was pale blue-gray now. It stood ten feet taller than any of the buildings around it.

A double door large enough to let a truck through gaped open onto the street. The marchers filed in through it into the big dim space inside. I thought for a moment that they might slam the doors behind them, but I was in luck. The doors stayed open. I went over and stood right outside, watching the Unies milling around. After a moment a skinny girl of eighteen or so with long dishwater blonde hair under her headband, wearing a thin loose knee-length green dress over nothing at all, noticed me and came over.

"Hi," I said.

"I greet you in the name of Planetary Unity," she told me. The whole time she had this blank look on her face, and the only thing that moved when she talked was her mouth.

"Can I talk to the Blue Elder?"

Her expression didn't change at all. "No one talks to the Blue Elder."

I didn't believe that for a moment, but it was pretty clear that she did believe it, so I didn't argue the point. "Is there anyone in your group who can get a message to him?"

"I can ask," she said, and went back into the group. I waited for a few minutes, and finally she came back leading someone else. "This is Angelo," she said. "He can help you."

Angelo gave me the creeps the moment I looked at him. He was in his thirties, maybe, with long black hair and a short black beard, and he had a blue headband on, like the rest of them. He wore a sleeveless tan shirt and trousers that might have been some color or other once but had turned something between grayish-brown and nothing at all. He had bare feet and a funny expression, but it wasn't the same funny expression. It wasn't half so sane. He was staring straight past my right shoulder, like there was someone behind me, which there wasn't.

"I greet you in the name of Planetary Unity," he said, still staring past me.

"Thanks," I said. "I'd like to talk to the Blue Elder if that's okay, or get a message to him if it's not. I used to know him a long time ago."

"You want to talk to the Blue Elder," said Angelo.

"Yeah."

"Why?"

"I work for the boss of one of the Habitats. She needs to know about something, and the Blue Elder used to know about it back in the day."

He stared past me for what seemed like a long while. "Come back here in two hours and forty-five minutes," he said. "I'll have an answer for you then."

I considered him and he stared past me. After a minute or so I looked at my watch and said, "Okay. I'll be back."

"Two hours and forty-four minutes," he said, and turned away from me.

The girl in the green dress had already wandered away by then, and the rest of the Unies were sitting on the floor in a loose circle, not saying anything. I figured they were meditating, the way Mom's disciples do every day, but something about them put my nerves on edge. I said something or other and went back out onto the street. As soon as I was outside the hall, two guys in thin ragged clothes got up and shut the big double doors in my face.

I HEADED DOWN TOWARD the water for the nearest salvage shops. Ernie Lobeck's been in that business longer than anybody else, but he's not the only one, and these days he buys mostly from scavengers instead of doing the work himself. I wanted to talk to the people who went out into the hills looking for stuff that nobody had found yet, and brought things back to sell. If the Merlin Project facility was anywhere close to Shoreside, I figured, that might be the best way to track it down. Of course I wasn't even planning on thinking the words "Merlin Project" too loudly in any of the shops, and I also wasn't going to assume that I'd get one honest word out of anybody. All I'd need was an extra bit of tension in the air or an uneasy look, and I'd know I was on the right track.

For all the good it did, I might as well have chucked all my clothes off and preached at them the way Ellie Kolchak used to do. I found five shops, chatted up the people behind the counter, and left more than half convinced that none of them had found anything out of the ordinary the last fifty times they'd gone looking for salvage. I kept busy at it until my watch said it was a little past two and a half hours since I'd talked to the Unies, and headed back up the hillside to their hall. The big double doors were closed when I got there, but before I could get close enough to knock on them, one side opened and Angelo came out. He smiled and looked past my right shoulder and said, "What's your name?" I told him, and he nodded slowly, like he'd heard it before.

"I've consulted with the Blue Elder," he said then. "He's willing to see you. Tomorrow, at two o'clock exactly. Not here." He motioned south along the street. "Go up between our hall and the next building, and you'll find a door. Knock there. I'll meet you and take you to him. We'll have to walk for an hour or so."

I processed that and then thanked him. He smiled again, turned his back on me and went back into the hall without another word. The door clicked shut a moment later.

I stood there thinking for a good long minute or so. Walking for an hour will take you right out of Shoreside into the hill country. I hadn't heard anything about the Unies having some kind of presence out in the hills, but it made sense if they were following in Ellie Kolchak's footsteps. Had they taken the step she never did, and tried to follow through on all that talk about building a new world, out there in the hills where nobody lives these days? I shrugged mentally and started back down toward the water.

I'd only been to half the salvage shops in town and I had some other ideas in case that fell flat, but just then what I wanted more than that was a beer and something to eat. I was strolling along, trying to decide between Rick's and one of the quiet dives where I like to meet Yanni, when I felt the prickle on the back of my neck that tells me somebody's watching me. That's not something I ignore, so I slowed down as though I was thinking about going into a dive, then used the glass in the window as a mirror to tell me who was close by. Things weren't that crowded yet, so I didn't have any trouble spotting the watcher.

It was Rex Samuels. He wasn't making an effort to stay out of sight. That interested me. I decided to see what would happen if I kept on walking. I went on another half block or so and found another window at the right angle. There he was again, closer. I couldn't tell if he had a gun or not, but I decided to take the chance. I slowed down a little more, walked a few more yards, and then turned to face him right about the time I figured he was in speaking range.

I was right. He was about ten feet away from me, and he didn't have any kind of weapon out. He wasn't expecting me to turn, and showed it, but the shock only slowed him down for a moment. He came up to me and said, "You've been following me around."

That shook me. No matter how street-smart you are and how well you know the place, you're going to get spotted tailing someone now and then, but Samuels didn't act like he knew enough to do that. I could tell from his expression that it was a waste of time pretending that I hadn't tailed him, though, so I nodded and said, "Yeah."

"Why?"

Across the street was a cheap bar, not one of the places I go much but quiet enough at that time of day. I gestured at it. Samuels looked at me and then at the bar, and nodded. So the two of us walked across the street and went into the bar. It was the kind of dingy little place that smells of cheap beer and alcohol fuel from the little stove behind the bar that cooks the bar snacks. There were red and white tablecloths over the little round tables, blotched with faded stains not even boiling had gotten out.

Once we were inside, Samuels looked at me again and I motioned to the back of the place. He nodded again. We went all the way to the back and found a little table in the corner. I sat down, and so did he. A waitress came by. I ordered a beer, and Samuels gave me an uncertain look and did the same.

I'd figured out what to say already, but I let it wait until the beers got there and the waitress headed off to another table. "There's been a string of armed robberies in Shoreside," I said then. "Couriers with the take from gambling and prostitution here, heading to banks offshore in the Habitats.

You look and act like two of the guys involved. So, yeah, I followed you."

That startled him. "I don't know anything about that."

"I know," I said, and drank some of my beer. "That's why I wasn't following you around today. False leads—" I gestured with my free hand. "All in a day's work."

"Okay," he said, watching me. "You're a detective?"

I thought of Sophie asking me the same thing, and had to fight to keep from grinning. "Not really. I work for the head of Habitat 4, Ruth Taira."

"Okay," he said again, and downed a swallow of beer.

I watched him for a while. He looked nervous, and not because he was a nervous type. He had something on his mind, something that excited and scared him at the same time. I decided to take a risk. "I'm pretty sure you're new in Shoreside. If you need something or land in trouble, talk to me. We might be able to work something out."

He considered it. I could see the idea circle around a couple of times behind his eyes. Then he shook his head and said, "Thanks, but I'm doing okay."

"Just thought I'd offer," I said. "If things change, let me know."

"Okay," he said a third time, finished his drink, and pushed his chair back. I put on a smile and gestured at the door, and he got up, paid for his beer, and left. I watched him go and wondered what his game was. Then I paid up and got out of there. I headed north, then up a few blocks toward the Unie hall, then back down and around, just in case Samuels or someone else was following me. I didn't spot anyone, but the fact that Samuels had caught me tailing him had my nerves on edge.

I WENT TO ANOTHER dive, a place where I know I can trust the food, to get something for lunch. Then I spent the rest of the day trying to find leads on the Merlin Project, and failing miserably. I even mentioned it by name in a couple of places, and got nothing more than blank looks and one old salvage hunter scratching his head and saying he thought he'd heard something about it a long time ago but he didn't remember what. If it still existed, and anybody knew where it was, they did a fine job of keeping me from getting a single clue about that.

If Fritz hadn't told me he'd seen paperwork that proved it existed, I'd probably have talked myself into believing that I was wasting my time. As it was, I visited all the salvage shops in town and a bunch of other places where somebody might have known something about it, and got nothing. I knew, too, that there was a pretty good chance that Max Bernard would hear that I was asking about it. If Bernard was talking to Big Goro, that might mean serious trouble for me, and maybe for the Habitats too. I gritted my teeth, and told myself that I was following my boss's orders and that she'd bail me out if it came to that.

It was getting on for six when I gave up. I was way up north by then, close to the warehouse district, but I went back to Rick's Cafe Américain as fast as tired legs and a lot of drunk sailors would let me. I hadn't forgotten that Roy Abeshima and I were going to meet there later that evening, but that wasn't the only thing that got me there fast. I wanted a double whiskey and a chair in a dark corner and the sounds of Sam Nakaichi's fingers pounding the ivories, playing one of her favorite Fats Waller jazz numbers.

I got there in good time, though I had to dodge two drunken brawls and a gunfight on the way. When I came through the door, Leo looked me up and down and stepped out of my way without a word the way he does, and I grinned up at him and went straight to the bar. The double whiskey made a prompt appearance, and sure enough, Sam was hammering away at a medley of Fats Waller pieces. The chair in the dark corner was harder to find, the place was that full, but George Morita was sitting by himself at a little table over toward one side, and jerked his head up to catch my attention and let me know that if I wanted company his was available.

George and I go way back, so I headed over, said hi in Japanese, and settled into the chair across from him. He was grinning from ear to ear and he had a tall glass still half full of some concoction of vodka and rum and I don't know what else. That told me right away that he'd played shoji with someone who was a lot better than he was, and got clobbered.

Of course I asked anyway, and he grinned even more, downed another swallow of his drink, and said, "Oh, yes. A gaijin woman, nobody I've met before. Young, too. She came into the tea house this morning around ten, watched a couple of games, and then sat down and played three games with me and won them all. She's a little unpolished, she needs more experience with good players, but she's talented, very talented, and she understands strategy." He talked on for a while, getting into fine points of shoji playing that are way over my head. I didn't mind. His voice, Sam's piano playing, and the harsh clean feeling of straight whiskey in my throat all turned into a nice steady soothing hum, and I didn't pay any attention until he mentioned the name of the woman.

I put my glass down a little harder than I intended. "Sophie Ames?"

That got me a quizzical look, though that drink of his was strong enough that it blurred around the edges. "That's the one. Know her?"

"Yeah. I didn't know that she plays shoji."

George tossed down more of his drink. When he spoke again his voice was a little more slurred. "You know, if I had to guess I'd guess she learned Western chess first. Some of her moves look like she's studied classic games. Chess games, I mean. Good, but not the same as shoji. A little more practice, though, she'll be very good. Very very good." He raised the glass like he was making a toast, and drained it.

I gave him a look. "George, you need any help getting back to the ferry?"

"Me? No, I'm fine."

"You're sure."

His grin told me he knew perfectly well that I was telling him he'd had enough and ought to go home. "Sure I'm sure." He hauled himself to his feet. I'll give him this, he didn't sway much. I said good night, and so did he, and he headed for the doors that opened onto the beach, which was smart, since sand is a lot softer than the wooden planks on the streets if you go down face first. I watched him go, raised my glass, and then sipped at my whiskey.

Minutes passed. It was mostly Shoreside regulars in Rick's that night, and the tension was thick enough to spread on toast. Old habits got me tuning in to what I could hear of the conversations, and the news wasn't good: four of Big Goro's boys had been found toward the north end of Shoreside that afternoon, their bodies practically torn apart. One big guy with an eyepatch who was sitting two tables from me told the story to some friends of his, louder than anyone else in the place, and in the process he dropped the detail that made sense of it all: somebody he knew heard a noise from that part of Shoreside, about the right time, that sounded like a sheet of metal getting ripped in half.

I knew that noise. I'd heard it too often when I was in the Army, and I knew that the thing that made it could shred somebody's body faster than fast. If somebody was bringing military-grade weapons into Shoreside, that was bad enough. If someone was prepared to use them on Big Goro's goons, that meant trouble on a scale bigger than I'd ever seen.

That was what the mood of the crowd told me, too. Once that sank in, I sat there feeling cold and edgy for a little bit. A waitress came around and I got another whiskey, and then I started making plans. I didn't have to work to remember what happened when Al Sakamoto, who was boss of Shoreside before Big Goro, got in the way of half a dozen bullets. It was more than two weeks before lead stopped flying all over Shoreside. You couldn't risk taking the ferry, not if any of the contenders thought the Habitats were trying to make a deal with one of the others, and of course all three of the would-be bosses thought that, probably because it was true. I'd had to go ashore twice during the troubles and both times I'd had to use roundabout methods to get there. I could do that again, no question, but it was going to be a real pain if I had to chase down the Merlin Project through the middle of something like that.

So THAT WAS WHAT I was thinking about when Roy Abeshima showed up. He had his lopsided smile on his face, so I knew he'd been drinking, but other than the smile he didn't look happy, which startled me. Usually he's fine as long as he's well sauced. He spotted me, came over, flopped down into the other chair and waved over a waitress. She was a big brown-skinned item in her fifties, maybe, with frizzy black hair standing out around her head like the halo in a picture of the Buddha. She and Roy tossed some words back and forth, she did the same thing with me, Roy ordered a drink, we both ordered some food and handed over money, and she went off toward the kitchen with a wiggle in her backside that said, clear as words, I've still got it and no, you can't have any.

As soon as she was gone, Roy leaned toward me across the table. "Where in the *hell* did you find that girl?" I gave him a blank look and he went on: "Sophie whatsername, the one you parked with me yesterday."

"Sophie Ames," I said, a little bemused. "Why?"

"Uh-uh." He waved a finger at me. "I asked first."

"She was around when somebody tried to rob Jim Nakano on the ferry dock. I asked her what she saw and got a lot more detail than I expected. She's got a photographic memory, or something like that. So I kept her in mind, and when I needed someone to watch your lobby I went and found her. Why?"

"Can you talk her into letting me hire her?"

It was my turn to wave a finger at him. "My turn. Why?"

"She balanced my books. In her head, sitting right there in my office. You ever seen someone add fifty, sixty numbers in their head and get it right? She did that. She found a couple of mistakes that had me tearing my hair out for a month before then. I had somebody else check her work today and she didn't miss a thing. Not one single thing."

"George Morita says she's good at shoji," I told him.

"I bet. Look, the next time you see her, can you put in a good word for me?"

The funny thing was, he didn't sound like he meant it. He sounded like he was going through the motions, saying something he knew he ought to say. The smile trickled away for a bit, and he looked tired and sad. I wondered what was going on in his head. "I already did," I told him. "After I picked her up yesterday we did dinner. She told me you'd offered her a job and I told her she should take it."

"Jerry, you're a good friend," Roy told me. "A really good friend." He put his smile back on the way you put on a raincoat, but he didn't sound any happier.

The waitress came back with Roy's drink and a bowl of edamame wrapped in a white cotton towel, leaking steam from a couple of places. Then Rick came by, doing the rounds, and we made a little conversation with him. That distracted us both for a little while, and by the time Rick headed somewhere else and Roy and I started talking again he was feeling nostalgic and started asking me about somebody we both knew in Habitat 4. That led to another old memory, and then to another, and by the time the rest of the food got there he was going on about some of the things the two of us got up to in the couple of years after his brother died. He didn't usually talk about that. Hell, he *never* talked about that, and I wondered where all this was going.

I sat back and padded my stomach with chicken yakisoba, since I figured I'd be drinking a lot more whiskey before the night was over, and fed him with details on the few occasions when the booze made his memories fuzzy. What he was saying stirred up a lot of old memories for me, too, but there was an edge to those that I wasn't used to. I thought about the way I used to run off to Shoreside when I was a kid, and I remembered Ellie Kolchak and some of the other people I knew back then, and wondered whether it was worth it. I thought of all the times I'd dodged bullets, and the ones I didn't dodge fast enough and left me bleeding here and there; I thought of fights I won and others I lost; I thought about the mess I'd had to deal with back in the days after Al Sakamoto got taken out, and the mess I'd have to deal with sometime much sooner than I wanted if Big Goro went the same way; and the whole time the thought that circled in the back of my head was that maybe I'd have been better off staying out on the Habitat and doing something different with my life.

All that was going through my head while Roy was digging through old memories, and then suddenly he stopped cold. I gave him a startled look, because he was staring at me with tears in his eyes, and I would have bet any amount of money until five seconds before then that never in my life would I see Roy Abeshima cry. "Jerry," he said, "I want to go back."

It didn't take me any time at all to figure out what he meant. "Back to the Habitat."

"Yeah."

The tears were enough of a surprise by themselves, but the fact that he'd been thinking the same kind of thing I was had me really unnerved. Still, he's a good friend, and I didn't have to wonder about what I should do. "Do it," I said. "Come on. Let's go. I'll walk with you as far as the ferry."

His mouth opened. He closed it, opened it, closed it again, and then forced out, "Yeah. Damn it, yeah."

I got up then, and he got up a moment later. I left a big tip for the waitress. We wove through the crowd to the door that opened onto the beach and went out onto the sand. There were plenty of tables and plenty of people on the beach, too, but we got past them soon enough, and then Roy started to talk to himself, low and soft, in broken sentences of Japanese. I couldn't follow it all but I caught the name of a girl we both used to know, and something about her father, and then "Pride, just stupid pride" in English, and I knew that I'd heard about as much as I was ever going to find out about what sent him to Shoreside for all those years.

We got to the ferry dock without running into any trouble. The whole way the Habitats stood there on the edge of the horizon, looming up against the first dim stars in a way that stirred a different set of old cold memories. There were half a dozen people waiting on the dock, so Roy clammed up for a while. Once the lights of the ferry came into sight, he turned to me and said, "What's the best place to stay on Ikkai these days?"

That's when I knew he meant it. He was going back to the Habitat, and I wasn't sure I'd want to bet that he'd ever come back to Shoreside again. "Kazuki-ya," I told him, after the moment it took me to remember what kind of place he'd think was good. "A little past Stair Twenty, right by the noodle bar Kenji used to work at. You remember the place?"

"Yeah," he said, and he managed a little smile. "Yeah, I remember. Is he still around?"

He was, and I told Roy where to find him and half a dozen of the other people we used to know. By the time I finished filling him in, the ferry was so close you could hear the diesel purr and smell the fried-food smell that came out of its smokestack. So I stood there with Roy until the thing docked, told him to drop me a line sometime soon, got out of the way of the people getting off, and watched him climb aboard the ferry with the other passengers, and the whole time I wondered if maybe if I was smart I'd get on the ferry with him right then and there, and never come back.

THE FERRY PULLED BACK from the dock and started for Habitat 5, and I turned around and started back toward the shore. Just at that moment I heard gunfire from the beach further north. Most of the people who'd just gotten off the ferry did the smart thing and got down flat on the boards, and I did that, too. More shots went off, pop-pop-pop, and some people screamed. By then I'd crawled over to the north side of the dock and looked off that way. It was a mess.

Some of the dives north of the ferry dock have tables out on the sand when the weather's good, the way Rick's does, and it was a busy night until lead started flying, so there were people flat on the sand, people crawling as fast as they could go toward the nearest door, and people who got up and ran for their lives, never mind the bullets. Then there were the guys with the guns. I couldn't tell at first how many there were, just guns going off and people moving fast or slow, but the running people got where they were going and I saw a bunch of people crouched behind tables and chairs, shooting at each other. It looked like three or four goons had opened fire on somebody at one of the tables, and the intended targets and his friends had returned the favor. I wondered at first if Big Goro might have been the guest of honor, but even if he'd been behind a table or flat on the sand bleeding his life out, he'd have been easy to spot.

I didn't stay around to find out the other details. Once there was a lull in the shooting I scrambled back over to the south edge of the dock, moved low and fast until I was over sand instead of water, and swung over the side and dropped. Once I had a whole bunch of wood pilings between me and the gunfire I relaxed a little, but I still moved fast until I was up close to the buildings along the shore. I heard some more gunfire behind me, and kept going.

Rick's was still pretty lively when I got there, though the tables out on the beach were mostly empty. Somebody else had grabbed the table indoors where Roy and I had been sitting, so I went to the bar and ordered another double whiskey. On the other side of the room, Sam was pounding away at some piece of Thelonious Monk's I used to know the name of when I was younger. I got my drink and took a sip of it, and right then Rick came over. "Hey, Jerry," he said. "Any chance you know somebody name of Sophie Ames?"

"Yeah," I said. "And you're the third person who's mentioned her to me tonight."

"Well, she's waiting up front," said Rick. "Walked in the front door and asked Leo if you were here. Said you'd told her this was the best place to find you."

"Yeah," I said. "I told her that." With a grin: "Are you complaining?"

"Nope." His grin more than matched mine. I raised my glass to him and went to find Sophie.

She didn't take much finding. Right by the front door of Rick's there's a bench where people wait sometimes when they want a table and it's too busy just then. That was where she was. She had on the clothes I'd bought for her, and she was sitting there with her hands folded tight in her lap, looking scared. I got most of the way over to her before she looked up, saw me, and relaxed a little. Just a little, so I wondered what she had on her mind.

"Hi," she said, and I said something similar and then, "What's up?"

She drew in a breath and said, "You said I should look for you here if I needed to find you. I—I'm in trouble, kind of. I need some help."

I considered that, and then said, "How about I buy you some dinner and we talk about it."

That got me a look that was half delighted and half scared. "Please."

So she got up and we went looking for a table. One cleared out right then over by the doors to the beach, so I headed there and she followed. I did the polite thing with her chair, then went around to the other side of the table, pulled out the empty chair with my foot, got into it, let myself slump for a moment.

"Are you okay?" Sophie asked.

She sounded like she actually cared about the answer, and that surprised me a little. "More or less," I said. "Why don't you tell me what kind of help you need."

"I need someplace to go," she said. "And—and I was wondering if you could take me out to one of the Habitats."

The waitress showed up then. It was the same woman who brought Roy and me our drinks earlier, and she took our dinner orders and headed off to the kitchen. Once was gone, I looked at Sophie and didn't say anything right away. Partly I was trying to figure out what she was up to, and partly I guessed she'd tell me more if I just kept my mouth shut. I was right, too. "It's kind of complicated," she said. "And there are some things I don't want to talk about, not now. But I don't have a place to stay any more and—and I don't think it's safe for me to stay here in Shoreside. People were shooting at each other up in the empty houses when I started walking down here."

I took that in. "There were people shooting down on the beach about ten minutes ago. There's going to be big trouble here in Shoreside sometime soon." I shook my head, let out a laugh. It sounded almost as nervous as I felt. "There's always plenty of trouble in Shoreside, but not like this. It feels like the place is going to blow up like Kikai."

"What's Kikai?" she asked.

I stared at her. If she'd asked me which way was straight down I don't think I'd have been more surprised.

"Assume I don't know anything," she said, with a hint of irritation.

I swallowed. "Okay. It's a big undersea volcano, a caldera, off the southern end of Japan." I wasn't sure if she even knew where or what Japan was, but she nodded, and I went on. "In 2062 it blew up. By the time it was all over a hundred million people were dead." She took that in and then nodded again, as though it was the most natural thing in the world.

I KNOW, IT WAS a feeble explanation, but how do you even put something like that into words? Like most people nowadays, I know more about Kikai than I want to. When I was in school, once a year we got shown the famous video from Mount Kaimon on the south end of Kyushu. NHK sent a cameraman and a reporter there to film an update when the eruption was just a column of ash clouds billowing up from the water off in the far distance, and the authorities were still saying it was going to be just an ordinary lava burp, nothing to worry about. So they were there, livestreaming the whole thing, when the caldera blew.

It's really something to watch. All of a sudden ash clouds come surging up out of the sea across a big chunk of the horizon, gray and black, rising like walls. Then there's a flash toward the middle like a nuke going off, because I don't even know how many million tons of cold sea water comes crashing down onto an even bigger lump of white-hot magma and they both go boom. A big seething mass of fire and smoke gets blasted twenty miles straight up into the sky, while the reporter tries to smile and talks at the camera and the eruption rumbles in the distance. Then you can't hear her at all for a while because the shockwave hits and she and the cameraman stagger and brace themselves against it.

By the time the camera's facing the eruption again the cloud is spreading out way up above them, and you can see big streams of ash and superheated gases coming down as the column collapses. They're really beautiful, like waterfalls or veils. They drop back to the sea and shoot out in all directions at hundreds of miles an hour. That's because of the steam explosions that go off when they hit the water, but you can't see those.

So the cameraman is filming and the reporter is talking when she can, and the air is shaking, and you can see in her face when she realizes that the stuff that came streaming down has turned into a roiling black cloud hundreds of feet high and it's rushing toward the two of them. It isn't until the cloud reaches land and things start going incandescent the moment it touches them that she really gets what's about to happen. She starts crying and the cameraman has time to repeat a prayer to Amida Buddha a few times as the pyroclastic cloud comes straight at them. Then the cloud hits and everything goes black and you know that every living thing on the southern third or so of Kyushu has just died.

In school they always followed that with pictures from a satellite showing the ash cloud streaming north-northwest over Japan, dumping its cargo on the islands. Then there was footage of towns on Kyushu and southern Honshu with the ash piled up ten feet thick while more comes sifting down from the sky, and people climbing up on roofs before their houses collapsed under the weight. Plenty of people didn't get out, but you can't see that, and after a minute or two the screen would switch to videos of the tsunami from all over the Pacific basin.

You'd think that would be what sticks in the mind, since the wave was more than a hundred feet tall when it slammed into Kyushu and the southern end of Korea. It was still forty feet or so when it raked the other Japanese islands and hit Shanghai head on, and when it got to the other sides of the Pacific, everywhere from Alaska to Australia, it piled up ten feet here and twenty feet there depending on the shape of the sea floor, and rolled back out to sea with its share of houses and cars and people. All of that got caught on camera. They always put a brief picture or two of a nuclear power plant in there somewhere around that point, too, and those are memorable in another way. All of Japan's nukes were on the seacoast and so were all the ponds where they kept spent fuel rods. The tsunami hit those, up they went, and that's the reason why nearly all of southern and central Japan is off limits for the next three or four centuries.

After that the teachers always showed pictures of the cold year that followed all over the northern hemisphere, snow in summer, long lines of hungry people, riots and revolutions, mass graves. They always wound it up with recent pictures from Hokkaido and the northern end of Honshu, which didn't get hit so hard and you've still got towns and farms that look Japanese. Of course nobody likes to admit that those are a Russian protectorate now, but it was that or let the North Koreans take over.

Those are the things you'd think I would remember from my school days, right? But what comes to my mind is always the reporter on Mount Kaimon right before the pyroclastic cloud hit. She was trying to say something into the camera, but you can't hear what it is, partly because she's crying and partly because of the roar. What I remember is her expression. I think it sank in just then, in the thirty seconds or so before the screen goes black, that there was nothing personal involved. There wasn't anything she'd done or left undone, it didn't matter if she'd been a bad person or for that matter a good one, and the universe didn't mean to kill her. She just happened to be standing in the wrong place when the earth cleared its throat, and the fact that she was about to die was just one of those things.

All this went through my head between when I stopped talking and when Sophie opened her mouth. "Oh," she said, and a moment later: "So that's what happened."

I looked at her and tried to make sense of that, and after a long, long moment I realized that it might make the kind of sense that could make me crazy rich, or get me and a lot of other people killed. That changed a lot of priorities in a hurry, and the one at the top of the stack was getting Sophie somewhere safe before anyone else caught on. "Okay," I said to her. "So you want to go to one of the Habitats."

"Please. I want that very much."

"I can take you to Habitat 4, where I live, but you're going to have to do exactly what I tell you." I could see a sudden flicker of nervousness in those wide brown eyes, and raised a hand, reassuring. "Nothing you don't want to do. It's just that there are a lot of rules and customs you don't know out there."

She nodded. "Then I'll do what you tell me."

The waitress came back with our meals then, made a little small talk, and headed off again. I downed another bowl of chicken yakisoba and she made serious inroads on a hamburger and fries. I watched her, wondering what she was thinking. She watched her plate. Neither of us said much until both our plates were pretty much empty.

"Ready?" I said then. She nodded, looking more than a little scared, and I waved down the waitress, got our bill, and paid up. Once that was taken care of, I got to my feet. "Let's go."

She got up and followed me out the doors and down onto the beach. The ferry dock stuck out to sea half a mile away. I motioned with my head. She caught up with me. The two of us walked along the sand past the gaudy clutter of Shoreside, past a few drunks lying passed out on the sand and a few people using the beach to get from place to place. I listened and didn't hear any gunfire, though I kept my hand close to my Browning the whole time. All the while Sophie stayed close and watched everything, from the drunks to the gulls circling overhead to the great silent shapes of the Habitats rising up from the horizon, black as night against the darkening sky except where windows let light splash out onto the sea. The shapes of the Habitats reminded me of the video I'd seen so many times at school, the black walls of smoke and ash rising up out of the ocean, and I thought about what people went through when Kikai blew up and the world changed.

Of course it wasn't just Kikai that happened. Things were falling apart for plenty of other reasons a long time before smoke started boiling up from that particular bit of ocean. They're still falling apart for plenty of other reasons now. It's just that back before Kikai, a lot of people all over the world talked themselves into believing that things couldn't fall apart, not really. The seas were rising, the deserts were spreading, the forests were burning, there was one shortage after another, one pandemic after another, one crisis after another, lots of people dying, lots of people losing everything they owned, and it just kept going. Every time the old governments tried a new gimmick to fix things, the gimmick just made things worse, but everybody still told each other that something or other would turn up any day now and solve all their problems. It took Kikai to make them change their minds, and by the time that was over and done with, a hundred million of them would never change their minds or anything else ever again.

Chapter 7

We boarded the ferry half an hour later, along with a few unlucky gamblers who'd already lost their stake and a couple of guys I know by sight who do the same kind of work I do for the boss of Habitat 2. Sophie sat next to the window with her hands folded in her lap and I sat next to her and tried to look nonchalant. She was scared and excited, and she glanced at me from time to time but mostly looked out the window.

By the time the ferry got us to my Habitat I'd worked out a plan and told Sophie what to do in a whisper. We climbed up onto the dock in the cold night air, and I walked straight toward the booth with Sophie following behind close as a shadow. I knew the guards and they nodded to me but one of them said, "Who's she?"

"Here on business," I said. "You can call my boss if you need to."

They were both big burly guys but they both looked scared when I said that. I could sympathize, because the thought of what would happen if they called my bluff was enough to put a chill down my spine. That night I must have been lucky, though. They looked at each other, and the one who'd opened his mouth said, "So long as she signs in."

I nodded, like it was the most ordinary thing in the world, and led Sophie to the booth by the elevator. She took the pen and wrote *Sophie Ames* in the kind of precise handwriting almost nobody seems to know how to do these days. The clerk in the booth was half asleep, and she faked a glance at the names and then picked up the phone to call the elevator.

A few minutes later we were on our way up to Ikkai. Sophie didn't have to be told what an elevator was but she stood very still in a corner until it rattled to a stop. We went past the guards up top and out into Ikkai. That startled her—Ikkai startles most people the first time they see it—but she stayed close to me and didn't say a thing while we wove through the narrow streets past bars and signs and night spots to Stair 11.

The noodle places on the landings were still open, and I turned to Sophie. "You want anything more to eat?"

"No—no, I'm fine," she said. She wasn't fine, not by any stretch of the imagination. She was scared half out of her wits, it didn't take any particular talent to see that or guess why, but she kept following me up the stair and down the hall until we got to my room and I let us both in.

Once we were inside and the little ceiling lamp was on and I closed and locked the door, she went further in and then turned to face me. She had her arms crossed over her chest and huddled behind them. "Please—please don't do anything to me."

"Not unless you ask me to," I told her, and she blushed hard and turned away. I expected that. The way she'd held her body on the ferry and in the elevator, about a quarter of her wanted me to scoop her up, plop her on the futon, and go from there, and the other three quarters were frightened half to death that I'd do that. I figured there was a pretty good chance those numbers would change in a day or two, and I was willing to wait. Partly I was tired, and partly I didn't want to mess things up between us by getting pushy. The thing was, I liked her. Damn if I could figure out why, but I liked her.

So I got some water heating for tea and said, "You ought to get some sleep. Here." I got a spare pair of pajamas out of the closet and handed them to her. "You can change in the bathroom if you like." She gave me a look that was wary and relieved and just a little disappointed all at once, mumbled something that might have been thanks, went into the bathroom, and came out again a while later with the pajamas on. They hung on her like a tent but the drawstring on the waist kept anything too embarrassing from happening.

I took her clothes and put them into the cloth bag by the door and hung them outside on the knob, then went back in and said, "They'll be clean by the time you wake up." She nodded without saying anything. I motioned toward the futon and she went over to it, and once she figured out that I wasn't going to come after her she lay down on top of the covers. I had to explain that those were supposed to go over her, and she nodded again, settled herself under them, and lay there with her face and her knees at the very edge of the futon and her back toward the other two-thirds of it. I fixed my tea and sat down at the table with a notebook and started writing down everything that had happened that day. Sure enough, the next time I looked at her she was sound asleep.

I finished taking notes and drinking tea at close to the same time, and then spent a while looking at her and thinking. I had a lot of questions and not many answers, but I'd realized back while we were sitting at Rick's in Shoreside that there was one possibility that made sense of all the odd things she'd said and done, and especially of the fact that she didn't know about Kikai but knew that the world had been different once. If Fritz was right and the Merlin Project actually existed, it would have to be really well hidden. That probably meant it was inland, in the hill country where not many people go, and it might be quite a ways inland, further than salvage crews generally get.

Suppose, I thought, the Merlin Project had been set up in some government facility back among the hills, someplace nobody else has gone since before Kikai. Suppose the people in it slammed the doors shut and went into hiding when things got crazy, and had enough supplies that they could stay hidden for a good long while. Suppose Sophie had been born there, and decided to leave and go find out what the rest of the world was doing. That would explain all the things she didn't know and all the things she wouldn't say.

I was feeling pretty pleased with myself when another thought surfaced: suppose that Big Goro knows something about the Merlin Project too.

That made sense, too, the kind of sense that set my teeth on edge. As boss of Shoreside he'd be in a good position to hear rumors and get scraps of information. A working supercomputer, or even the spare parts of one, would be much too sweet of a plum for him to resist. It was worth enough that if he could control access to it he'd have the money to buy the Habitats and sell them for scrap if he wanted to. That made it all the more urgent for me to figure out how to make contact with the Merlin Project facility before Big Goro did, assuming he hadn't managed it already.

It also made me all the more certain I had to keep Sophie safe in the Habitat for the time being. If I was right, she was the only person outside of the Merlin Project facility who knew where it was and how to get into it. I had to make sure Big Goro didn't find out about her, and the same went for Huddon, who'd claim the whole thing for the federal government as soon as he had the chance. The feds would probably get it anyway, but if that happened, the choice would be up to my boss, and she'd be able to extract plenty of benefits for the Habitat in exchange. And my boss? That was easy enough. She would find out about it the moment I had some evidence that I wasn't just shoveling more moonbeams.

Beyond that, a dozen half-formed plans tumbled around in my mind, but sleep came first. I washed up and got into my pajamas and crawled under the covers on the other side of the futon, moving slow and quiet. Sophie didn't stir. I settled down with my back toward her and was asleep in minutes.

THE NEXT MORNING I had time to shower and shave and get into clothes before Sophie woke up. She blinked and sat up slowly, like she didn't know where she was at first, then tried on a little tentative smile. I said good morning and she said the same thing, and I went and got her clean clothes from outside the door and handed them to her and then sat down again and started looking over the morning paper, taking in the latest on the not-quite-war between North and South China. She took the hint and went into the bathroom. I heard water running, and a while later she came out looking less feral than she had the day before.

"Breakfast?" I asked, and she nodded and started to say something, and then looked past me at the oval window and her eyes went round. She went straight there and stood facing three miles of water and the blurred gray line of Shoreside and the green hills off beyond it, while I watched her and wondered what she was thinking.

After twenty seconds or so, she turned around with an embarrassed smile. "I'm sorry. I didn't realize last night that there was a window, and—and it's a nice view. And you were saying something, weren't you?"

"Breakfast," I reminded her, and she said "Please" and sat down on the chair facing me across the table with her hands folded in her lap. So I got up and got water going for noodles and tea, and got a couple of fish cakes warming up, and went back to the table. I'd had some time to think before she woke up and I knew what I needed to do.

"I have some things I have to get done today," I said, "and you should stay safe here in the Habitat." She nodded. "So I'd like to introduce you to my mom. She'll make sure you're fine and answer your questions while I'm gone. Okay?"

Sophie nodded again and said, "I'd like to meet your mother."

"She's a little strange," I told her.

That got me a little smile. "So am I." I managed to stifle a laugh, but not by much. "I know I am," she said, with the solemn look that I was getting used to. "And you've been very nice about not making a fuss over it."

That called for a long explanation or none at all, and I settled for going to the phone and calling Mom. She picked up on the first ring, the way she always does, and the first thing she said after she finished with the moshi-moshi was, "So who is she?"

I wasn't sure whether someone had spotted us on the way through Ikkai or Ame no Kokoro had been unusually chatty that morning, but I improvised. In Japanese—it occurred to me only later that I didn't know what languages Sophie did or didn't speak—I explained that Sophie was someone from Shoreside with information my boss needed, and asked her if she'd be willing to take care of her while I was busy that day. Of course she said yes, and I told her, "Her name is Sophie Ames and she's a little strange."

"Please bring her to the worship hall," Mom told me. "I'm sure she's a very nice girl and today isn't a busy day."

By the time I finished the call the water for the noodles was boiling, and I went ahead and made breakfast. I had most of it on the table before I wondered whether Sophie knew how to use hashi, and remembered about half a second later that I didn't have anything else but a couple of soup spoons, which won't do much good with noodles.

"No," she said when I asked, "but show me." Okay, I thought, I'm in for it, but what I was in for was a shock. I showed her how to hold the hashi and move them, she watched my hand with those wide eyes, and then picked up her hashi and used them. There's always a learning curve with them. For kids it's usually a couple of years, for adults it's a couple of weeks, and for her it was a little over a minute. I think I managed not to stare, but it took a serious effort.

So we ate breakfast, and she thanked me very nicely for it, and then I threw on a jacket and got my Browning settled, and we left the room and headed up the stair to Nikai. Of course Mom was standing in the doorway when we got to the hall, and welcomed Sophie like a long-lost daughter. Her English is pretty good even though she gets the grammar mixed up sometimes. The two of them got to talking right away. I hung just long enough to make sure I wasn't needed and then left Sophie to Mom and the Mushukujin.

Half an hour later I was on my way to Shoreside. I didn't take the ferry. I had a bad feeling about that, with so much lead flying over the days just past. I didn't have a reason to think any of it would be headed my way on purpose, but you never know. That's why I caught one of the freight elevators down to a different dock, where the lighters stop on the way out to the ships and back into the freight docks on the north end of Shoreside. They know me there. Like most of the people who work for my boss, I cross the water that way sometimes, and a few of the older guys who work there remember when I was a kid dodging school so I could go to Shoreside and get into trouble.

It only took a few words and a couple of bills handed to the crew boss to get me aboard a lighter full of crates of machine parts from some Congolese factory or other. The lighter trudged in through the sunken ruins to a big wooden dock full of crates and longshoremen and crew bosses yelling at the top of their lungs. I got past the dock quickly enough, went south past the warehouses where the guards keep watch with shotguns in their hands, and then veered uphill a couple of blocks into the quiet part of Shoreside.

That was a little risky, partly because there aren't many people there at that hour and I'd be easier to spot, partly because I was only a block or so from the first row of abandoned houses. I knew better than to assume that they were all still abandoned just then. Maybe Big Goro had his people up in there, maybe it was whoever was gunning for him, maybe both: there's been more than one pitched battle uphill from Shoreside in my time. Risky or not, there were too many people I didn't want to meet just then and most of them would be close to the water.

Maybe I was lucky, or maybe Ame no Kokoro was looking out for me. I didn't run into any trouble on the way to the Unies' hall. I didn't run into anyone at all. Nobody was on the streets just then, and I thought I could guess why.

I COULD SEE THE Unies' hall well before I got there. The big double doors in front were closed tight. I remembered what Angelo said, though, and went around the far side where a narrow street went further uphill. The door he'd mentioned was there, probably salvaged from some abandoned house further up. It had a peephole in it, the old-fashioned kind with a little glass eye set in yellow metal. I checked my watch, made sure I wasn't too early or too late, and tapped on the door three times.

Angelo opened it a few moments later. He had the same clothes on he'd worn the day before, complete with the blue headband, and they looked like he'd slept in them. I gave him as thorough a once-over as I could without making it obvious. He didn't have a gun on him, which made me a little less edgy. He gave me the same odd look as before, like he was looking off past me toward something I couldn't see, but he put on a smile after a moment. "Mr. Shimizu. You want to see the Blue Elder."

"Yeah," I said. "If that's okay."

"You want to see the Blue Elder," he said again. "Tell me why."

"Told you that yesterday," I said, with a grin I didn't feel.

"Tell me more." His expression didn't change.

"Okay. I knew him a couple of decades ago. We both used to know somebody else who used to talk about something my boss needs to know about. I think it's worth talking to him, seeing if he remembers anything about what she said." I shrugged. "And it'd be nice to catch up for old times' sake."

He was still looking past me. "Who was the person you both knew?"

"An old lady named Ellie Kolchak."

"Ah," he said, like the name meant something to him. "And what was the thing she used to talk about?"

I couldn't think of any way to get around telling him, or I would have. "Something called the Merlin Project. I don't know what it was."

"Ah," he said again. "Come with me. We have to take a little walk."

"About an hour, you said."

"Yes. About an hour." The way he said it gave me the creeps, though I couldn't have told you why.

He went past me to the street and started walking north, the way I'd come. I followed him and tried to figure out where we were going.

Where we were going, to begin with, was all the way along the street until it guttered out into bare dirt a good dozen blocks or so further north. On that side of town the ground slopes down for a ways and then rises up again into low hills covered with grass and scattered pines. Something you could call a trail, if you were feeling charitable, led further north from the end of the street. That way there were only a few abandoned houses and then not much of anything but hills, wandering back out of sight north and west.

We went further, and the trail ducked down into a fold of the land, so you couldn't see it unless you were close to it, and it stayed there. It wasn't much more than a thin place in the grass, but I noticed as we went further that wherever the dirt showed, bare feet of more than one size and shape had left tracks there. The tracks were fresh, too. I was pretty sure they hadn't been there for more than a few hours.

After a while, we passed a place where some animal or other had dug into the ground and splashed dirt all over the trail, and somebody with small delicate feet had left a good clear print in it. I pointed to it and said, "Busy day here?"

Angelo gave me the same right-past-me look. "Yes. The others went ahead at dawn."

That made me uneasy. I gave him a look I hoped he couldn't read. He just kept walking.

Time passed. The trail ducked and danced this way and that way, staying out of sight in little valleys and folds of the hills. We must have gone a good three or four miles from Shoreside before the trail veered through a gap between two hills and went down into the valley on the far side of them. There were old buildings in the valley, gray and flat-roofed, and after a little while we came to an old rusting chain-link fence with a gap in it. On one side of the gap was a little sign, not quite rusted enough so you couldn't read it. It said NO TRESPASSING—GOVERNMENT PROPERTY.

That got my heart beating just a little fast. If the Merlin Project still existed, I knew, it might be in a place like this one. It hadn't occurred to me before then that the Unies might know something about it. Was that what they were hiding out here? A supercomputer, or maybe some way to make contact with the people who had it?

We kept going. Past the chain-link fence the trail turned into something more like a proper path, leading straight between pines and shrubs to one of the gray concrete buildings. There was a door in the wall ahead, and it was hanging open.

ALL MY NERVES WERE on edge when we got to the door, but Angelo went straight in like he didn't have a thing to worry about. I followed him. Inside was an empty room. I couldn't see much of it. There were a few windows high up on one wall with glass still in them, but the glass was filthy with a good many years of dirt and dust, and not much light got through.

If there had been anything else in the room, somebody had hauled it off to sell to Ernie or his competitors a long time ago, but an intact metal door still barred the way further in.

Angelo went over to the door and pulled a key out of one of his pockets. The lock made a muffled click. He pulled the door open, motioned toward the space beyond, and stood there waiting for me to go past him.

I went past him and stepped into the room. It wasn't any better lit than the one I'd just left, just one window up high on the wall letting in a little daylight, but I wasn't paying a lot of attention to that. My attention was on Angelo. My nerves were on edge already, as I said, but he was one of the main things keeping them that way. So once I was past him, I wasn't too surprised when I heard the little scrabbling noise of Angelo picking something up off the floor, and then a quiet little click, not at all muffled. It was the sound of somebody clicking off the safety on a pistol.

Reflexes took over. I spun around and knocked the muzzle away from me with one hand. The gun went off so close to me that I could feel the heat, but the bullet missed me and then my other fist got up close and personal with Angelo's face. He didn't expect that, which told me he didn't know how to fight. I grabbed the wrist of his gun hand and then socked him again in the midsection. He doubled over, and I didn't have much trouble after that getting the gun out of his hand and forcing him down to his knees.

"Cut the crap," I told him. "I want to talk to the Blue Elder."

Angelo started laughing. It wasn't a laugh you'd hear from anyone even slightly sane. It came out in little puffs, high and shrill and sharp-edged. "I tried," he said, forcing the words out through the laugh. "I tried, I tried. But you wouldn't let me take you there. I tried."

That was when I realized he was staring past me, and not the way he'd done earlier. He was looking up at something on the other side of the room. I aimed the gun I'd taken from him straight at him, backed away to one side, and looked.

Mike Glaskey was there, all right, or what was left of him. He was sitting in an old half-rusted metal chair, wearing a long filthy blue robe and a scrap of blue cloth tied around his head, and he still had the shaggy hair and long beard I remembered. His mouth was open and so were the places where his eyes had been. He'd been dead for a good long time, long enough that there wasn't enough stink to notice, long enough that somebody had to tie him in a couple of places to the chair to keep his corpse from tumbling down. You could see the bullet hole in his chest, too, where he'd been shot.

I turned to Angelo again. He was still mumbling "I tried, I tried, I tried" in a low voice. I went to him and jabbed him with a shoe, none too gently. "Who killed him?"

That got me a look that still gives me nightmares sometimes, a grin that showed every one of Angelo's teeth and a stare that went right through me all the way to outer space. "The Elder? He's not dead. He talks to me all the time, just like he always did. He's not dead. He told me to bring you here, he told me to send you where he is, the way I sent the others, the way I sent him when he told me to." His voice rose into a shriek. "He *told* me!"

I pulled the trigger.

Once he stopped moving I wiped the pistol grip on my vest to get rid of the prints, put the pistol in Angelo's right hand, got the finger through the trigger guard, and twisted the arm around so it looked as though he'd shot himself. Out in the Habitats, that wouldn't fool anybody for ten seconds, they'd do some kind of test on his hand and figure out it didn't have any burnt powder on it, but the only people who might find him this far out were from Shoreside. The nearest thing to police I'd ever seen in Shoreside was Bill Takagi, and he wasn't the kind of guy who knew anything about lab tests.

I hadn't heard anyone else moving in the building on the way in. That didn't change while I was backing away from poor Mike Glaskey and the man who'd killed him. It didn't change, either, when I noticed the other door out of the room.

It was open just a little bit, so I went over to it, listened for a moment, kicked the door open, and wished I hadn't.

The rest of them were in there: all the Unies, as far as I could tell. They'd gone ahead of him, all right. From the blood and the stink, he'd shot them earlier that day and laid them out neatly in two rows, the same way they'd marched through the streets of Shoreside. I saw the skinny girl with the dishwater blonde hair close to the door. She was lying there with her eyes closed and a blank look on her face. You'd have said she was sleeping except for the bullet hole in her chest and the half-dried blood all over the thin green dress.

I GOT OUT OF the building as fast as I could. Outside, where the air smelled of pines and dry dirt instead of gunfire and blood, I stopped, spent a few minutes steadying myself, and then made myself search the buildings. They were all just as empty as the one I'd left—well, to be honest, they were emptier, because none of them had a bunch of dead Unies in them. Whatever the old government had been doing there, they must have stopped when I was a kid if they'd even kept things going that long. The Merlin Project? If it had been there, I decided, Max Bernard and Michael Huddon were both in for a disappointment.

With that in mind I started back toward Shoreside. I'd paid attention to where the sun was on the way out, so I knew the general direction to go, but the trail wasn't easy to follow. After half an hour or so I was pretty sure I'd gotten away from it, because the hills around me didn't look quite the same shape as the ones I remembered on the way out, and I hadn't seen a footprint for a while. I muttered a bit of profanity under my breath, made sure from the sun's angle that I was still pointed more or less south and east, and kept going.

More time passed: most of an hour, or so my watch said. Finally, off through the pines ahead, I spotted a little cluster of buildings. That cheered me up but it also put my nerves on edge, because I knew I might be seeing some of the abandoned houses up the slope from Shoreside. I made sure my Browning was loose in the pocket holster and went closer.

It wasn't too many more minutes before I knew that they were abandoned houses, all right, a little group of three of them off by themselves. By then I could see more of them further to the south, and the long brown shape of an armored truck cheered me even more as it came briefly into view even further away, marking the road that linked Shoreside with the inland cities. I knew I could still wind up dead if I got a little too stupid, but I'd never been that far into the hill country before and I'd started to get nervous about finding Shoreside ever again.

So I went a little closer to the three abandoned houses, staying in among the pines, and I kept my eyes and ears wide open. I didn't get far before I knew that the houses weren't as abandoned as they should have been. There was somebody lounging out in front of one of them, smoking a cigarette—I could smell the tobacco smoke before I could see him. That got me moving low and quiet through the pines, circling around until I could see whoever it was.

I saw him, all right. I had to work my way about halfway around the houses, but there he was, sitting on the steps of one of the houses, dressed in a plain cheap sleeveless shirt and trousers the color of dried mud. One glance told me who it was, but I moved a little closer and watched him from another angle for a while just to be sure.

It was the man who'd called himself Richard Dart, the one I'd watched being dragged off by Big Goro's boys the night I spotted Sophie for the first time.

I crouched behind a tree, watching him, for a good long time. He finished his cigarette and went back inside the house, and I heard voices through the open door, though I couldn't make out what they were saying. That was enough. I got away from there as fast as I could. I didn't try to make sense of what I'd seen. That was for later, when I didn't have to worry whether some of Goro's toughs might notice me and decide they needed some target practice.

So I went straight toward the water, or as close to that direction as guesswork could manage, and after a little while I spotted my own shoeprints in a patch of bare ground and knew I'd found the trail again. From there a few more minutes brought me back to Shoreside. My heart was beating hard and I felt a little wobbly, which isn't normal for me. The few people I passed didn't seem to notice anything. I kept walking, and turned down toward the busier parts of Shoreside as soon as I felt steadier.

I went straight to Rick's, nodded to Leo the bouncer on the way in. At the bar I ordered a whiskey and downed it, then got another and went to a little table in back. Yeah, I was shaken. It wasn't because I'd killed Angelo, or because I'd seen all the other Unies lying there with bullet holes through them and blood all over. Counting Angelo, I've killed eleven people: shot seven, knifed three, and pushed one off the old helicopter deck on Gokai on top of Habitat 4 and watched him fall all the way down until he hit the sea, and the first time I ever had to kill a guy was the only one that left me shivering. As for corpses, shot or otherwise, you don't spend much time in Shoreside before you get used to those.

No, one part of the problem was Mike Glaskey. I remembered him from back when I was a snot-nosed kid running loose in Shoreside and he was Ellie Kolchak's number one follower, naked the way she was but muscled and suntanned and bright-eyed, always full of stories about the wonderful future that was always about to show up. Yeah, he was basically crazy, but he was nice to me when I was young and stupid, and he deserved better than a bullet in the chest from somebody who was even crazier than he was.

The second part of the problem was the guy who'd called himself Richard Dart. If he was still alive, smoking a cigarette up there among the abandoned houses, the whole business around the armed robberies of couriers had just twisted around in a direction I didn't like at all. Either Big Goro or one of his top people must have let Dart go, and that meant that somebody in his organization knew about the robberies. It might mean that Big Goro or one of his top people was behind the robberies, and that raised questions I couldn't begin to answer yet. Then there was the third part—

The third part was that I was losing my edge. I could feel that. Sure, I came out of Angelo's little trap alive, but that's not the thing that mattered. A couple of years back I would have beaten Angelo good and hard, gotten him to spill everything he knew, and then shot him if that seemed like the right thing to do. I wouldn't have shot him dead on the spot, and lost whatever chance I might have had of getting a clue or two about the Merlin Project. I shook my head, downed the rest of the whiskey, and wondered what I was going to do with myself if I really was getting too old for my job.

MAYBE I SHOULD HAVE kept hunting for clues to the Merlin Project, but I'd had enough for one day and I honestly couldn't think of any other way to track it down just then. I considered trying the ferry but my gut instinct said stay away from it. So once I got my nerves settled down I headed back to the docks and waited for a lighter. It took more than an hour to find somebody going the right way, but finally I climbed aboard a lighter on its way out to Habitat 4.

Once the little engine started up, I sat on the hard wooden seat and watched the waves turn concrete back into gravel a little at a time as Shoreside slipped away behind me and home got closer. The septic tank that came up the morning Huddon and I rode the ferry to Shoreside, when he talked about warlords and kings and the world of light where we came from, had done the sensible thing and come unstuck from the ruins. It was drifting slowly northward with the current as the lighter passed it. I wondered where it would end up, and then spent a while wondering where I would end up, and pulled myself back from that overfamiliar topic by thinking about Sophie.

I'd spent more than one set of spare moments thinking about her already. As the lighter wove its way past the last of the ruins and made for deeper water, I finally had a while when I didn't have anything else I had to think about, and my thoughts circled around her in a way that startled me at first. She wasn't particularly pretty, if by pretty you mean either the blowsy charms of girls from Shoreside or the polished look you see so much of in the Habitats. She was odd and gawky and vulnerable, and that was part of what I liked about her.

It occurred to me while I watched the waves splash against concrete that if I liked either the Shoreside type or the Habitat type I could have had as much of either one as I wanted, and it's true. I'd had my share of Shoreside girls when I was young and dumb, and spent time with a couple of women from Nikai when I wasn't much older or smarter. The sex was fun but that's as far as any of it went. I'd be lying if I said I wasn't thinking about having the same kind of fun with Sophie, but there was more to it than that.

With the Shoreside working girls, you know exactly what you're getting and what it's going to cost you. Out in the Habitats, it's not so cut and dried, but the principle's the same: you want something, they want something, you both know what the deal is. Whether it ends up being half an hour of fun, or a relationship that goes on for a couple of months or years, or you get married and have some kids and live in the same three rooms together until you get old and die, don't expect any surprises, because you're only going to get so much.

With Sophie, I was already pretty sure that rule didn't apply. I was starting to figure out that she wanted to offer me everything she had, and by that I don't just mean her body. What exactly it did mean wasn't something I could figure out in advance, and what she might ask from me in return, that wasn't any clearer. Maybe that's why my thoughts kept circling around her, and around what I was going to do once I went to Mom's worship hall to meet Sophie again.

I was still thinking about that when the lighter went under Habitat 4 and pulled up to the cargo dock. I got out, said hi to the dock boss, and took the freight elevator up to Ikkai. Fifteen minutes and a few hundred steps later and I was back in my room. I picked up the phone right away and called Fritz, and got him on the fifth ring.

"Your timing is excellent," he said. His voice was higher and scratchier than usual, which means that he's excited about something. "How soon can you get here?"

I gave him an estimate and beat it by two minutes. For a change, I didn't have to wait a long time at the door, and it wasn't Fritz who opened it. It was Susan Ono, the same one of my boss's assistants who'd been there the day I met Michael Huddon. If she wasn't wearing the same black suit I couldn't tell you the difference, and she had the dour look on her face she usually puts there. "Shimizu-san," she said, with a little forward shift that might have been third cousin to a bow. "Please come in."

I followed her into Fritz's sitting room. Fritz beamed at me and waved me toward the little table with tea and cookies. I wasn't particularly interested in those, but Fritz gets sulky if you turn down his hospitality, so I got a cup of tea and a couple of cookies while Susan sat down. Once I was settled in the third chair, Fritz said to her, "Tell him."

Susan glanced at him, then at me. Her face didn't change at all. "Starting about two years ago the salvage dealers on Sankai started getting inquiries from overseas firms about electronic components. Not general inquiries. They were looking for specific items, fifty, sixty, seventy years old. Of course the dealers let the appropriate people know."

"Any connection between the overseas firms?"

That got me a look that wasn't quite so dour as before. "Yes, though it took some finding. We're pretty sure they're controlled by the Bureau de Sécurité Extérieure."

I nodded. The EU has half a dozen intelligence agencies but the BSE is the one you mostly hear about outside its borders.

"Ms. Ono brought me into this just over nineteen months ago," Fritz said. "To identify an electronics technology from a shopping list of components, that can be easy, or it can be hard. In this case it was hard. The people involved were clever enough not to do all their shopping in one place. So I called in a few favors and had a very pleasant correspondence with salvage dealers in New Guangzhou and Dar Es Salaam. I'll dispense with the story. The only technology that uses all the components in question is one of the old supercomputers."

I took that in. "You think they're trying to build one?"

"Repair, not build," Susan said. "They have at least one, maybe two. There are rumors that they need more spare parts than they have. Nobody can make chips to those specifications any more, and none of the salvage dealers have them for sale."

I glanced at Fritz, then, and he grinned and sipped his tea and said, "I've told her about the Merlin Project. So has Mrs. Taira, if I understand correctly." Susan nodded, and he went on. "So. I think we now know who may be after it. Have you found anything relevant?"

That was exactly what I didn't know. If I was right about Sophie, everything I needed to find out about the Merlin Project might be sitting in Mom's worship hall at that moment, but I couldn't be sure that I was right. "I'll tell you everything I've found," I said. To Susan: "How much do you know about what I've been chasing?"

"Only the basics."

"Brace yourself," I said, and she allowed a thin little smile and got a pen and a notepad from inside her jacket.

THE DOORS OF THE Mushukujindo were open when I got there a couple of hours later, after I visited my room for a quick shower, a change of clothes, and a phone call to my boss to tell her about Dart. Inside the worship hall I could hear voices repeating prayers in unison. I recognized the words after a moment: the prayers for the muenbotoke, the ghosts who didn't have any descendants to say prayers for them. There were a lot of voices saying the prayer, most of them old and female. I put my shoes in the shoe rack, rinsed hands and mouth, went in, said hi to the kami and settled on the tatami mats in the anteroom to wait for Mom to show up.

I didn't have to wait long. Mom came down the little narrow stair from the office after maybe a minute. After we'd said the usual things and I bent down to let her hug me and kiss my cheek, she said in Japanese, "Sophie is in the office. We've been drinking tea and talking just now. She's a very pleasant girl and I think you should marry her."

You're not supposed to roll your eyes and laugh at your mother. Part of me wanted to, and part of me didn't, so I shelved the whole question and let her take me upstairs. When we got there Sophie glanced up at me with a smile a blind man could have read. I sat on the floor with the two of them and drank a cup of green tea and made a little conversation. After that Sophie and I left the hall. Out on Nikai I turned to her and said, "I hope Mom fed you lunch."

"We had soup and sushi." With a sidelong glance and a smile: "It was a while ago."

I know how to take a hint. We went down to Ikkai and I took her to a pleasant little place over by Stair 4, the kind of restaurant that's quiet and dimly lit and the food's good in the kind of understated way that won't distract two people from each other. I knew exactly what was going to happen between us as soon as we got back to my room, and I was pretty sure she knew the same thing. We both talked about other things and ate and sipped a little sake, and I honestly don't remember a thing about the food.

I don't remember much more about the conversation, either, but one thing sticks in my mind. I asked her what she and Mom had talked about, and that got us discussing Mom's religion. "I don't know if there are gods," Sophie said. "Do you?"

"I wish I did," I admitted. "The one thing I'm sure of is that if there are any, they don't spend a lot of time taking care of us."

"Of course not." She looked startled, like nobody had ever thought that before. "Why should they care more about us than we care about them? But if there are gods, what your Mom's doing seems reasonable. She helps them, and so maybe they'll help us."

I agreed that it sounded like a good plan, and the talk spun somewhere else. We spent quite a while there. Finally I paid up and led her through Ikkai to Stair 11 and then to my room.

Once we were both inside and I'd locked the door, she turned to me with the kind of unsteady smile that means just one thing. About a quarter of her was still scared, I gathered, and the other three quarters were hoping that we'd end up on the futon as soon as possible. So I smiled at her, and she said, "You said I should ask you if I—if I wanted you to do something," which is just about the clumsiest proposition that's ever been sent my way. I didn't care. I wanted her, and she wanted me, and the other details didn't matter too much just then.

I put a finger under her chin and raised it up to the right angle, and then kissed her. I'd have bet good money just then that she'd never been kissed before, but she understood the idea in the abstract and her learning curve was almost as fast as it had been with hashi. She followed that first kiss up with another one, and put her arms around me and clung to me, a little awkward and a little scared and much more than a little willing. So I led her over to the futon, and she started fumbling with her clothes. I helped her out of them and then got out of mine, and we lay down on the futon and went from there.

By the time I got her clothes off I knew part of what it was that made me want her so much. No, it wasn't her body, at least not in the usual way. It was a pleasant body, with more curves than I'd guessed from the way her clothes fit her, but it wasn't the kind of body that makes guys' heads whip around so fast they sprain their necks. No, it was something else that had me feeling better than usual as I got her kindled.

There's a word you hear old-timers use sometimes. I think it was slang back toward the beginning of the century. The word's "adorkable," and it means something like awkward and endearing at the same time. What it meant that evening was Sophie. She was clumsy and uncertain, she had only the vaguest idea of what we were going to do, and that's part of what made her adorkable. I went slow and gentle, and she gasped and held onto me as though everything that happened was a total surprise. I guessed she'd read about sex in romance novels or something like that, but she was a virgin, and not just in the technical sense. I don't think she'd ever even touched herself before.

When we finished I lay on my back and pulled the covers over us, and she slid over tentatively and settled her head on my shoulder. "Thank you," she said after a little while.

"Thank you," I said. "That was really sweet."

"Yes." She shifted her head, and I could feel her lips press against me. A moment later: "I want to stay here if I can."

"We'll see what we can work out," I said. It wasn't what I was thinking. What I was thinking was something closer to "you know, I could get used to this." I gather she was thinking the same thing, because she sighed and nestled up against me. I put an arm around her and squeezed, and she planted another kiss on my shoulder. Somewhere in the minutes that followed I drifted off to sleep with her body pressed against mine.

When I woke the next morning she was gone.

Chapter 8

I didn't realize that at first. I woke up more slowly than usual, remembered only after a minute or two that there should have been someone else on the futon with me, and assumed that she'd gotten up to use the bathroom. It was early, with just a little diffuse gray light filtering in through the window, so I wasn't too worried.

Another minute or two passed, and I realized she wasn't making any sounds at all. I blinked, sat up, and then got off the futon, and saw two things. One was the empty space where her clothes had been once I finished getting them off her. The second was one of my notebooks, open, with some writing that wasn't mine in it. I went over to it and looked. It was Sophie's handwriting, tense and unsteady in a way I hadn't seen before. This is what it said:

Jerry please help me my life is in danger. I have to go. There's a house marked 318 it's red brick and it's up against the hill not far from where we meet. I'll meet you there. Please hurry. Bring a gun if you can.

Thank you for last night. I'm sorry I have to go right now. Please hurry.

I read it again. The first thing that went through my mind was that she might have been dangled in front of me as the bait for a trap. That didn't seem likely, but I'd be lying if I said I didn't think about it. The second thing that went through my mind was that if it wasn't a trap, she must have gotten a message somehow in the night, and that thought made me stop cold for a moment. I thought of the way she knew the time without having to use a watch, and what George Morita said about her shoji playing, and what Roy Abeshima said about how she did math in her head, and wondered: was the Merlin Project supercomputer still working—and was there some way she could talk to it?

I considered all that, then washed up fast and started getting dressed. I knew it might be the smarter option to go straight to my boss, tell her everything, and see if I could arrange to go to the house marked 318 with a half dozen guys packing serious firepower to back me up.

That's not what I did, though. I figured that I could handle whatever trouble she was in, and I didn't want to spend time explaining all about Sophie and my guess about the supercomputer to Mrs. Taira, and then to whoever else had to hear about it before she made a decision. Besides, I like to do things on my own. That's nearly gotten me killed before, and it nearly got me killed this time, too, but I didn't know that yet.

I pocketed my Browning and my yawara stick and got a knife strapped to my leg right around sock level, where I could get it fast if I needed it. That was enough, I figured, and I left my room and headed for the elevator as fast as I could without attracting anyone's attention. I knew there was a pretty good chance that she hadn't been able to leave the Habitat yet: she might be down at the passenger dock, waiting for the ferry, and if she wasn't quick enough to figure out how to handle the guards they might have put her in a holding room while they called someone and figured out what to do with her.

My luck didn't reach that far. She wasn't at the passenger dock when I got there, and a glance at the sign-in book in the little office by the foot of the elevator showed where she'd signed herself out more than an hour before. I stifled something colorful and went back up to Ikkai, then down again to one of the freight docks. The ferry wasn't an option, not with Shoreside ready to blow up like Kikai, and I didn't plan on going in on one of the lighters this time unless I had to. There was another way and I meant to use it.

Once I was on the dock I went over to the shift foreman, a big beefy guy who's half gaijin and has the red hair to prove it. He's not really a friend of mine, but I buy him beers from time to time, and so he always gives me this gap-toothed grin when we meet. "Hey, Jerry!" he said. "Long time no see." He always says that, even when we just talked fifteen minutes before.

"Hi, Bill," I said, and slapped him on the arm like I meant it. "Any travelers around?" There usually are, the travelers make spare change running stuff to and from the freighters, and of course a lot of the stuff in question isn't the sort of thing you want to show to the people in the customs office. The dock crews don't argue because they get a cut of the proceeds, and my boss doesn't argue because she gets her cut, too.

He gave me the same grin. "Yeah, you're in luck." He turned. "Steve? Get one of the traveler boats right away." Steve was a nanmin kid of eighteen or so, thin and wiry, with the kind of tattoos that tell you he was born on Ikkai and doesn't plan on going any higher. He went to the other side of the dock to get the signal flags they use to talk to the lighters and travelers and the other small boats. Bill and I made small talk for a few minutes. Then a traveler boat came skimming along with its sail full of air, turned smoothly, did something clever with the sail to spill the air out, and nosed right up to the dock not twenty feet from where I was standing.

"Jerry!" Bear called out from the bow. "Good to see you, man."

I thanked Bill, said hi to Bear, and climbed aboard. Bear didn't have to say anything to his crew; they did something with the sail, the woman at the rudder swung it around, and about the time I got settled on whatever you call the seats on a travelers' boat, we were skimming away from the Habitat. "So where're you headed?" Bear asked.

"On the beach a little south of Shoreside," I said. "Someplace I won't be spotted."

"Easy peasy," Bear said, and turned aft. Don't ask me to tell you what he called out to the crew, it was a mix of boat talk and travelers' slang and I can't follow either of those, but the boat turned in a nice smooth arc and headed south past a couple of big three-masted freighters at anchor. I sat there watching the morning turn the landscape from dim gray shapes to the greens and browns and gaudy colors of Shoreside and the land behind it. Minutes slipped past, and then Bear called out something else and the boat turned in toward the shore.

We got to the beach at the foot of the hill a little before the sun came up. The beach was gray and empty, without even a footprint on it, which pleased me. I'd already asked Bear if anybody needed anything, the way you do with travelers, and handed over a couple of good-sized bills, so I didn't have anything else to do but jump. I landed in a foot or so of water and went up onto the beach. I turned and waved, Bear and the others waved back, and then they did something fast and clever with the sail and the rudder and went skimming back out to sea.

North of me, Shoreside slept off the bender of the night before. The beach was as empty as it ever gets, which was some consolation. I headed up along the edge of town, moving fast.

A red brick house with the number 318 on it, up against the hill, not far from the concrete block where I'd met Sophie a couple of times: that's what was circling in my thoughts just then. There weren't a lot of brick buildings in the town that used to be where Shoreside is. Most of them got demolished a long time ago because twentieth-century brick is better than the stuff that gets made these days and you can sell it for a decent price, so I didn't expect any trouble finding the place. Going up into the abandoned houses could be trouble all by itself, and I knew that, but I didn't have much choice. Besides, I told myself, that early in the morning all Big Goro's boys would be sleeping.

I was wrong. I hadn't yet gotten to the abandoned houses when I noticed movement further uphill, and got out of sight as fast as I could. A quick glance that way showed me I wasn't mistaken. There were guys up there in the empty places, moving quick and quiet. Big Goro's? That seemed much too likely.

If I'd been smart I would have gone straight back to Habitat 4, said a prayer for Sophie at the worship hall, and called it good. I wasn't that smart. I'd spent so many years ducking and weaving through Shoreside's back alleys that I thought I could get past whoever Big Goro put there to stand guard, and I was entirely willing to leave a couple of bodies for the crows to eat if that's what it took. So I doubled back a block and started back uphill a different way, staying out of sight as much as I could.

I was a couple of blocks into the abandoned houses before I realized I was in deep trouble. There weren't just a few guys standing guard among the houses. There must have been more than a dozen of them, they were armed to the teeth and they were obviously looking for someone. Even if the someone in question wasn't me, I didn't expect to have an easy time of it. That was my second chance to turn around and get out of there in a hurry, but like I said, I wasn't that smart. It wasn't just that I thought I could get past them. I was thinking of Sophie, and what they'd do to her if I was right about the Merlin Project and they had any idea just how valuable the information she had might be.

So I kept going. I got another three blocks uphill before they caught me.

It happened fast. That kind of thing usually does. I ducked into a gap between two ruined houses to dodge somebody who was on his way down from further up the hill. The next moment I heard the click of a safety going off and a voice, low and nasty: "Freeze."

I froze, because I recognized the voice. It was Bill Takagi's.

"Hands way up," he said then. "Mako, search him."

Mako said, "Okay, boss," then came up behind me, patted me down hard and fast, and got my gun and knife and yawara stick. By then I'd managed to move my head slow enough not to notice until I could see Bill. He was standing half a dozen yards away with a pistol in a two-handed grip, aimed straight at me. I suppose I should have been happy that he was that scared of me, but at the moment I was mostly annoyed that I'd been stupid enough to get caught.

"My, my, my," Bill said once Mako had me disarmed. "Jerry Shimizu heading uphill from Shoreside at the hairy crack of dawn. I wonder why. I know lots of people who'd wonder the same thing." Then, in a hard voice: "Where's the girl, Jerry? Tell me where the girl is and you might even get back out to your goddamn drilling rig alive."

I KEPT MY FACE from showing anything. It took hard work. If Bill knew about Sophie, she was in at least as much danger as I was, and probably a lot more. "Tell me which girl you have in mind," I said, trying to sound bored. "I'll see if I remember anything about her."

"Don't be stupid," he snapped. "You went out to the Habitats night before last with a girl. Thin face, brown hair, light blouse and brown slacks. She's worth a couple of million at least."

I gave him the kind of look you point at someone whose brains have gone south for the winter. "You're crazy."

"Uh-uh," he said with a short hard shake of his head. "And you know it, Jerry."

"Stone cold crazy. If a girl I pick up in a Shoreside bar for the night is worth a couple of million, maybe you should try a cute little blonde I know in a brothel downhill. She ought to be worth a lot more than that."

He just laughed at me. "Jerry, you're funny. Seriously funny." He looked past me, at Mako. "Get his hands."

"Okay, boss," Mako said, and hauled my hands in back of me. Coarse rope slid around my wrists. I tried the old trick of tensing them to get some wiggle room for later. Mako knew the same trick; he jabbed me hard in the back and pulled the rope good and tight. It's what I would have done, so I wasn't too surprised.

Bill lowered his gun then, though he didn't put it away. "No more jokes," he said to me, and came closer. "You know what? You got a choice, Jerry. You can keep pretending you don't know a thing about this Merlin Project business, and Mr. Omogawa's gonna get it out of you. Or you can tell me. Maybe we can cut a deal, Jerry. Just you and me and Mako here."

All at once a gun went off right next to me, three times, loud enough to jolt me and leave my head ringing. All three bullets slammed into Bill. His eyes bugged out, he tried to say something, and then he was down on the ground spilling blood everywhere. I tried to twist around but Mako grabbed one of my arms and jammed the hot muzzle of his pistol against my back just long enough to give me a nasty little burn. He didn't say anything. Neither did I.

Pretty soon I heard the sound of people running. By then the pool of blood around Bill Takagi was getting close to my shoes. I looked back over my shoulder at Mako, then down at the blood. He looked at me, nodded, and pulled me back a foot or two.

By then the first couple of Big Goro's boys showed up at one end of the gap between the houses. A little later some more showed up at the other end. They didn't come any closer, just stood there and waited. A couple of minutes passed, and then

I heard a heavier and more leisured rhythm. I didn't have to wonder who it was.

The boys on the end of the gap I was facing got out of the way fast. Big Goro filled the space where they'd been. He sized up the situation and then came walking up to me and Mako.

"You were right, boss," Mako said past me. "Bastard tried to double-cross you."

Big Goro took that in. "Mako," he said, "thank you. I mean that. You've done me a big favor and I don't forget favors." He turned toward me. "Jerry. Tell me why you're up here."

"Looking for clues," I said. "My boss wants to know who's behind those robberies. I got a lead from somebody—maybe relevant, maybe not. You tell me to get lost, I'll get lost."

I thought for about five seconds I was going to get away with it. Then Big Goro shook his head. "No, Jerry. You don't get away that easy." He leaned a little toward me. "Tell me about the girl."

"What's this business about a girl?" I said, trying to sound a lot more baffled and a lot less worried than I was. "Takagi was going on about that too."

"You're lying, Jerry. Talk."

"I can't tell you what I don't know."

Big Goro laughed. He's got a high-pitched laugh, soft and shrill, and when you hear it you know you're in deep trouble. "Oh, yes," he said. "Yes, you can." Then, past me: "Jake, Rudy, take him. You know what to do."

Two guys grabbed my arms and hauled me out into the street, then up onto the porch of one of the houses. The door was hanging open. They dragged me through it and straight to a back room. The light wasn't good but I could see dark stains on the floor I didn't like at all.

"Put him against the wall," Big Goro said. "Hold him there."

The two goons who had hold of me got the rope off my wrists and backed me up. They each took an arm and held onto it, leaving me flat against the wall facing Big Goro.

I was going to be dead soon. That was the thing that went through my mind first, and it's what I came back to once my thoughts finished scurrying around in a circle. Big Goro couldn't risk a fight between the Habitats and Shoreside, since the Habitats could cut off the flow of cargo in a heartbeat and leave Shoreside to starve. That meant my boss couldn't find out that he'd grabbed me, and that meant that my corpse would have to go into an unmarked grave somewhere so nobody found out. Was that what happened to Jason Fujita? I didn't expect to find out, but it seemed unpleasantly likely.

That I was about to die didn't bother me as much as I thought it would. What bothered me was what he'd do to Sophie if he caught her. If I was going to end up dead either way, damn if I was going to help him get his filthy hands on her.

"The girl," said Big Goro. "Start talking."

You can't start talking. I knew that. If you talk at all, once the pain starts up, you'll end up babbling what you know. I made my face blank, and inside my mind I started repeating the one norito I know by heart, the one you use to pray for purification when you really need it: *Kiwamete kitanaki mo tamari nakere ba—*

"You're not listening to me, Jerry." His voice was still soft.

I ignored him, or tried to. *Kitanaki to—*

His fingers jabbed hard into my right shoulder, hitting a nerve point. Pain spiked all the way down the arm.

—wa araji uchi to no tamagaki—

"It doesn't matter," Big Goro said then. "It really doesn't, Jerry. I'll get her with your help or without it. You can make it easy on yourself, or ..." Another jab, another nerve point. That one hurt even more.

—Kiyoku kiyoshi to maosu. Kiwamete—

"Talk," he said. His voice was deeper and louder. That was what I wanted. My best bet was to get him to lose his temper and kill me before the pain got too bad.

—kitanaki mo tamari nakere—

"Talk!" he shouted, and jabbed. That one was much harder to ignore. I had to fight down panic, keep concentrating on the words of the norito and hope it would be enough. I began to wonder if it was going to be enough.

Then the door behind Big Goro opened. Someone I couldn't see said, "Mr. Omogawa, sir," in an agitated voice.

Big Goro turned. Low and hard: "Don't interrupt me."

"There's trouble, Mr. Omogawa. Bad trouble."

Louder: "I said—"

"It's the Feds."

That got a moment of dead silence. If anything moved closer than the Habitats I didn't hear it. Then Big Goro spat out something impressively obscene in Russian under his breath, and turned to the guys who held me. "Hold him right there," he said. "I'll be back." He went out the door and slammed it shut behind him with a bang.

A moment later a much louder bang shook the house. It sounded to me like a twelve-gauge shotgun, and it was close enough to leave my head ringing. Another round went off a moment later. Before that happened the two guys who were holding me dropped me, drew a couple of pistols, and went for the door, fast. More gunshots sounded as they flung it open and lunged through it, and one of them staggered back with a couple of holes in him and fell onto the floor. He didn't look like he was going to move again.

I didn't take the time to find out. When they let go of me I dropped down onto the floor, but I scrambled up off it right away. There was a window on the far side of the room. I would have gone straight through the glass if it was still there, but somebody had stripped it out a long time ago and it was just an open square with sky on the other side. I hauled myself up and through it, twisted around, and let myself drop.

I LANDED HARD, BUT the pain barely registered. I was outside on a patch of bare ground that probably had grass in it back in the day. None of Big Goro's goons were in sight and I didn't see anything between me and a fair chance of getting away but some empty space. I broke into a sprint and kept going as fast as I could until I was out of sight of the house. It didn't matter that my head was still ringing from the sound of the shotgun blasts or that I could feel every bruise Big Goro had laid on me. When lead starts flying that close to the boss of Shoreside you can take it for granted that a lot of people are going to be dead soon, and I didn't want to become one of them by accident.

Once I got a couple of houses between me and the place Big Goro had taken me, I ducked into the gap between two tumbledown buildings. By then I was gasping for air, but it didn't take long for me to catch my breath and find my bearings. I didn't like being anywhere near Shoreside without a weapon, but I knew better than to try to head back home—if Big Goro wasn't on the receiving end of that shotgun, he'd have his boys waiting for me at the ferry dock with guns out, and they wouldn't bother asking questions. That left one option, and it was the one I'd already decided to take.

I listened for a moment to make sure that nobody seemed to be headed my way. The gunshots had stopped, and everything had gotten very quiet. I left my hiding place and headed for the edge of the old ruins up against the hill, weaving in among the abandoned houses so they'd have to work to spot me. I wasn't going to give them a second chance. Besides, I had an appointment to keep.

The street ended where the side of the hill rose up in a mess of greenery and gray rock. I had to backtrack a bit, go a little closer to the water, and try a couple more streets before I found the red brick house with the number 318 on it. The front door was barricaded shut—I could see where nails had been pounded through it from inside to hold the bars in place—but I went around to the back and found a door that would open.

Inside was what you expect in an abandoned house near Shoreside, nothing left but a few scraps of broken furniture, some empty beer bottles in a corner, and a variety of stale smells. About the time I got to the middle of the room I was in, though, I heard a low buzzing sound start up. I froze. The buzzing got a little louder, and then a machine came floating through a doorway, hovering about five feet off the ground. It was black and angular, about two feet across, and it had four little ducted fans at its four corners, like miniature versions of the ones you see on government aircraft. It had things like claws dangling down below it and other things like tools sticking off it at various angles. A drone? I'd never seen one before, not outside of photos in old books, but that was what it looked like.

I considered screaming and running away, and decided against it. About the time I finally made up my mind it stopped in front of me, hovering, and something pivoted up from its upper surface: a screen, I realized after a moment. Letters appeared on it: JERRY

"Yeah," I sald out loud. An improbable guess elbowed its way forward. "Sophie?"

YES THANK YOU FOR COMING HES ASLEEP THERES STILL TIME

"He?"

LATER NO TIME NOW PLEASE FOLLOW

The drone went back through the doorway and I followed it.

On the other side of the doorway was what was left of a kitchen, and on the far side there was an open door and a stairway. It looked pretty dark down there, and it smelled like mildew and wet dirt, but the drone turned on a light on its underside and headed down. The light wasn't much, but it was enough that I could find the steps. Another drone was waiting down below, and it went back up the stair I'd just come down and closed and locked the door up top—I heard the deadbolt click into place. It wasn't a comforting sound.

By then the first drone brought me to another door, which had some kind of electronic lock on it with a little red light below the knob. The light turned green and the door unlocked itself as we got near. OPEN IT, the screen said to me. JERRY PLEASE TRUST ME THE DRONES WONT DROP YOU THERES NO OTHER WAY

That was even less comforting, but I'd already decided to go wherever all this led. "Okay," I said, and opened the door. On the far side was the kind of echoing darkness that tells you there's a lot of empty space, and the light on the bottom of the drone didn't touch anything I could see. The air smelled different, mostly of dust and old metal. Besides the smells, the only thing that came out of the darkness was the buzzing of more drones.

HOLD OUT YOUR ARMS, the screen told me. I drew in a breath and raised my arms, and six drones came out of the darkness and grabbed me. Three of them took each arm, and they rose and I went up a few inches with them. They turned so I was side on to the door, and then flew me straight out through it into the deepest darkness I'd ever seen, with nothing below my feet but too much empty space.

That went on, and on, and on. Whether I was going one direction, or more than one, or rising or falling or just hovering in place, I had no idea. Finally my feet came to rest on a floor I couldn't see. The drones let go of me and all but one of them flew away. Letters blinked into existence on a screen near my face: HE DOESNT KNOW ABOUT THIS WAY HES STILL ASLEEP FOLLOW ME THERES STILL TIME

Following her involved picking my way after the screen as it slid away in front of me, and hoping that I didn't lose my balance or run into anything. I managed it, and was rewarded finally with a dim light from somewhere ahead of me. I kept going, following the drone, and when I could see my surroundings my heart started pounding, because I was pretty sure I'd found the Merlin Project facility, and it wasn't miles away in some hollow in the hills. It was right next to Shoreside, underground, tucked away inside the hill just south of town.

I was in a corridor in some kind of old facility. The floor and walls and ceiling were bare concrete. Conduits, a couple of dozen of them, ran along both walls. Near them, every few yards, words and numbers I couldn't interpret had been stenciled on the concrete in faded yellow paint. Light filtered down the corridor from somewhere up ahead. A faint smell of ozone joined the dust-and-metal scent in the air, and that put the hair on the back of my neck up hard. There aren't many things that make that smell underground and all of them mean you're going to be dead soon if you aren't careful.

The corridor finally opened out onto a big room, a couple of hundred feet each way and a couple of stories high. It had lights up above and steel grilling for a floor. Down about twenty feet I could see eight big gray-white cylinders, each of them a hundred feet long and twenty feet across, with cooling fins on one end and blinking lights close by the fins. The ozone was stronger there in the room, and a dry harsh heat came up from the fins. I stared at the cylinders for a moment and hoped I wasn't already dead.

I MONITOR THE RADIATION THERES NO LEAKAGE PLEASE HURRY, the screen spelled out. I swallowed, nodded, and followed the drone across the room to an open doorway on the far side. The whole way I was aware of those big cylinders down below me. They were loaded with used nuclear fuel rods. If nothing broke into them, the thermodynamic generators on one end would churn out electricity for a couple of thousand years, but they lost a big chunk of Nashville in 2072 when a quake cracked one open, and enough water got in to cause a steam explosion and spray bits of fuel rod all over a couple of neighborhoods. I wondered how far down the water table was here, and hoped I wasn't going to find out.

The doorway on the far side led into another room, just as big, with more steel grilling for a floor but huge masses of conduits and cables down below instead of radiothermal generators. Long tall cages ran in rows all through the room. Inside the cages were big complex metal boxes with flickering lights on the front. Each of the boxes was twice my height and covered with black metal fins, lots of them, and they pumped out heat like furnaces. No, I'm not exaggerating. To judge from the little lights, they were busy with something, too.

THIS WAY, the drone told me. I followed. Something broke the flat surface of one of the cages: a mess of circuitry bolted onto the outside, with an antenna sticking up out of it. I got closer and spotted the oblong blue plastic shape at the center of it all: a Morningstar mine. I handled those in the Army. They're like your old-fashioned Claymore mines, but with some neat ballistic tricks worked in; you can literally hold one in your hand and set it off, and it'll blow a hole in whatever's in front of it, with no more recoil than a pistol. This one was pointed inward, toward a place in the middle of one of the boxes where a lot of lights were busy.

THE BLUE THING IN THE MIDDLE IS A BOMB, the drone told me.

"An antipersonnel mine. I know the type."

GOOD HERE ARE THE TOOLS

Another drone came buzzing into sight, carrying a bag of some old-fashioned plastic in its claws. It hovered next to the one that was talking to me, and let me take the bag. Inside were screwdrivers, wrenches, wire cutters, that sort of gear.

NOW DO EXACTLY WHAT I TELL YOU

I did exactly what the screen told me. It took some doing, too, but five minutes later I'd gotten the mine out of the middle of the circuitry and handed it to the second drone, which flew away with it. THE NEXT ONE IS THIS WAY, the drone said, and I gathered up the tools and followed.

THERE WERE ELEVEN OF the mines in all. Somebody had boobytrapped the facility so that they could blow chunks of the computers to scrap with a single radio signal. I don't know much about computers but I was pretty sure whoever placed the mines knew exactly where to put them. I got all of the Morningstars out, though halfway through I started shaking and had to stop for a few minutes to get my nerves under control. But I got them all, and the other drone flew away with them one at a time. The rest of the gear stayed bolted to the cages, and a casual glance wouldn't show anything missing. I guessed that was deliberate.

When I was finished the drone spelled out THANK YOU THANK YOU THANK YOU.

I drew in a long unsteady breath, let it out. "What next?"

COME THIS WAY LEAVE THE TOOLS THERES ONE MORE THING I NEED YOU TO DO

The drone led me back into the room with the big gray cylinders under the floor, and then out again by a different doorway. That opened onto another long corridor with no lights, and that ended in a cluster of smaller rooms that looked meant for people to live in. BE VERY QUIET, the drone warned me, and I went through those as silently as I could.

On the far side was a short corridor and then a door with an electronic lock on it, like the one I'd seen in the basement. Its light turned green and it clicked open and I went through. Inside was a bleak little room with a bed in it. Sophie was on the bed, dressed in a flimsy little medical gown that barely covered the territory. She was out cold, and I didn't have to wonder why. There was an IV bag on a pole next to her and it was letting a drip of something through a needle in her arm.

TURN OFF THE VALVE AT THE BOTTOM OF THE BAG, the drone told me, THEN TAKE THE NEEDLE OUT PUT IT IN THE BEDDING BY THE ARM

I got that taken care of, and made sure it looked to a casual glance as though the needle was still in place.

THANK YOU NOW ALL WE NEED the drone began to say, and then paused. A moment later. NO NO NO HE IS AWAKE HE MUST HAVE HAD HIS OWN ALARM SYSTEM THIS IS BAD DO YOU HAVE A GUN

I winced. "I had trouble on the way here and lost it."

THIS IS VERY BAD YOU MUST NOT LET HIM FIND YOU HERE HURRY

"Can you stop him?"

NO HE HAS OVERRIDE CONTROL HURRY ILL TRY TO GET YOU OUT

I hurried. Out in the corridor I paused, heard the faint sound of footsteps back the way I'd come. THIS WAY, the drone told me, and went away from the sound. I didn't need the encouragement. I went as quickly as I could without making noise.

We made good time down that corridor, around a corner, and into another room that looked like it was made for human beings, about ten feet by twenty feet with marks on the floor where there might have been furniture once. On the far side was one of the doors with the electronic locks. I headed straight for it and waited for the little light to go green.

It stayed red.

I turned to the drone, but at that moment the screen went black, the buzzing stopped, and the drone sank down and landed on the floor, inert. Override control, I guessed, with the part of me that wasn't repeating some of Mom's choicest Russian swear words.

Movement in the distance caught my attention. Before I could get out of sight in one of the corners of the room close to where the corridor came in, a guy came into sight. He could see me just as well as I could see him. More to the point, I could see something in his hand that was probably a pistol, and he had it pointed straight at me. I put on the most nonchalant look I could manage and waited.

It took some effort to keep that look on my face when he came close enough for me to recognize him. It was Rex Samuels, but he wasn't dressed like a Shoreside gambler. He was wearing the same kind of flimsy light blue things Sophie had worn the first few times I saw her, with a white lab coat over the top.

"You," he said, as he came into the room. "Give me one reason why I shouldn't blow you to hell right now."

Maybe there was something less risky to say, but I couldn't think of anything. "Do that and you won't find out what I've already done."

That shook him. "I can find out."

"You don't have the time," I told him, trying to sound a lot more confident than I felt. I could see sweat bead on his forehead, and he tensed. Before he could shoot, I went on. "You want my cooperation, you can earn it. You know who I work for. She's interested in the Merlin Project." That got a sudden sharp inbreath from him. I knew I'd hit the bullseye. "Very interested, and willing to deal with you. The Habitats aren't short on money. You tell me what I need to know, I'll tell you whatever you want and then put you in touch with her. You could cut a much better deal with her than with Big Goro or the Europeans."

Had I hooked him? I couldn't tell. He looked at me for what felt like a long time, and then said, "Keep talking."

"Nope," I said. "Your turn. This is the Merlin Project facility, and it's got one of the last working supercomputers in the world. It's worth more than all five Habitats put together, and then some, but you've got the computer boobytrapped with Morningstar mines." His eyes narrowed, and I went on in a hurry. "My boss is going to want to know why. There's someone else down here with you, and my boss is going to want to know about her, too."

That got me another long hard look. "You're not as stupid as I thought," he said then.

"I'll take that as a compliment."

He laughed. It sounded like someone pulling nails out of a board. "Okay," he said then. "Goro's a cheap thug and I don't like working with him. The Europeans are a lot smarter and have more money but I don't trust them as far as I can throw them. If your boss can make it worth my while we may have a deal." I started to shift, testing the waters, and he said, "Uh-uh. Move an inch and I'm going to waste you. Got it?"

"Have it your way," I said. "What's with the Morningstars? And what's with the girl?"

"The girl," he said, and his face twisted. "That's not a girl. It's a human body with a computer wired into its brain. That's what the Merlin Project was about—trying to integrate a human brain with a high-speed supercomputer to make an AI capable of independent thought. A really bad idea. I just wish we'd realized that at the beginning."

"You've been here for a while," I said.

"I came here as a grad student in 2057. It was a job, the whole country was going crazy back then, and I thought the project team knew what they were doing. Then Kikai happened and a little after that one of the hemorrhagic fevers came through, the old government fell apart, a lot of the project staff bolted once they weren't getting a paycheck, and I ended up as the youngest member of the team by twenty years. The rest of them aged out. That left me to take care of the monster we'd created."

"Go on," I said after a moment. "A monster?"

"They wanted to create a computer that had a human being's creativity and empathy. They got something that had a human being's overinflated ego and all the compassion of a machine. It's way too smart and way too dangerous to let loose. The old guys who ran the project couldn't accept that. They kept on trying to reprogram it, with zero results. But the last of them died a couple of years ago and I started trying to figure out how to do what's got to be done—break the connection and turn the machine back into an ordinary supercomputer. In the meantime—" He shrugged. The gun didn't waver. "I need money like everyone else, and I rigged a neural link to one of the ordinary computers down here so I could run numbers while I was at the gambling tables. That's how I figured out you were following me, too—I just had the computer file away every face I saw and let me know if one of them showed up too often." His short sharp laugh echoed off the concrete. "I can do all kinds of useful tricks. So, yeah, I'm willing to talk to your boss if she's prepared to be reasonable."

"And the girl?"

"I told you it's not a girl. The brain and the computer are too tightly integrated to just terminate the body, or I'd have done that years ago. That, and there are defenses." Sweat was beading on his forehead again. "I rigged the Morningstars and programmed in some brute force overrides to keep the machine from using those defenses to kill me. It'll do that in a millisecond if it ever gets the chance. That's why you're going to tell me how you got down here and what you're doing here and what you've done, and then we're going to go outside, take the ferry out to your Habitat, have a good long talk with your boss, and see if she can come up with the funding to help me draw a line under the Merlin Project once and for all and give the Habitats access to a supercomputer that'll do what it's told."

I nodded, and pretended to be thinking it over. I didn't want to say anything in response, because I'd already heard something I'd been listening for, and as far as I could tell Samuels hadn't heard it at all.

The faint whisper of bare feet coming down the corridor behind him.

I DIDN'T HAVE TIME to come up with anything to say before Sophie spoke. "Dr. Samuels." Her voice sounded thin and brittle. "I heard everything you just said."

I've never actually seen anyone else go white as a sheet, but that's what Samuels did. His gun shook a little, though not enough that I could risk jumping him. He half-turned and backed over toward one side of the room, getting out from between me and Sophie, while his left hand fumbled in one of the pockets of his lab coat, grabbed something, jerked down hard as though he'd slammed a button with one thumb.

Dead silence followed. One second, two seconds, three, and then he let out a panicked sound from down in his throat and turned toward Sophie with his gun leading the way.

That was all the opening I needed. I went at him fast and hard. He saw me and started to swing back around, but by then I was on him. I grabbed his right wrist and twisted it to lock the joint, got my left leg in front of his right, and slammed my body weight into him. He went face down on the floor and landed hard, I landed on top of him even harder, and something he had in his left hand went skittering across the concrete.

Sophie let out a sudden cry and sprang for it. I wasn't paying a lot of attention just then, because Samuels was trying to get out from under me, so I had to keep his gun hand pinned and still stop the rest of him from getting loose. That meant slamming his face into the concrete a couple of times to get his attention. By the time I had the chance to look up at Sophie again, she had the thing in both hands and was doing something to it. It looked a little like one of those dead remotes you find so often in abandoned houses and trash heaps, but I was pretty sure that it wasn't dead and she didn't plan on using it to turn on a teevee.

Samuels made another try at getting out from under me, and I got tired of it and hit him again. He tensed to try something else, and just as I was getting ready to hit him another time he sagged and mumbled something that sounded pretty desperate. I tried to process that, and then noticed that the drone he'd shut off had started buzzing again. A moment later I heard a fainter sound coming down the corridor, and a moment after that I realized that more drones were on their way, lots of them.

"Jerry," Sophie said then. "You can let go of him."

I looked up at her. She was standing there, still wearing the flimsy little medical gown I'd seen on her when she'd been on the bed, and not a stitch else. Her face was alight with an expression I'd hate to have to describe in detail, furious and elated and shaken and half a dozen other things all at once, and she held the remote-thing in both hands like it was the scepter of the entire world. Maybe it was, for her.

Samuels lay sprawled under me. He looked like the fight had gone completely out of him, and so I rose to a crouch. I decided I wasn't willing to take any risks, slammed the heel of my hand down onto his right wrist, and got the gun out of his grip that way. It was a nice little .357 revolver, not really fair trade for my Browning but good enough, and I grabbed it and kept it pointed straight at him as I stood up and backed away.

Then the drones came streaming down the corridor, setting the air shaking. There were two columns of them, and they swept past Sophie on either side and went for Samuels. Three of them grabbed each of his arms, and hauled him to his feet. I pocketed the gun and went over to the other side of the room. From the look on Sophie's face, Samuels was in deep trouble and I didn't want to be too close to whatever she had in mind.

"Dr. Samuels," she said. Her voice was as clear and hard as ice, and not half as warm. "You lied to me, over and over again. You told lies about me just now, ugly hateful lies. You threatened my life, and you just tried to kill me. You won't get another chance."

Another drone came down the corridor behind her. I saw the blue rectangle it had in its claws, and felt sick. Samuels saw it too, and started to blubber in sheer terror, but the other drones held him. The drone with the Morningstar mine flew past Sophie and hovered in front of Samuels' face. I turned away, clenched my eyes shut, covered my ears with my hands, and waited for the thing to go off. I didn't have to wait long.

When it was over, I opened my eyes and looked toward where Samuels had been, and wished I hadn't. His body was a crumpled headless mess on the floor, and what was left of his head was sprayed across a concrete wall maybe ten yards behind where he'd been standing.

I turned toward Sophie. The light I'd seen in her face earlier had gone out. She was staring at what was left of Samuels, and she looked huddled and fragile and sick. Then she doubled over and vomited. I went over and put a hand on one arm, steadying her. When she was done, she glanced up at me the way she'd done the first time we'd talked, or the first night she'd slept in my room. She swallowed visibly and said, "I want to go outside."

"Sure," I said. "You should probably get some clothes first, though."

That earned me a little faint sound in her throat that might have been a laugh's third cousin. "Yes, I probably should."

We went back through the corridors to what I guessed was her room, a little bare place with a bed and a closet and not much else. She smiled at me when she took off the little medical gown, and I smiled back. Then she put on the clothes I'd bought her in Shoreside, drew in a long uneven breath, and said, "Okay, I'm ready."

"Show me the best way out," I said.

I was glad that we didn't have to go past what was left of Samuels. Instead, we went another direction, down a long bare corridor with lights every so often, and then to another of the doors with the electronic locks. The little light turned green the moment Sophie got within sight of it. Out we went, with one of her drones to escort us, into a concrete room with no lights but the one from the drone. Sophie closed the door behind us and the light went red. "This is the way Dr. Samuels went out," she told me. "He had an alarm on it, but—" She shrugged. "That doesn't matter any more."

She led the way across the room to a stair that angled up into not-quite darkness.

"Do you know where it lets out?" I asked her.

"Somewhere on the beach. I don't know anything more than that."

I thought about that as we went up the stair, and drew Samuels's gun. A quick check with my fingertips found bullets in all six spots in the cylinder. A quick movement with one finger—it was a right-hander's gun, but I'm used to those—clicked off the safety. I was thinking of Big Goro and his boys, and how much lead might be flying in Shoreside just then; I was thinking of the warning Fritz gave me and the last conversation I'd had with Michael Huddon. I'd already managed to get through two messy situations that day with my skin more or less intact but I wasn't ready to take a chance on my luck holding out a third time.

The stair ended in another bare concrete room, smaller than the one below. A big irregular gap in the far wall showed a narrow passage between walls of rock, and then daylight. I could hear the rush and hiss of waves on the beach echoing off the rock, and the air had an edge of salt to it.

A moment passed, and then something moved in the darkness just this side of the gap.

"Mr. Shimizu," said Max Bernard's voice. "Good. Excellent, in fact."

Chapter 9

SOPHIE LET OUT A LITTLE frightened cry and stopped. I got in front of her and had the gun pointed at Bernard before he finished getting the first word out. "Your lucky day," I said.

"Oh, it is," said Bernard. "Yours, too. And your very interesting companion. I don't think we've met."

"No," said Sophie. "Who are you?" Her drone rose up and hovered over her head, splashed light over him.

He looked up at it, smiled. "Call me Max. That fine old machine is yours, I presume?"

Before she could answer, I said, "No more questions. Why are you here?"

"Waiting to take delivery of a very rare artifact. You are here, and therefore Dr. Samuels is no longer available to sell it to me. That does not concern me. I can deal just as well with you." His smile broadened, put on an edge. "Please lower the gun. It will not help you. I have men outside, plenty of them. If you shoot me, or if I call out, they will respond at once, and they're very well armed. No, Mr. Shimizu, what you're going to do is put that gun away, and the two of you are going to come with me on a little voyage. A chance to see a little more of the world, let us say. The boat's waiting close by. Shall we?"

"I can't leave the area," said Sophie then.

"Oh, but you can," said Bernard. "And you will. I'm sorry to say there isn't an alternative."

There was an alternative, and I knew that if even if he didn't. A quick glance at Sophie told me she'd thought of it, too; she had that tension you see in people who don't know how to fight and are getting ready to do it anyway. I didn't know how long it would take her drones to pick up more Morningstar mines and come swarming through the door, but I knew I had to stall for time. "Not so fast," I said. "You said it's my lucky day. Why?"

I could see his teeth gleam in the light from the drone. "Your boss wouldn't deal with me. Mine is more than willing to deal with you. I can promise you plenty of money and certain other benefits. If you're willing to consider taking a new position in your current line of work, you can expect more. Much more."

That was when I knew for sure who he was working for. I wanted to spit in his face and tell him he could take Patrice Malinbois's money and put it someplace other than my wallet. I didn't do anything of the kind. I stood there, my gun aimed at the center of his body mass and my nerves wound up as tight as they could go, trying to think of what to say next.

I didn't have to say anything. A sound from outside did the job for me. It sounded like a sheet of metal being ripped in half. I recognized it right away, and so did Bernard.

His smile went away fast. He tried to lunge out of my line of fire and get his gun. I turned and aimed, but Sophie was faster than I was. Her drone went at his face, moving so quick it was gouging him with its claws before I'd processed that it was moving. I didn't want to risk shooting it, and it was buzzing all over him like one of those giant hornets you see in old scroll paintings of Buddhist hells, so I jumped him.

I don't think he saw me, but then he had blood all over his face by the time I got there and he was flailing with both hands to try to keep the drone off him. That made it easy for me to get behind him and bring down the butt of the .357 hard on the point of his right shoulder, where a good solid hit makes the whole arm numb.

I'll say this much for him, he was tough. He whipped around and lunged at me, pulling back his left hand to throw a punch. The drone got there first, grabbed his arm and yanked it back, and I took advantage of that to land a good hard gut punch with my right fist. Bernard doubled over, and I grabbed him, hit him again a couple of times, and checked his right side. His gun was still there, a nice little Beretta automatic. I tossed that out of reach and then threw him to the floor, where he landed hard.

"Roll over," I told him, and got the .357 in a two-handed grip pointed at him. "Keep your hands where I can see them."

The drone came and hovered a foot or so from my right shoulder, buzzing. It sounded pleased with itself. A moment passed, and he rolled over. His face was a mess and so were his hands. I considered shooting him dead, but the sound from outside had already told me that his friends weren't going to be coming to his rescue anyway, and that meant I could do something a lot more useful instead.

"I've got six bullets left," I told him. "Let me know how many of them you want through your brain." Out on the beach, the ripping-metal noise sounded again, as if somebody wanted to underline the point. Bernard didn't try to move. He lay there with his face bleeding, not saying anything, waiting. I figured he had other weapons on him. The question in my mind was simply how soon he'd try to kill me again.

Then something blocked the light from the beach, and I let myself glance past Bernard.

It was a big black guy wearing a flak vest over a dark blue jumpsuit. He had a close-fitting helmet on his head and a clear plastic visor over his face, and he carried a gun I recognized at once: black and angular, with two pistol grips front and back and a collapsible stock behind. That was the thing that made the tearing noise I mentioned. I carried the same model of flechette gun when I was in the Army, and I knew exactly what would happen if he pulled that trigger. If you've never seen someone hit by one of those guns, be glad. Flechette guns spray out steel darts with inch-long fins, and the edges of the fins are sharp enough to shave with. A light squeeze on full auto can rip someone in half.

I met the guy's gaze, and very slowly moved my left hand off to the side and dropped the .357. The guy with the flechette gun nodded and stood there, covering all three of us, as another big guy in the same outfit came up behind him, carrying another gun of the same make. Bernard had seen them, too, and his face looked a lot paler.

I glanced at Sophie, who was watching the two newcomers with a baffled look. "Put your hands up," I told her, "and then don't move." She looked at me, nodded uncertainly, and then raised her hands. I did the same thing.

Another dark shape blotted out part of the sunlight. This time it was more familiar: Michael Huddon, with that walking stick of his in one hand and the inevitable smile on his face. "Excellent," he said to the guys with the flechette guns, and jabbed his stick at Max. "There's the man we want. Get him out of here and patch him up. I know people in New Washington who will be very happy to see him."

One of the guys moved to cover Bernard from one side. The other slung his gun behind his shoulder, dropped to one knee, flipped Bernard over and got his hands cuffed behind him. He stood and hauled Bernard to his feet, while the other guy made sure Bernard knew exactly which parts of his anatomy would get shredded first if he did anything stupid.

"What about these?" the second guy said, with a motion of his head at Sophie and me.

"On our side," said Huddon. "I'll see to them." The guy nodded, and the two of them marched Bernard out of there without another word.

"You can lower your hands," Huddon said then. "Thank you, both of you. You disarmed our quarry, didn't you? You've been of great help to the United States."

"Is it okay to ask how?" I said.

Huddon aimed that insufferable smile of his at me. "Of course. I might even answer." Then, with a laugh: "Tell me this. The man you caught. What name did he give you?"

"Max Bernard."

"His real name," said Huddon, "is Ferdinand Beissel. He's one of the top field operatives in the European Union's Office of External Security. His specialty is technological espionage. The federal police have been after him for years, but he's always been able to stay ahead of them, until now." His smile didn't change at all, but his tone was suddenly all business. "Tell me this. Was he after the Merlin Project?"

"Yes," said Sophie. "He was after me."

That got her a long considering look from Huddon. "I think we need to have a conversation sometime soon," he said. "First things first. Is the Project facility secure?"

"It is now," Sophie told him. "I've activated the defenses. I'd like to send this drone back to join the others, if things are safe outside."

Huddon considered that, too, and nodded. "By all means." The drone spun around in the air and went back down the stair, leaving us in near-darkness.

"Perhaps we can discuss this further outside," Huddon said then. "You can pick up your gun if you like, Mr. Shimizu. It would be a shame to leave it to rust." He turned and started toward the daylight. I got Samuels's gun and pocketed it, and then found Bernard's pistol and pocketed that, too. Then I turned to Sophie. I couldn't see enough of her expression to matter, but she slipped her hand into mine as we started after Huddon. It felt cold, and trembled.

OUTSIDE THE DAY HAD turned bright and warm, with a light breeze off the ocean to keep things comfortable. The tide was out, and there on the sand sat a big gray airplane with the stylized eagle emblem of the federal police on it. It had its four big ducted fans turned to horizontal. The door in the side of the fuselage was open. More guys in blue federal police jumpsuits and flak jackets were marching prisoners onto the plane, and some guys who didn't live long enough to get taken prisoner were sprawled on the beach with blood around them. A quarter mile or so down the beach, another federal plane sat waiting.

I was taking that in when a guy in blue with officer's bars on his collar came up to Huddon and said, "Team Two's still busy in town, sir. Mathers says another half hour, maybe. He wants to talk to you."

"Of course." Huddon turned to us. "Might I ask you to find a place to sit and enjoy the beach for a little while? It isn't safe to go back into town quite yet."

That seemed reasonable, not that I was going to argue with someone who had the federal police on his side. Sophie and I both said something more or less agreeable, and walked a little further south, to where a bunch of big lumps of concrete lay sprawled across the sand at the foot of the hill. By the time we got there, the last of the prisoners had been marched into the plane, its engines woke up and rose to a strident whine, and it took off straight up, then tilted the fans and headed west out of sight over the hill.

Sophie and I found a concrete block that was low and flat enough to serve as a bench, and sat down. "Is it okay if we talk?" she asked me.

I was pretty sure what she had in mind wasn't idle chitchat, so I made sure there were no federal police close by. The nearest ones were down by the second plane, and then there were two up north where the hill ended and Shoreside began, far enough to be out of earshot. "Sure."

She sat there huddled and silent for a while. "It wasn't all lies," she said finally. "The things Dr. Samuels said, I mean. You should know that. You should know about the Merlin Project, and—and about me. Before anything else happens."

I nodded, and she glanced at me and went on. "The name of the project wasn't casually chosen. In the legends, Merlin was supposed to be half human and half spirit, and the goal of the Merlin Project was to make someone who was half human and half computer. They tried the protocol first with adults, but the ones who survived went catatonic. Some didn't come out of it even after the neural link was shut down. It also caused incurable nonstop epilepsy in eleven percent of the test subjects who survived the procedure."

"Ouch. How many people did they go through?"

"Sixty-one adults. After that they started using infants instead, even though it was illegal. The first tests were promising, but it took them a long time to work out the details, and they ended up having to bribe two local hospitals to induce labor at seven months and tell the mothers their babies had died. They did that to thirty-seven women. Twenty infants survived the electrode implant procedure, but more problems came in when brain development started, and only one of the infants made it past the age of eight."

"And that one was you."

"My human half."

I nodded again, and she went on. "So I grew up in the project facility and was raised by the project staff. Some of them treated me like a child and some treated me like a computer and so one way or another I got the care I needed. I didn't know about any of the other test subjects yet. By the time of my first memories there were only four of us left and we were kept separate. I didn't even know that there was anything unusual about me until I was in my early teens. I used to think that the project staff had their computer halves down in the deep levels where I wasn't allowed to go, and it was a real shock when they let me figure out, a little at a time, that they didn't have computer halves and I really was different.

"My human half was one of the last infants they harvested, and so I was still very young when most of the project staff left and the rest sealed the facility from the outside world. I didn't know there even was an outside world for a long time, and when I figured that out, they told me that society had fallen apart but we were safe inside the hill. Most of the people that stayed with the project were old, and they died one by one. The last except for Dr. Samuels was Dr. Ames, whose last name I took, and she died just over a year ago.

"That left Dr. Samuels. He kept telling me that the world outside was a wasteland full of roving bands, but I tracked his movement patterns and finally realized that he was going outside three or four times a week. So I spent some time finding out how he did it—the exits weren't included in the data on the facility in my drone management program—and finally worked up the courage to go outside myself by a different door, the one I had you use. The first time I was outside for maybe five minutes and I was scared out of my wits the whole time, but nothing happened to me, and I went out again and again to try to understand the gap between what he told me and what I saw. It took a long time for me to accept that he was simply lying to me.

"That was after you and I met. It was when I realized that he'd been lying that I decided to go with you to the Habitat. I thought I could simply walk away from him, and—" Her voice caught, and it took her a moment to go on. "He rigged the Morningstar mines the way you saw, used his override control to keep me from disarming them with my drones, and sent a message by way of my computer half to tell me he would set them off and kill me if I didn't go back to the facility. That's why I left this morning. I knew he'd be waiting at the ferry dock and if you came with me he'd kill you, so I came up with the best plan I could and left you the note."

"Why did he make you come back?"

Sophie huddled a little further into herself. "Because he knew I could kill him otherwise. I can flood the whole facility with inert gas. It's part of the fire prevention system and

I control that. The only way he could be sure I wouldn't do that was if I was there too, so I'd die along with him. If I'd turned on the gas as soon as I left to meet you none of this would have happened, but I—I didn't want to kill him. I didn't think he'd try to kill me."

Then, in a sudden outburst: "And the thing that made all of thus such a waste is that the Merlin Project failed. They wanted a superintelligent AI that could think creatively so they could figure out how to solve the world's problems. What they got was an idiot savant. Do you know what that is? I've got a perfect memory and I can do calculations a lot faster than you can, but most of my processing capacity has to go into running the brain-machine interface. If there's a way to solve any of the world's problems I don't know what it is. I couldn't even anticipate what Dr. Samuels was going to do, and we'd both be dead now if you hadn't handled things the way you did."

"You did a pretty good job on Beissel," I said. "Thank you—it could have gotten really messy if your drone hadn't gone at him."

That got me a smile. "I'm glad. I thought it would help." She paused, made herself go on. "But now you know what happened and what I am. That I'm—not all human. I don't think I'm a monster, but—" With a little bitter laugh: "Maybe I'm wrong. An artifact—that's what Beissel called me. A very rare artifact." She closed her eyes and hunched her shoulders upwards, harsh and angular as the concrete blocks around us.

I knew before she'd finished that the smart thing to do was to say something that didn't promise too much, and hand her over to Huddon as fast as I could. No, she wasn't a monster, but I knew I was way out of my league trying to deal with a human-supercomputer hybrid, and the smart thing to do was to back away.

That wasn't what I did. What I did was put one hand on her shoulder. She looked toward me, startled and red-eyed, and I held out my other arm, inviting. She closed her eyes again and then slid over to my end of the concrete block and buried her face in my shoulder and clung to me, shaking hard. I put my arms around her and held her. Yeah, I stroked her hair, too.

That took up a while. Finally the shaking stopped and she whispered, "Thank you. I should have known that you had an answer."

"Okay," I said. "What was my answer?"

I could feel her face shift into the first rough draft of a smile. "Nobody hugs an artifact."

She had me there. I stroked her hair again, and she let out a long ragged sigh and nestled her head into my shoulder. That bumped against one of the bruises I got from Big Goro, and it took an effort not to wince.

"When all this is over with, can I go back to the Habitat?" she asked then. "I like it, and—and I need a place to stay." She glanced up at me with one eye. "I turned on the inert gas as soon as we got outside and my drones are busy right now welding shut the doors to the outside. I don't want anyone else to get access to my computer half ever again."

"Of course you can come to the Habitat," I told her. "Once it's safe to go through Shoreside. I had some trouble with Big Goro's boys this morning—that's why I was late, and why I didn't have a gun. There was shooting going on when I left his place. I don't know how things stand right now."

Sophie looked scared. "I don't know how to deal with that."

"You don't have to. We're going to wait until Huddon tells us it's safe, and then head for Rick's and find out what's happened. We can wait there for a travelers' boat if we have to."

She nodded, closed her eyes again, and settled her head against my shoulder. I sat there with one arm around her, and wondered why I'd let myself get into the situation I was in and why it felt like the best thing that had ever happened to me.

WE SAT THERE FOR fifteen minutes, maybe, while waves rolled in from across the Atlantic and the sun swung over toward the middle of the sky. Sophie stayed huddled up against me, and I kept an arm around her and left it at that. Finally Huddon came strolling back our way from somewhere over by the other plane. A couple of federal police came part of the way with him, but stopped half a dozen yards back. They didn't have their flechette guns pointing anywhere in particular, which was encouraging.

"Thank you for waiting," he said. Sophie blinked and sat up straight when he spoke; she'd had her eyes closed. "Everything's cleared up now, and all of Beissel's people who are still alive have been rounded up. A very successful operation, all things considered, and you deserve a good part of the credit for that, Mr. Shimizu." I thanked him, and he turned to Sophie. "We haven't properly met, have we, Ms.—"

"Ames. Sophie Ames."

"Is Ames really your family name, by any chance?"

"No. The last name they gave me was a fourteen-digit alphanumeric code."

That apparently meant something to Huddon. He reached out his hand, and Sophie took it a little awkwardly, pressed it and let it go. "Dr. Michael Huddon," he said, "Department of History, National University. If I told you that I've read the classified papers dealing with Project CS3-22881, would you know what I was talking about?"

"If you mean the original proposal by Sleave, Gellman, and Kurojima," Sophie said at once, "or the amended proposal by those three and Capoferro, yes, of course. Have you read the interim reports by Capoferro and Ames?"

"No," he said, considering her. "No, the file I located in the old National Archives didn't include any of them."

"My accession number is ninety-five. It's the only active number."

Huddon winced visibly. "I'm sorry to hear that. Did you know the others?"

"No. I just got their records afterwards."

He nodded. "Well, I suppose that's something." I was still trying to work that out when he turned to me. "Shoreside is secure now. You shouldn't have any trouble getting back to the Habitat. That said, I'm going to suggest that you wait in Shoreside for a little while."

I gave him a wary look, and he smiled. "I'll be flying to Habitat 4 in a few minutes, and I need to have a conversation with Mrs. Taira. Give me an hour, say, and then take the ferry out to the Habitat. Will that work? Excellent. I'll see you there." He turned and started up the beach, and the two guys in blue went with him. A moment later the officers he'd stationed at the southern end of Shoreside came walking back past us, with their flechette guns slung behind their shoulders, and the look of guys who've finished work and are on their way home.

Once they were past, I turned to Sophie. "Ready?"

"I think so," she said. I got up and gave her a hand, and the two of us left the concrete blocks and walked down onto the sand.

Once we were close to the water, she said, "Just a moment," reached into a pocket and pulled out the remote thing she'd gotten from Samuels. She went to the water's edge, ran out onto the wet sand as a wave slid back out to sea, and threw the thing good and hard into the ocean, where it hit the face of a wave and vanished. She scampered back up the beach just ahead of an incoming wave, looking shaken but pleased with herself. "I already deactivated it," she told me, "but I've been scared of that thing since I was little."

"The override control?"

She nodded. "Now it's gone for good."

We started walking north toward Shoreside. Behind us, the other airplane took off from the beach, tilted its fans, and went zooming out across the water toward Habitat 4, flying low and fast. I watched it pop up once it got close to the Habitat, and land on the old helicopter pad on Gokai. Sophie watched them too, and about the time the plane landed, she said, "They're tracking me, you know."

I looked her way. "The federal police?"

"Yes. I'm pretty sure they've figured out a frequency that resonates with my antenna."

It took me a moment to process that. "The one that connects your halves."

She nodded. "I can—hear, more or less—radio frequencies. The plane's got a transmitter aimed at me, and I'm pretty sure the people on board have a receiver picking up the harmonics. If I go anywhere but the Habitat they'll know. I don't want to go anywhere else, but—" She shrugged. "I thought you'd want to know."

"Yeah," I said. "Thank you." She smiled and we walked on. It made sense, of course. The federal police have all kinds of limits on what they can look into, on account of the way federal power got abused under the old constitution. They make up for it by being tougher than anybody else, and having the best technology you can get these days. The flechette guns and the aircraft are part of that, since nobody else but the military can afford those, but you never know what else they're going to pull out of their packs and use on you.

I had that in mind as we went toward Rick's, but I didn't let it distract me. Every step of the way I had my eyes and ears wide open for any sign of trouble. I hoped that Huddon was right about things being settled; I hoped that just this once I'd be enough of my mother's son to tap into whatever whisper from Ame no Kokoro tells her what's going to happen. The whole way, too, I had to work to ignore the trembling happy look on Sophie's face or the echo of it inside me, where I tried to convince myself it didn't have any business being.

Gunfire popped in the distance as we got to the place where the hill goes away and the buildings start. It wasn't as far away as I would have liked. You hear shots pretty often in Shoreside, but this was a lot more than usual. I got the .357 out of my pocket just in case, then thought of Bernard's gun and turned to Sophie. "Any chance you know how to shoot?"

That got me a scared look. "No." Then she drew in a breath and said in a small voice: "I can learn if I have to."

I thought about how fast she'd learned to use hashi, and decided she was right. "Later on, it might be a good idea. For now, let's just get to Rick's."

We got to Rick's. It could have been any other day, except the gunshots kept up and I heard people shouting in the distance. They didn't sound frightened or angry, for whatever that was worth. The bars between Rick's and the place where I'd first met Sophie were closed up tight, no surprises there, but we didn't have to go far before I knew that Rick's was wide open. The people who worked for him had hauled tables and chairs all over the dry part of the beach, and most of the chairs were full. It was a big crowd, drinking and whooping. From the empties all over the sand it looked like they were having a hell of a party.

Rick was going from table to table as usual. He spotted me and Sophie as we got near to the southern end of the tables, and came over. "Hey, Jerry! Beer for you, and something for the lady? First one each is on the house."

I glanced at Sophie, who nodded tentatively, and then turned back to Rick. "Two beers, please and thank you. What's the occasion?"

"Big Goro's gone over the mountain."

A knot came untied south of my floating ribs. "No kidding. Any idea what happened?"

"The way I heard it, a couple of shotgun slugs said hi while they were passing through. Hey, lemme get you those beers." He headed off to the building, and I steered Sophie over to an unoccupied table, did the polite thing, and sat down in a chair close to hers.

The moment I got settled, she turned to face me. "Does 'gone over the mountain' mean dead?" I nodded and she went on. "That's good news, isn't it?"

"Might be. Depends on who replaces him and how soon."

Rick came back with the beers, handed them over. "Here you go."

"Any word yet on who's taken over?" I asked him.

"Oh yeah. It's Jim Nakano's beach now. You know Goro was trying to off him, right? Apparently Jim decided he was tired of it and returned the favor. That's why everybody's partying."

I gave Rick a blank look and then said, "Damn." He grinned at me and went to the next table, and I took a good solid slug of the beer and then said to Sophie, "Really good news."

One of her hands wrapped around one of mine. "I'm glad."

Glad? To judge by her face that was the understatement of the decade. If I'd used the word it would have been the same thing. Jim was tough enough to keep Shoreside in line but he was fair and he didn't like to bully people, and having him in charge would put an end to a lot of things that needed to stop. I thought about what Huddon had said about warlords and kings, and wondered if this was the change he'd talked about.

THE FERRY SHOWED UP nearly on time and Sophie and I got on it without any trouble at all. From the dock I could see people partying up and down the beach. A couple of bars south of Rick's opened up by the time we headed for the dock and I'd figured out already that the gunshots were people shooting into the air to celebrate. I kept my eyes and ears wide open anyway while we stood waiting.

Once we got on the ferry and settled on a bench seat next to each other I let myself relax a little. Sophie took one of my hands in both of hers and sat there with her face lit up, watching the waves splash against what was left of the ruins to either side, then watching the Habitats once we went out past the ruins, taking it all in. Me, I closed my eyes for a little while and let some of the stress of the morning drain away. I could feel every bruise I got from Big Goro, and the muscles I used to fight Rex Samuels and Max Bernard were yelling at me in chorus. Maybe Mom's right, I thought. Maybe I really do need to find something else to do for a living, and—

I could feel Sophie close by, and finished the thought: maybe.

The ferry took its usual time to get to Habitat 4 and the two of us climbed up onto the floating dock. The two guys in flak jackets were expecting me, which didn't surprise me at all. The kid in the booth who had us sign in told me, "Mrs. Taira wants to see you right away."

"I want to see her right away," I told him. "Call her office and let her know I'm on my way, with someone she needs to see."

The kid agreed to call, and Sophie and I went to wait for the elevator while he got busy with his phone. The elevator didn't come down any sooner than usual. Once the door rattled open and we climbed inside, Sophie asked, "Who's Mrs. Taira?"

"My boss," I said. "Her official title's President of the Community Council of Habitat 4. What that means in practice—well, do you know the Japanese word *daimyo*?"

She paused for a fraction of a second. I got the impression that she was looking something up. "Yes. So she rules the Habitat."

"Yeah, basically. You'll need her permission to move here. You'll be able to get it, but you'll have to tell her about the Project and about yourself."

"I can do that," she said. "I wonder how much Dr. Huddon's told her."

I shrugged. "We'll find out."

The elevator rattled to a stop and let us onto Ikkai. I said hi to the guards there and they told me that my boss was waiting. I nodded and took Sophie straight to Stair 3, which is the closest stair to the elevator. We went up to Sankai; I led her to the familiar waiting room, where Louise Yoshimitsu gave me a sudden startled look and then sent another, uncertain, toward Sophie. She picked up the phone, punched a couple of numbers, and said "Mrs. Taira? They're here." A moment later she motioned us toward the door.

Inside Mrs. Taira was sitting behind her big desk, silhouetted against the view out the windows. Huddon was sitting in a chair over to one side of the room with his hands folded over his shillelagh. Two other people, both old men, were waiting with them. One of them, a plump smiling guy in a fussy ice cream-colored suit, sat on a chair not too far from Huddon. I recognized him after a moment as Frank Yukihira, the guy who runs Habitat 5.

I didn't need to make an effort to recognize the other. He was a lean stooped man with a face like a tired scholar's, dressed casually in slacks and a plain shirt, a brown tweed jacket and no tie. He was standing by the window looking out toward Shoreside, his hand on a chair. I tried not to show my reaction, though under the circumstances I doubt I managed it. The thought that Sam Akane was involved in this business was unnerving enough, but I couldn't think of the last time he'd left his penthouse on Habitat 2 for any reason at all.

I went to the center of the floor and bowed, and Sophie surprised me by coming along with me and doing the sort of old-fashioned curtsey you never see outside of old movies any more. The old woman behind the desk nodded precisely, motioned us to chairs facing her and the windows. "So," she said, once we sat down. "Dr. Huddon has been telling us about the Merlin Project and Ferdinand Beissel." She glanced at him. "Perhaps you can finish."

"Of course." He was wearing that insufferable smile of his, but this time I figured he'd earned it. "I don't need to say anything about the Merlin Project, since Ms. Ames knows more about it than any of us and I'm fairly sure Mr. Shimizu has heard a good deal from her by now. As for Beissel, I don't expect to get much out of him. Where and when he heard about the Merlin Project, why he or his superiors in the EU decided to follow up on it, how they figured out it was here—I doubt we'll ever know. Some of the Shoreside people he hired and two of the agents he brought with him have already talked, though. It was that or face capital charges and a firing squad, so they didn't argue much.

"As near as we can tell, though, the EU sent a different agent here two years ago to sound out Goro Omogawa and see if there was any trace of the Project facility in the area. The agent went back to Brussels with a favorable report. My guess is that he detected radio waves coming from the top of the hill, and a little too much heat radiating through the rock from down inside. So Beissel was sent here as soon as all the preparations were in place. The robberies of the couriers were his idea, and the people who carried them out were his agents. He thought he'd need power equipment to dig into the hill, and that meant he had to get money in some way that wasn't obvious, buy the equipment here in the United States under false pretenses, and bring it to Shoreside. Smuggling it in from overseas would have been too risky without cooperation from the Habitats, which he knew by then he wouldn't get."

"Thank you," said Mrs. Taira.

"You're welcome. When he and Omogawa figured out that Rex Samuels had access to the facility is another question I can't answer. Late in the process, certainly. Omogawa seems to have guessed first, and I don't think he told Beissel right away. These last few days, certainly, Beissel knew. It's pretty clear that Beissel and Omogawa meant to double-cross each other, and both of them were planning to kill Samuels and take control of the Project facility. Beissel meant to strip the place and smuggle it out piece by piece at night—there was a ship waiting for him off Habitat 3. The federal police have it now. Omogawa meant to use Beissel to get into the facility and then kill him, and sell access to the computer for whatever he could get. Neither of them knew about you, Ms. Ames, and I don't think Beissel figured it out until you showed up with a drone. And of course neither of them had figured out what kind of backup I could call in."

Mrs. Taira nodded once, acknowledging. Sam Akane turned away from the window. "Ms. Ames," he said, "we've heard some interesting things about you." His voice was higher-pitched than you'd expect. "You're in mental contact with the supercomputer?"

"It's a little more than that," said Sophie. She gestured at herself. "This is my human half. The computer is my other half. The two halves are both me, just—just connected by radio waves. I know that probably sounds strange."

Akane took that in, nodded once, and glanced at Mrs. Taira, whose face stayed serene and impenetrable as a porcelain mask. "I see," the old man said. "But I have no way to put what you're saying to the test."

I'd seen him deploy that trick before, the one time I'd encountered him, and heard plenty of other stories about times he'd used it. Those words were the test. I knew people who'd failed it, and not all of them survived the experience, but Sophie passed easily. Her face lit up and she said, "Oh, that's a fun problem. Anything I proposed, you could assume that I'd just prepared and memorized the answer."

His eyebrows rose fractionally. "You enjoy problems like that."

"Yes," said Sophie. "Very much. They give me something to think about."

Huddon cleared his throat politely, and said, "I might be able to help." He got up, went to Mr. Akane, handed him something small and black, and said something in a low voice. Mr. Akane nodded. Huddon returned to his chair, sat down, and pulled a sheet of paper from inside his jacket. "Mr. Shimizu, maybe you could show this to Mr. Akane, Mrs. Taira, and Mr. Yukihira, and then take it to Ms. Ames."

I left my chair and got the paper from him. Sam Akane took it from me, glanced at it, and handed it back. My boss gave it a quick assessing look, and Frank Yukihira went over it carefully, then gave it to me. I didn't glance at it until they'd seen it, but I gave it a quick once-over once I got it back from Yukihira. It had a long complicated equation written on it by hand, the kind of thing Fritz likes and I can't do at all, with x raised to the 0.348th power and divided by the cube root of $4\pi - 3$ and fun things like that.

Sophie took the paper from me, gave it an intent look for a moment and then said, "The answer's forty-two. That's a joke, isn't it?"

Huddon's face betrayed nothing. He glanced at Mr. Akane, who gave him a nod in response. "Yes, that's the answer," said Huddon to Sophie. "And yes, it's a joke. But it's more than that. While you were solving it I had Mr. Akane watch the radio signals you were sending and receiving. Your computer half, as you call it, has some very sophisticated weak-signal capacities."

Sophie looked pleased. "When I was younger I spent a lot of time running antenna simulations, trying out different geometries and frequency patterns. I ended up rebuilding my antennas a couple of times. Not the one in my spine, unfortunately. It could be improved but there's not much I can do about that."

Huddon turned to the others. "I hope that's satisfactory."

Mrs. Taira glanced at Sam Akane, who nodded. "Yes," she said to Huddon. I let myself breathe again.

A MOMENT PASSED, AND then Mrs. Taira went on. "Perhaps you can advise us as to what your superiors expect in this situation."

Huddon put on the familiar smile. "Obviously it's of concern to the United States that no foreign power gets access to the Merlin Project. Beyond that, it's an interesting legal question. The Merlin supercomputer was built with federal funds so it's technically US government property, but human beings can't be anyone's property under either the old or the new constitution. Since Ms. Ames is both, her status would keep lawyers awake at night for quite a while if it became public."

"That doesn't seem wise," said Akane.

Huddon shook his head. "Not at all." He turned to face Sophie. "Ms. Ames, how many people know about your two halves?"

"The people in this room," she said. "And Beissel." Then she put her hand on my arm and said, "Please don't do anything to him."

I gave her a startled look, and then realized what she meant. The other four people in the room were silent for a moment. "There's no question of that," my boss said to Sophie then. "Mr. Shimizu has been a personal assistant of mine for many years now. I have every reason to trust his discretion."

"Thank you," I said.

Mrs. Taira nodded, acknowledging, and went on. "We'll take it as given that to everyone outside this room, except for those of Dr. Huddon's superiors who need to know, you're simply a young woman with certain unusual talents. I trust that's acceptable to you."

"Yes, of course," Sophie said.

"It would be helpful," Sam Akane said then, "to know where you will live."

Sophie swallowed visibly. "I need my two halves to stay within radio range, or they'll both stop working. So if it's okay, I'd like to move here, to Habitat 4." With a glance and a smile toward me: "I know people here. And—and if the European Union knows about me, I know I need to be somewhere safe."

My boss allowed a little precise smile. For her, that's the equivalent of whooping for joy. "We would be delighted to welcome you here." She glanced at Akane and then at Yukihira, got a nod from one and a little half-disappointed shrug from the other. "Do you have any special requirements?"

"Well, it would be helpful if I could set up a repeater station," Sophie said. I got the impression that she'd thought about it hard, for a hundredth of a second or so. "It would work best if I put it on the west side of the Habitat on an outside wall. It wouldn't take more than six watts of power, and I could make do with less than that. But I'm running a little slow right now because the signal here's kind of faint."

"That can be arranged."

"Thank you. That's very nice of you."

"Once you have settled in, perhaps we can talk. I have—" She allowed another smile, equally precise. "Problems that might interest you."

Sophie beamed in response. "Thank you. I'd like that very much."

Huddon said, "Perhaps you could also help the federal government out with a few things now and then. For example, I know people who'd like to learn a little about those antenna geometries you mentioned."

"I'd be happy to," Sophie said. "If I can get some paper and a pen I can draw up the plans and specifications. I have a drafting module. It took me the longest time to figure out how to get it to interface with the muscles of my hands and arms, but I did it."

Huddon processed that. "Thank you. I'm sure you can get what you need."

"If I may," Frank Yukihira said then. It was literally the first thing he said, and his deep soft voice nearly made me jump. "Ms. Ames, do you by any chance know accounting?"

"Oh, yes. I have a full charge bookkeeping module. I've only used it once outside of school, but I know how it's done."

"I'm glad to hear that. When you're not otherwise occupied, perhaps I might interest you in something along those lines. The banks in my Habitat do a great deal of foreign trade and things get—" He gestured, one palm up. "Perplexing at times. I'd like to be able to have their accountants consult with you from time to time."

Sophie had the good sense to glance at my boss and get a nod from her before answering. "I'd be very happy to do that," she said.

Yukihira gave her a big smile and thanked her. Sam Akane, watching them both, nodded once, as though that settled everything that had to be said.

A couple of minutes of polite noise later, Sophie, Huddon, and I got up, thanked the others, and headed for the door of the office. As we were leaving, my boss said in Japanese, "Before you go, Shimizu-san."

I smiled at Sophie and said, "I'll be with you in a moment." She nodded uncertainly and went out after Huddon. The moment the door clicked shut behind them, my boss got out the little clutch purse she uses for petty cash. "Get her suitable clothes, anything else she needs." She handed me a stack of bills, and they weren't small ones. "And keep her safe and happy. That's your chief assignment now; anything else can be reassigned. She's a remarkable asset."

I grinned. "I'm on it."

She gave me a smile in response, and then it faltered. "You should know this. I found out what happened to Jason Fujita. He was shot by Bernard's people. They thought he was protecting Huddon." A fractional shrug lifted her shoulders a little. "I've made arrangements for his family, and for a proper funeral."

I bowed to her and left.

Sophie was standing outside in the waiting room, looking uneasy. That went away as soon as she saw me come through the door, and she beamed and took my hand as I came over to her. Louise, sitting at her desk, glanced up and then away, hard, with the kind of stiff look on her face that tells you somebody from Sankai or Yokai is upset and doesn't want to show it. I had other things to think about just then. It wasn't until later, when Sophie and I were crossing Nikai to Stair 11, that it occurred to me that Louise's parade of not liking me was her idea of flirting. I shook my head, half baffled and half amused. Fortunately Sophie was walking a little ahead of me and so I didn't have to explain why.

We went straight to my room—our room, I reminded myself, since I had no questions about what Mrs. Taira's last comment to me meant, and it was what I wanted to do anyway. Once we got inside and I shut the door, Sophie turned to me. "Do you think that went well?"

"Really well. You've got a job and an income now, you know."

I could see the tension drain out of her. "Oh, good. I didn't even think of that."

"No worries either way. I make plenty."

Sophie nodded, and went over to the window at the far end of the room. "I should call Mom and let her know we're both okay," I said, "and there's a friend of mine named Fritz, someone you should meet soon, and I should call him, too. After that Mrs. Taira wanted me to take you shopping and get you some clothes and things."

She glanced back over her shoulder at me. "That's very nice of her." Putting on a smile: "And you."

Behind the smile was a whole boatload of uncertainties, and I thought I could guess where most of them came from. I went over to her. "You said the repeater ought to be facing west. Is the outside wall here a good place for it?"

Sophie turned. "A really good place." She closed her eyes. "I meant it last night when I said I want to stay here."

"I want you to stay here," I told her.

She put her arms around me and buried her face in my shoulder. I held her, and after a while she made a muffled noise that was probably "Thank you." Then she drew in an uneven breath, looked up at me, and asked: "Do you think we could get married?"

"You know," I said, "I was just going to say something about that."

Of course that was a barefaced lie. I hadn't been thinking anything of the kind just then, but by the time she finished mentioning it I'd thought of three things. The first was that Mrs. Taira would be pleased to hear of it, and when she's pleased she gets very generous. The second was that Mom would be even happier, since she's been bugging me to settle down and get married for years now. The third thing—well, I could still feel the bruises I'd gotten from Big Goro and the way my muscles yelled at me after two not especially long fights, and there were all the other thoughts I'd had over the days just past. Maybe it really was time to do something else with my life. There was something else, too, something that didn't sort itself out into words as easily as the others, something that made me feel like Sophie and I were on one side of a line and the rest of the world was on the other, and that meeting her might just be the one piece of genuine good luck that I'd ever had. Maybe that's why I answered her the way I did, but we'll let that pass for now.

"Good. I'd like that." Her face went solemn and she took my hands in hers. "Jerry, please be patient with me. I'm not very good at human things."

"We'll manage," I told her, and reached for her.

Of course that led to a kiss, and then to another, and one way or another it was a while before I had the chance to make those phone calls and take her shopping. The whole time, though, a little part of me was thinking about what Huddon said about the old Gnostics and deciding that maybe he was right. Maybe we really are homeless gods, all of us. Maybe we left the world of light so long ago that we don't even remember it any more. Now here we are in a world that doesn't happen to make sense to us and we just have to get by as best we can.

Sometimes the world brings knowledge and a lot of times it brings death and every so often it brings love, and there's nothing personal involved. There wasn't anything I'd done or left undone, it didn't matter if I'd been a good person or for that matter a bad one, and the universe didn't mean to bring me and Sophie together. I just happened to be standing in the right place a couple of times when Sophie showed up, and the fact that the two of us ended up alive and happy and together was just one of those things.

GLOSSARY

Amatsu no kami: the gods of heaven
Ame no Kokoro: heart of heaven
arigato: thank you
daimyo: feudal warlord
Daishizen: Great Nature
do: hall
donburi: rice bowl with meat and vegetables
edamame: steamed green soybeans in the pod
En no Gyoja: legendary Japanese wizard, the Merlin of Japan
gaijin: people from Western countries
Gempei wars: wars in early feudal Japan between the Taira and Minamoto clans
gokai: fifth floor
gyoza: Japanese dumplings
Hakata ramen: Japanese noodle dish from Hakata prefecture
hapi coat: hip-length, short-sleeved garment
hashi: chopsticks
Hokkaido: northernmost large island of Japan
Honshu: largest, central island of Japan
ikkai: first floor
kami: divine beings
kana: Japanese syllable writing, easy to learn and read

kanji: Japanese characters derived from Chinese, much harder to learn and read
Kunitsu no kami: the gods of earth
Kyushu: southernmost large island of Japan
michi: way, path, road
moshi moshi: traditional Japanese telephone greeting
muenbotoke: ghosts who have no descendants to perform rites for them
Mushukujin: homeless gods
nanmin: refugee; in the story, anyone of Japanese ancestry
nenju: Japanese rosary of 108 beads
Nihon: Japan
nikai: second floor
norito: formal prayer to the kami, in archaic Japanese
ramen: noodles in broth
sake: Japanese rice wine
-san: suffix for names, equivalent to "Mr." or "Ms."
sankai: third floor
Shinihon: Little Japan, slang for the five Habitats
shoji: Japanese chess
tabi socks: Japanese stockings with a gap between the big toe and the other toes
tama: soul
tatami: mats made of rice straw, used as floor covering
temizu: water fountain used to rinse hands and mouth before entering a holy place
tempura: any battered and deep-fried food
torii: ritual gate outside a holy place
-ya: suffix for any place of business
yakisoba: Japanese fried noodle dish
Yaoyorozu no kami: gods not of heaven or of earth
yokai: fourth floor

www.ingramcontent.com/pod-product-compliance
Lightning Source LLC
Jackson TN
JSHW031339130125
77033JS00025B/986

* 9 7 8 1 9 1 5 9 5 2 1 2 7 *